BOOK YOUR PLACE ON OUR WEBSITE AND MAKE THE READING CONNECTION!

We've created a customized website just for our very special readers, where you can get the inside scoop on everything that's going on with Zebra, Pinnacle and Kensington books.

When you come online, you'll have the exciting opportunity to:

- View covers of upcoming books
- Read sample chapters
- Learn about our future publishing schedule (listed by publication month and author)
- Find out when your favorite authors will be visiting a city near you
- Search for and order backlist books from our online catalog
- Check out author bios and background information
- Send e-mail to your favorite authors
- Meet the Kensington staff online
- Join us in weekly chats with authors, readers and other guests
- Get writing guidelines
- AND MUCH MORE!

**Visit our website at
http://www.kensingtonbooks.com**

The Most Dangerous DUKE in London

MADELINE HUNTER

ZEBRA BOOKS
KENSINGTON PUBLISHING CORP.
http://www.kensingtonbooks.com

ZEBRA BOOKS are published by

Kensington Publishing Corp.
119 West 40th Street
New York, NY 10018

All Kensington titles, imprints, and distributed lines are available at special quantity discounts for bulk purchases for sales promotion, premiums, fund-raising, educational, or institutional use.

Special book excerpts or customized printings can also be created to fit specific needs. For details, write or phone the office of the Kensington Sales Manager: Attn.: Sales Department. Kensington Publishing Corp., 119 West 40th Street, New York, NY 10018. Phone: 1-800-221-2647.

Zebra and the Z logo Reg. U.S. Pat. & TM Off.

First Printing: June 2017
ISBN-13: 978-1-4201-4390-4
ISBN-10: 1-4201-4390-5

eISBN-13: 978-1-4201-4391-1
eISBN-10: 1-4201-4391-3

10 9 8 7 6 5 4 3 2 1

Printed in the United States of America

This book is dedicated to my husband Warren,
whose love and support made all of this possible

Chapter One

The Dowager Countess of Marwood could be a formidable enemy if she so chose. Her mere presence dared one to take her lightly so she might have an excuse to rain destruction, just for fun.

Adam Penrose, Duke of Stratton, knew at once what he had in her.

He had called at her grandson the earl's country estate at her request. *Let us attempt to bury the past,* she had written, *and allow bygones to be bygones between our families.*

He had come, curious to see how she hoped to accomplish that, considering that some of those bygones were not gone at all. One look at her and he knew that whatever plan she had concocted, it would not benefit *him*.

The lady kept him waiting a half hour before entering the chamber herself. She finally sailed into the drawing room, angled forward, head high, her ample bosom leading the way, like a figure on a ship's prow.

Mourning for her son, the late earl, forced her into black garments, but her crepe ensemble must have cost hundreds. Abundant gray curls decorated her head, suggesting that she also mourned the dead fashion for wigs. Shallow, large, pale blue eyes examined her caller with a critical gaze while an artificial smile deepened the wrinkles of her long face.

"So, you have returned." She announced the obvious when they sat on two sturdy chairs, after his short bow and her shorter curtsy.

"It was time."

"One might say it was time three years ago, or two, or even several years hence."

"One might, but I did not."

She chortled. Her whole face pursed, not only her lips. "You have been in France a long time. You even look French now."

"At least half so, I assume, considering my parentage."

"And how is your dear mother?"

"Happy in Paris. She has many friends there."

The dowager's eyebrows rose just enough to express sardonic amusement. "Yes, I expect she does. It is a wonder she did not marry you off to one of her own kind."

"I think a British match would suit me better. Don't you?"

"Indeed I do. It will help you enormously."

He did not want to discuss his mother or the reasons why a solid match would help. "You wrote of bygones. Perhaps you will enlighten me regarding that."

She opened her hands, palms up, in a gesture of confusion. "The animosity between our families is so old that one wonders how it even started. It is so unnecessary. So unfortunate. We are county neighbors, after all. Surely we can rise above it if we choose to."

Unable to sit and listen to her blithe references to that history, he stood and paced to the long windows. They overlooked a spectacular garden and on to the hills beyond, not far away. The house and its immediate grounds occupied a shallow valley.

"How do you suggest we do that?" He asked the question while he corralled the bitterness in his mind. The dowager knew damned well why the recent animosity had started and probably knew about the older history too. To acknowledge any of that would make her peace offering peculiar, however. *We stole your property and savaged your mother and helped drive your father to his death, but you should rise above that now.*

He turned to see her watching him. She appeared puzzled, as if he had done something unexpected and she could not determine if he had won a point without her knowing it.

He raised his eyebrows, to encourage her to speak.

"I propose that we resolve this the ancient way. In the manner of political dynasties down through time," she said. "I believe that our families should join through marriage."

He barely avoided revealing his astonishment. He had not expected this, of all possible overtures. She did not merely suggest a truce, but rather an alliance bound by the strongest ties. The kind of alliance that might keep him from pursuing the truth about this family's role in his father's death, or seeking revenge if he learned his suspicions about the last earl were correct.

"Since I do not have a sister for your grandson, I assume you have set your sights on me."

"My grandson has a sister who will suit you perfectly. Emilia is all any man could ask for and would make a perfect duchess for you."

"You speak with great confidence, yet you have no idea what *this* man would ask for."

"Do I not? As if I have lived this long and learned nothing? Beauty, grace, demure obedience, and a fine settlement. Those qualifications are high on your list, as on all men's."

The temptation to add other requirements, ones that would shock her, almost conquered his better judgment. He only won the battle because he had learned never to let the enemy know his thoughts.

"I can find that in many young women. Shall we be honest with each other? What is it about this particular match that would be to my advantage?"

"A bold question, but a fair one. We will be allies instead of enemies. It will benefit you just as it will benefit us."

"Well, now, Countess, we both know that is not true. I have been invited to negotiate peace now when my father never was in the past. I would be a fool if I did not wonder why you think I would be agreeable. Considering the rumors regarding my activities in France, I can surmise how you may think this will protect your grandson, but not how it will help me."

Her eyes narrowed. Her skin's wrinkles froze like stone carvings. She displayed no fear. Adam admired her strong poise, but then she was not the one she assumed to be in danger.

She stood. "Come out on the terrace. I will show you my granddaughter. Once you see her, you will understand how you will benefit."

He followed her out into the crisp April air. The garden spread below them like a brown and red tapestry, punctuated by small new leaves and early flowers of yellow, pink, and purple. Bulbs, he assumed. They had not yet begun blooming when he left Paris.

A girl sat within the reviving growth, on a stone bench thirty feet away. She had a book open, held up so her face did not angle down. The dowager must have given her a reprieve from mourning because the girl wore a pale blue dress. She was pretty, and perhaps sixteen years of age. Her blond hair sparkled in the sun, and her fair skin and lovely face would appeal to any man. Add a fine settlement and she would do well enough.

The dowager stood beside him, her expression one of supreme confidence. He did not trust her, but he admired her skill at this game. He admitted to himself that her offer did have its advantages, and not because the girl was lovely. His father's name and his family's honor had been badly tainted in the best circles, and if he wanted to overcome that curse, this marriage would definitely help.

It would mean forgetting the reasons he had turned his back on England as well as his only good reason for finally returning. Which was why the dowager had invited him here in the first place, he assumed.

"Emilia is as sweet in disposition as any girl I have known. She is of good humor too and has a fair amount of wit, lest you worry that she might be dull," the countess said.

Sweet Emilia pretended not to see them, just as she pretended to read, posed so he could see her face and form. No wrap warmed her, and no bonnet protected that fair skin. He wondered how long she had been sitting like that, waiting for her future intended to inspect her.

He did not know why she held no appeal. Perhaps because while she might be lovely and witty, she was too young, and from the look of her compliance with her grandmother's instructions, probably lacked spirit.

The doors opened and the earl strode out. Tall and blond, he had not yet completely shed the gangly thinness of boyhood. He glowered at his grandmother while he passed her. She pursed her face in return. His arrival apparently had not been part of the dowager's plans.

He advanced on Adam like a man greeting a friend, but his rushed, loud welcome and the glisten of sweat on his brow told another story. Theobald, Earl of Marwood, was afraid of his guest. Many men had shown the same reaction since Adam arrived back in England two weeks ago. His reputation had preceded him, and society apparently expected him to issue challenges left and right at the slightest provocation.

Adam had done nothing to correct their assumptions. For one thing, he might very well issue a challenge or two, depending on what he discovered about events five years ago. For another, there were men, like Marwood here, who were more pliable when motivated by fear.

"I see Grandmother has already broached the idea of this match," Marwood said heartily. He looked down at his sister Emilia, still posed in the garden. The two of them looked much alike—fair, pale, handsome, and young.

The earl could not be more than twenty-one. Adam wondered if Marwood knew about the rumor that had haunted Adam's father to his grave. Marwood's fear suggested he might, and that Adam's long-held suspicions about these old enemies might be true.

"Are you amenable to the idea?" Marwood asked.

His grandmother drifted closer. "Forgive my grandson. He is still young enough to think impetuous impatience is a manly virtue."

Marwood looked to heaven as if praying for that patience. "He knows by now if the notion appeals or if it does not."

"The notion appeals, in a general way," Adam said. He did not lie. He still weighed the implications of the dowager's plan. This offer to simply turn the page on the past tempted him more than he expected.

The young earl shot his grandmother a glance full of bright optimism. The dowager managed more circumspection.

Adam focused his gaze on the girl. The dowager retreated. The earl sidled closer. Eager to complete negotiations, the earl extolled his sister's charms, man to man. Out of the corner of his eye, Adam saw the dowager shaking her head at her grandson's lack of finesse.

A movement on the hill beyond the garden caught Adam's eye. A flash of black streaked along the crest, took flight over a large, fallen tree, then abruptly stopped. A woman all in black, on a black horse, looked down on the house.

"Who is that?" he asked.

Marwood squinted and feigned lack of recognition. He glanced sideways at Adam, and thought better of it. "That is my half sister, Clara. She is the daughter of my father's first wife."

The black spot named Clara managed to communicate a good deal of hauteur even from this distance. She paced her horse back and forth on the hill's crest, watching the show below as if the rest of them put on a pageant for her amusement.

He remembered Lady Clara Cheswick, although they had never been introduced. She had been out in society before he left England, though. Bright-eyed and vivacious. Those were his impressions absorbed in passing.

"She does not allow mourning to interfere with her pleasure in riding," Adam said.

"She would probably say she honors our father this way. They liked to ride together."

"Since she is the eldest, why am I not being offered her hand?"

Marwood glanced askance at the dowager, then smirked. "Because the goal is to keep you from killing me, isn't it?" he said in a low voice, with unexpected bluntness. "Not give you another reason to want to."

Adam chose not to reassure Marwood about the killing part. Let this pup of an earl worry. "You are intriguing me now, not discouraging me."

Marwood bent his head closer and spoke confidentially. "I am doing you a great favor now in speaking honestly. My father spoiled and indulged her and allowed her to build notions unfitting for women. He never demanded she marry, and now she thinks it beneath her. He left her a good bit of property in her own name, a handsome tract with rich farms." His voice turned bitter on the last sentence. "She is my sister, but I would be no friend to you if I sang her praises when in reality she is something of a shrew."

Clara was the old earl's favorite child, apparently. Adam wondered if the recently deceased father still had the ability to turn over in his grave. With a nudge or two, perhaps. "How old is she?"

"Far past marrying age. Twenty-four."

Old enough to remember. She might even know a great deal, if her father kept her close. "Call her down here. I would like to meet her."

"Truly, you do not want to—"

"Call her. And tell your other sister to put the book down. Her arms must feel like lead by now."

Marwood scurried to his grandmother to share the request. The dowager sailed over to Adam while trying to appear calm. "I fear you misunderstand. For this match to come to a satisfactory conclusion, the bride must be Emilia. Clara's character is above reproach, but she is not suitable for any man who desires domestic harmony."

"I only asked to meet Lady Clara. Nor have I agreed to any marriage yet."

"Before he died, my son specifically spoke with me about this alliance. I am only executing his own intentions. He said it should be Emilia—"

"He wants to meet her, Grandmother." Exasperated, Marwood raised his arm and gestured to his sister Clara to come in.

The horse ceased pacing. The woman had seen and understood the instruction. She sat on that hill, her horse in profile, her head turned to them, gazing down. Then she pulled the reins hard. Her horse rose on its back legs so high that Adam feared she would slide out of her sidesaddle. Instead she held her seat neatly while she pivoted her horse around. She turned her back on them and galloped away.

The lady had just slapped him in the face from a distance of six hundred yards.

The dowager's expression showed smug triumph beneath its veil of dismay. "How unfortunate she did not see my grandson's signal."

"She saw it well enough."

"She is a bit willful, I will admit. I did warn you," Marwood said.

"You did not mention that she is rude and disobedient and quick to insult others if she chooses."

"I am sure she did not intend to insult you." He gave his grandmother a desperate glare.

"Sure, are you? Then please tell the grooms to bring my horse to the garden portal over there immediately. I will go and introduce myself to Lady Clara so I do not brood over her unintended cut and allow it to interfere with our families' new friendship." Adam bowed to the dowager. "Please give my regards to Lady Emilia. I am sure she and I will meet soon."

Chapter Two

Clara galloped a good two miles away from the house. What had Theo been thinking, hailing her and gesturing for her to come in? She was hardly dressed to meet his guest. From Grandmamma's stiff pose, she suspected only Theo thought it a good idea.

She pulled in her horse and walked it over to a copse of trees. Putting Theo out of her mind, she dropped off the saddle onto a tree stump, hopped down, and pulled a sheaf of paper out of her saddlebag. She found a good spot beneath a tree, sat, and turned her attention to the pages. Her friend Althea had sent this yesterday, and she needed to read through it and send back her thoughts on it.

She immersed herself in the prose, making a few marks with a pencil she had tucked in her bodice. Absorbed by her reading, she did not look up for at least a half hour. When she did she saw that she was no longer alone.

A man watched her from a hundred feet away. His white horse contrasted with his dark coat and dark hair. The latter ended past his collar and bore none of the signs of being styled by a hairdresser aware of the current London fashions.

She recognized him from the terrace. A notion nudged at her that she had perhaps seen him before that.

Theo's visitor had followed her. She thought that very bold. The way he just sat there and observed her only confirmed that he had no manners.

She considered returning to her reading, then decided that might not be wise. It was one thing to pretend you had not seen your brother's gesture for you to ride in, and another to pretend you did not see a man right in front of you.

He paced his horse closer. She could see him better now. Displeasure hardened his mouth, which emphasized its sensual full lips. Dark eyes took her measure quite thoroughly. His black coat was not fashionably cut for London, but she knew French fashions well enough to recognize it as most appropriate for Paris. He wore a casually tied dark cravat.

She thought him very handsome in a brooding, poetic way. Having known a few men of dark humor in the past, she had little interest in making another's acquaintance, no matter how handsome he might be.

He stopped his horse ten feet away. He did not dismount but towered above her. She considered standing, to bridge the distance, but decided not to. If he meant to frighten her, he would have to do better than this.

"Good day, sir." She allowed her voice to convey how unwelcome she found his intrusion.

He swung off his horse. "Please forgive me the lack of a formal introduction, but I doubt you will mind since you are a woman who does not bother with such things overmuch."

"I am sure I do not understand what you mean."

The corners of that mouth turned up enough to indicate he knew she was lying. Indeed, that half-smile implied he knew everything about her.

"You cut me back there, Lady Clara. That is what I mean."

"It is not possible to cut someone you do not know."

"You managed it all the same."

High-handed would be too kind a way to describe him. "You mentioned an introduction," she said through a tight smile.

He made a short bow. "I am Stratton."

Stratton? The Duke of Stratton? *Here?* Had Theo gone mad?

No wonder he looked vaguely familiar. She had seen him years ago, across ballrooms, before his father died and he left England. When last in London ten days ago she had heard a mention or two that he had returned, but it was beyond comprehension that Theo had allowed him on the estate.

He sidled over and assumed a casual stance right next to her, with one of his shoulders propped against the tree trunk. He folded his arms like a man who expected a lengthy chat.

She scrambled to her feet, clutching the papers close to her chest so they did not fly across the hill.

"I had no idea who you were. Even if I had tried to guess the identity of the man with my brother, your name would never have entered my head."

"Assuredly not. Our families have been enemies for decades."

"Theo is letting his new title go to his head if he received you. My grandmother must have been apoplectic."

"It was your grandmother who invited me here."

"That's not possible."

"The letter was from her, in her hand. It was most unexpected," he said in a sardonic tone.

She narrowed her eyes on him. "Yet you accepted her invitation."

"Your grandmother has been one of society's bulwarks longer than I have been alive. The patronesses of Almack's quake in her presence. I would never insult someone with such influence."

He teased her now. She doubted that he cared a fig for Grandmamma's social influence. He did not look to be a man who would set aside his family's pride and seek Grandmamma's good word on his behalf.

She should pack up Althea's article and leave. Curiosity got the better of her, however.

"Why did she invite you?"

"She proposed a dynastic marriage with your sister, to end the animosity. To bury the past." That half-smile again. "You can imagine my astonishment. It was much like your own right now."

Astonished hardly did her reaction justice. This only got odder and odder. Also increasingly annoying. She experienced a double feeling of betrayal. First on behalf of her father, who would have never approved of this idea. And second for herself, because she was not told, let alone consulted. Grandmamma must have used the full force of her will in keeping this a secret from her if even Emilia had not confided in her.

"So when will the engagement be announced?" She let her high skepticism into her sarcastic tone.

"I have not agreed to the match yet."

"My sister is both lovely and bright. She would make a splendid duchess, of course, only not for you. I am relieved you lacked decisiveness."

"Do not blame me for the delay in knowing my mind on the matter. There I was, making my decision about a lovely dove, when a black crow flew by and distracted me."

Crow? Why, the—

"Then the crow flapped her wings in my face and turned her tail to fly away." He walked over until he loomed above her. "I never stand down from a challenge, Lady Clara."

If he thought she would tremble and blush, he was wrong. Except she did tremble a bit, while she noticed that his demeanor exuded a good amount of mystery and excitement and that his dark, deep-set eyes held layers that drew her in to the point of almost drowning. His proximity and his gaze left her tongue-tied for an embarrassing moment. Perhaps she did blush a little too.

"Better if you had snatched up the dove while you could," she said. "Now I have time to remind my grandmother that you will never do."

"I will do very well for her purposes."

"What are those?"

"Don't you know?" He cocked his head a fraction. "Perhaps you don't."

It grew awkward, standing so close to him. She experienced a mix of alarm and . . . exhilaration. She stepped back and fussed with the stack of pages in her arms. "Excuse me."

She walked toward her horse. His tall, lean form soon warmed her side and his boot steps paced alongside her. "You are leaving without even a good day? You are determined to insult me, I think."

"I would be within my rights to shoot you, let alone insult you. You are trespassing on this property, no matter what else my grief-stricken grandmother may have said. You crossed the border between my brother's land and mine a quarter mile back."

"And I would be within my rights to use my crop on your pretty tail in response to your behavior."

She stopped walking and glared at him. "Such a threat

is beyond the pale. Try that and I will certainly shoot you. Do not doubt it. I am not a woman who quakes when faced with stupid masculine bravado. Any gentleman with proper breeding would have allowed the misunderstanding regarding my brother's instructions to pass. It is outrageous that you felt entitled to follow me and then berate me. Now, I will be on my way, and you can be on yours."

She strode on to her horse. He paced alongside her again. She wanted to hit him with Althea's manuscript, he annoyed her so much.

"Are you a writer?" His hand reached out and he flicked the corners of the pages. That brought his arm close to her body. An inner jolt almost had her jumping away.

"A friend wrote this. It is an essay on—" She caught herself. "I am sure it would not interest you."

"Perhaps it would."

"Then I am sure it is *none of your business*."

"Not a writer, but a bluestocking."

"Oh, how I hate that word." She stuffed the pages into the saddlebag. "You just spent years in France. They are reputed to celebrate cultural women. If you give me that moniker simply because you found me reading, apparently you did not learn much while you were there except how to be irritating."

She picked up the reins and positioned her horse.

"Allow me to assist you." He moved closer.

"Please, just go away." She quickly stepped onto the tree stump. With a jump and a pull she got herself back into the saddle.

"Admirably done, Lady Clara. I see that you are independent in all things."

She swallowed a groan at his comment. "Do you think I am so witless as to get off a horse if I had no way to get back on?"

As she turned the horse to ride away, she saw the duke's

expression. Humor softened that face somewhat, but within the mind behind those dark eyes, calculations formed.

Adam watched Lady Clara ride away.

What a provocative woman. Bright-eyed and vivacious still, but also more lovely, with a creamy complexion and strands of flame mixing with her brown hair.

Spirited. Too spirited, most men would say. He was not one of them. He liked highly spirited, self-possessed women. He preferred if they did not treat him with disdain, of course. He would excuse her. This time. The dowager's plans had taken Lady Clara unawares—as they had him—and the enmity between their families made her rudeness understandable.

He would also excuse her because he had wanted her immediately on seeing her under that tree, and more by the time they parted. Desire always encouraged generosity.

He mounted, but rode east, not back to Marwood's house to the west. There was no need to return there and to the road. If he continued this way for several miles, he should soon be on his own land.

He crossed well-tended farms and passed through one hamlet of houses. Was this still Lady Clara's property? If so, her father's legacy had been significant. No wonder Marwood spoke of it with resentment.

Only when he crested a low rise in the land did he realize just where he was. He recognized the town he approached from its mill. He could barely make out the wide stream that snaked north and south. Marwood's property met his own in places along that stream.

He trotted his horse forward, thinking about the dowager's offer, as dictated by the late earl. The earl had reasons for seeking a peace treaty. Adam thought he knew what they were. But even near death, a man's character did not change, it appeared.

The last earl had schemed to ensure he won an old contest, even while having his mother offer an olive branch in the hopes of protecting his son.

Clara tied a ribbon around Althea's essay, and tucked her page of notes on top. Althea was a fine writer. However, when she cared deeply about a cause or event, she veered from opinion into polemic. It would not take much to change this so it did not display that failing.

She set it into a low drawer in the writing table she used in the library. While she did, her brother Theo entered the chamber, saw her, and glared. Then he went to the decanters and poured himself some brandy.

"You ruined it," he said through clenched teeth. "All was well in hand, and you had to insult him to the point he forgot everything else."

She had seen neither Theo nor her grandmother upon returning, so this was the first chance her brother had to upbraid her. Not that she would allow that.

"If you had told me you would be receiving Stratton, I would have kept well away, I assure you."

"It was Grandmother's idea, but sound in its own way."

"Papa would never have approved. If there is to be a rapprochement between our families, let them take the first step."

He smirked down at his brandy, then at her. "You have not been in London much the last half year. You have not been partaking of society at all while in mourning. So you have not heard about him, have you?"

"I would not have paid attention anyway, because he has nothing to do with me. With any of us. That is how it has been since at least Grandfather's time." She had been raised with the lesson. Her father—dear Papa—had not had to speak of it much to pass on the tradition of family acrimony.

"Unfortunately, he is not like his father. Or any of the others. He is . . . dangerous."

She laughed. "He did not appear dangerous to me." Except he had. All that brooding had a lot to do with it. If she ever saw him again, she would be tempted to tickle him until he laughed like a fool, just to defeat the power of that dark mood he carried.

"He is not dangerous to *women*." Theo's voice dripped with sarcasm.

Well, now, she was not sure she agreed with that either.

"He duels, Clara. He has killed two men, and almost a third one. In France. The slightest provocations and he calls men out. He will not stand down. It is rumored he had to return to England because the French authorities told him to leave their country." Theo threw back the rest of his brandy. "He is a killer."

Theo's posture shrank while he spoke. His brow furrowed. His blue eyes took on a distant gaze toward nothing. Clara was older than Theo by three years and had watched him grow up. She could tell that her brother was afraid.

She stood and walked over to him. "He is hardly going to kill *you*, Theo. Not over some old family argument begun before either of you were born."

"What better way to win that argument? One wrong word, one bad look, and he will have his excuse."

"You are being too dramatic."

"Grandmother agrees. Mock my judgment if you want, but will you so quickly mock hers?"

Stratton's explanation of his visit made sense now, but

in a most ridiculous way. Grandmamma's grief had taken an unfortunate turn if she saw such a threat in the duke. As for Theo . . . He was brave when there was little danger, but less so when threats flew.

"I assume the thinking was if you are his brother-in-law, he would never want to duel with you," she said. "That is a high price to pay for peace, brother. And what of Emilia? If he has such a temper, is it fair to tie her to him?"

"I said he is not dangerous to women, didn't I?"

"You do not know that for certain. If we do not even sit at a table with that family, we should not arrange matches with them."

"Grandmother—"

"You are the earl now. You must think for yourself."

"What ridiculous advice, Clara. He is barely out of school." Grandmamma entered the library as she spoke. "I'll not have you further complicating the matter by urging Theo to an unseemly independence from my advice."

"I am twenty-one," Theo muttered, flushing.

"Are you? Well, a year more or less hardly signifies."

"I am not complicating anything," Clara said.

Her grandmother sat down. Back straight and head angled just so, she assumed the pose of the queen of all she surveyed. At the moment that included Clara.

"Your behavior today meant the duke left before I— we—could settle things. If that is not a complication, what is it?"

"A reprieve. For Emilia. For all of us, while you reconsider this extraordinary notion of marrying her to that man."

"He seemed suitable enough to me. Too French, but what can you expect with that mother of his, and the way he stayed abroad all this time. Still, a few weeks and he will step into his correct role in life and do what he must to reclaim his place among us. He knows that he needs to wed a girl with your sister's impeccable breeding, and we will benefit by having him close, where we can keep an eye on him so the past cannot harm Theo."

"You cannot also think he is dangerous to my brother. Has everyone here lost all sense?"

"As always, you assume you know all of it because of how my son favored you. However, there is much you do not understand. I do not take this step lightly. I will not have anything happen to Theo, especially with his heir presumptive being that insufferable cousin. Leave this to me, Clara. Emilia will marry Stratton, and all will be well."

Lest Clara not appreciate how the last word had been given, her grandmother lifted a book, opened it, set her spectacles on her nose, and began reading.

Clara looked at Theo, hoping to find an ally for her objections.

He turned away to pour himself another brandy.

Chapter Three

Adam handed his hat and crop to the servant at the door of White's. He strode through the club's salon.

Glances shot his way. Heads bowed to each other. Enough silence fell that he heard the low buzz of whispers.

He proceeded on, nodding acknowledgments to men who could not resist looking more directly. A few returned smiles far too hearty for casual acquaintances.

He exited the salon through a door at its end and sought the back stairs to the second level.

"Sir, I am afraid that all of the chambers are in use." The servant's gentle rebuke caught him halfway up the stairs.

He turned. The servant saw his face and flushed. "My apologies, Your Grace. I did not realize it was you. Welcome back, sir."

"They are above, I assume."

The servant nodded. Adam climbed to the landing.

Sounds came from behind one of the doors. Male voices, and laughter. He pressed the latch and walked in.

Two men stared at him, struck mute with surprise.

"Hell," one of them finally muttered. "Brentworth here speculated that you might show up today, but I told him you would never come."

"Then he was right, Langford, and you were wrong." Adam threw himself into a chair and looked around. "It appears not much has changed."

"Very little." Gabriel St. James, Duke of Langford, threw him a cigar. He grinned with delight and his blue eyes sparkled. "Damn, but it is good to see you. Word was you came back a month ago. Where have you been?"

"Getting my affairs in order. Examining the estate books." He reached for a candle and held it to his cigar. "Sacking the steward who was robbing me. That sort of thing."

He had been doing a few other things too. One had been investigating a woman named Clara Cheswick. He had learned some things about her that only piqued his interest all the more.

"In the country, then. No wonder the only indication of your return has been the gossip and rumors." Eric Marshall, Duke of Brentworth, got up to get the whiskey decanter. He came over with a glass, poured Adam some, then topped off his own glass and that of Langford. No grin from him, but only a subdued smile on his severely chiseled face. No sparkle in his dark eyes, either, but rather deep scrutiny.

Both men were the epitome of fashion, but in ways as different as their demeanors. The amiable Langford's cropped curls always looked as if he had just been in a wind, while the more serious Brentworth's locks never dared such exuberance. Langford wore a casually tied dark cravat this evening, while Brentworth's white linen neckpiece appeared as if his valet had starched it five minutes ago.

It was not that Brentworth lacked spirit or was a slave to convention compared to Langford. Rather he prized discretion and did not flout either his appetites or thinking. The same could not be said for Langford.

Adam appreciated how his two friends performed the old rituals and took his return in stride. He had not missed that the chair he sat in—his usual chair—had not been in use by either of them, despite its proximity to the comforting low fire. He sipped some whiskey and puffed on the cigar and allowed nostalgia and familiarity to seep through him. He had been back in England for over a month, but right now he finally felt he had come home.

"What kind of rumors and gossip?" he asked, allowing the last comment to penetrate his peace.

His friends exchanged hooded glances. "While you were gone, your reputation visited England, even if you did not," Brentworth said.

"You mean the duels."

"One is understandable for any gentleman. Two might be excused. Three, however . . ." Langford said.

"No man in the salon below would have allowed any of those insults to his family to stand unchallenged. I did what anyone would do."

"Of course, of course," Langford soothed. "The question, however, is whether you have now returned to do it here as well. There are some fellows who are remembering every small slight they may have given you, and any whispered criticism of you or your family. I am sure that within a few weeks, once you are back in society and spreading your charm, that will all be forgotten."

"It may be better if it is not."

That took Langford aback. "You cannot want to be thought of as dangerous. No one will treat you honestly."

"If being seen as dangerous keeps stupid men from saying stupid things that force my hand in the name of honor, then let them think me dangerous." He set down his glass by way of ending that line of talk. "I am glad I found you both here."

"Where else would we be on the first Thursday evening of the month?" Brentworth said. "As it was in the beginning, so it still is. You may have abandoned us, but we are still the Decadent Dukes Society."

Adam smiled. The three of them had been youths at school when they gave themselves that name. All heirs to dukedoms, they had formed a bond at once. The school set them apart, and the other boys did too. They had all learned fast that the only person who would treat a duke normally was another duke. Thus a long and fast friendship had formed.

This chamber, and its monthly meetings, began once they all left university and came to town to enjoy their privileges. For a long while the Decadent Dukes Society had been more than a clever title made up by schoolboys. Many times they met here but soon left to go and explore just how decadent they could be.

Langford had found his second calling in those debauches. A way of life. Decent families only received him now because he was a duke, although his considerable charm might have bought him a few reprieves in any case.

Brentworth, on the other hand, had outgrown such excess first, at least regarding behavior others might see or report. It was one more example of how he managed without effort to be the public's notion of a duke, in appearance and demeanor. Superior, arrogant, and confident in his privileges, he towered over the world in both stature and aloofness. Adam did not mind just how ducal this one friend had become. He knew Brentworth well enough to comprehend how different the man truly was from his public persona.

"So why did you return?" Brentworth asked. "After so many years, I assumed you never would."

"I would like to say that I merely concluded it was time, but it was not that simple. The French government also decided it was time. Complaints were made, and as a result the king also decided it was time. I received a summons to court."

Langford laughed. "How old-fashioned. Almost charming."

"Since it was in the king's own hand, and things were getting a little warm in France—well, here I am."

"Have you attended on him yet?" Langford asked.

"As soon as I arrived. We drank a good deal of wine together. He asked about the ladies in Paris. I might have been gone on a grand tour, it remained so friendly and chatty."

"So your English half responded to the command of your English king," Brentworth said. "If not for that—was it in fact time?"

"Yes." And it had been. The fury that drove him away had finally eased over a year ago, replaced by more deliberate thoughts, and acknowledgment of his obligations. There were duties that could not be forever conducted long distance from France. One in particular.

"It is good that you finally came up to town," Langford said. "We will go and have some new coats made for you tomorrow. A trip to a hairdresser might be in order too. You can't go around looking like one of those French counts who seduce widows to their eternal regret."

"A few were not so regretful, as I recall." Adam gazed down at his frock coat. Cut in the French manner, a bit longer and tighter than English fashions, it probably did make him look foreign.

"We will get drunk and you can tell me about them and make me envious," Langford said.

"Unless something has indeed changed, there is little I can tell you about widows."

"So, what are your plans?" Brentworth asked.

"I expect that my plans are much like yours now. Tend my estate. Vote in Parliament. As I said, the usual sort of things."

"That is all?" Brentworth asked. "You leave England and stay away almost five years, and upon your return all you want is to be a country gentleman who comes to town for the sessions?"

"I intend to find a rich and lusty wife too. It is also time to marry."

"Speak for yourself," Langford said.

"Ignore him," Brentworth said. "There are two mammas who have Langford squarely in their sights, and he is running out of places to hide. Unfortunately, it is doubtful either girl is lusty enough, or I am sure he would gladly hand one over to you."

"If there are two, he should send one in your direction," Adam said. Oddly enough, mothers almost never targeted Brentworth. Rumor had it that he terrified ingénues so much that their mothers looked elsewhere. "As for the lusty enough part, have you found out yet, Langford?"

Langford laughed. "Perhaps in France all kinds of explorations are made on the subject when it comes to girls, but lest you forget, here in England we just hope for the best and almost never get it."

Being half French, Adam found the strangled sensuality that had plagued the English these last few decades both odd and curious. It was as if mothers and grandmothers had all convened a conference early in the war and decided that, in the name of rejecting all things French, their daughters should not have as much fun as they had enjoyed in their own youth.

A stillness fell in the chamber. He looked up to see Brentworth eyeing him, and not kindly.

"Say it," Adam demanded.

"Hell, yes, I'll say it—"

"Leave it alone, Brentworth," Langford urged.

"No, I insist," Adam said.

Brentworth stood and went to the whiskey decanter again. He took long enough there that Adam thought perhaps the rancor had passed, or been swallowed for now.

Brentworth abruptly turned on him. "I understand that you were grieving. I understand that there were things being said that were—scurrilous and damaging and—"

Adam bolted to his feet and hurled his glass into the fire. Flames jumped. "Scurrilous and damaging? *He killed himself* because of it!"

"*I know that*. But you never spoke to us. You never allowed us to help. You just disappeared with your mother without a word, and there has been no word since, and you walk in here as if the last years never happened. Hell, Stratton, we have all been friends for years and you acted as if the two of us were lined up against your family."

"I never thought that."

"The hell you didn't."

Langford shook his head. "Sit down, both of you. I have told you before, Brentworth, that under the circumstances, whatever he did was a choice made in anger and grief. Who knows how you or I would have acted?" He offered Adam a smile of—what? Forgiveness? "You do not have to explain anything to us."

Except he did. Brentworth was right. He had turned his back on everyone and everything in his anger. He could not leave England fast enough. Not because of the implied disgrace behind his father's death, and not because he could not trust anyone.

"I left as I did because if I had not, I would have surely killed someone out of rage, without even knowing whether I blamed the right person."

Brentworth sank back into his chair. Neither friend's gaze met his for a long time.

"And do you know now? If you blamed the right person?" Brentworth asked.

"Not yet."

Langford tapped the ash off his cigar. "An interesting answer. I guess now we know why he has really come back, don't we, Brentworth?"

Clara quickly read her morning mail while eating breakfast in Gifford House, the family's London home. Two letters in particular received very brief attention.

Her grandmother had written a scold. *I am told that you have refused to receive Stratton twice since you went up to London ten days ago. I must insist that you cease such provocations.*

Theo's letter said much the same thing. *We are unlikely to make progress with Stratton if you continue insulting him. Think of Emilia's future. Think of mine. Surely you can find a modicum of gentility where he is concerned.*

She *was* thinking of Emilia's future. And the family's. This whole idea of bridging the divide between her family's and Stratton's struck her as ill-advised and disloyal. Let them try it if they wanted to, but she was not going to cooperate. Grandmamma knew that. It was why no one had told her about this plan before embarking on it.

Donning her pelisse and her bonnet, she lifted a wrapped

package and descended to the reception hall. Eschewing the family carriages, she told a footman to get her a hackney.

She took some air on the portico while she waited. Unfortunately, while she did, a carriage pulled into the drive. She cursed under her breath.

Stratton again. And here she was in plain view. She could hardly have the butler tell him she was not at home.

On the other hand, it should be obvious she was leaving. A few polite words and he would be on his way.

The duke stepped out of his carriage and approached her. After a greeting, he stopped with one foot on the lowest step of the portico and eyed her.

"You go out a great deal."

"I may be in mourning, but I am not dead."

He gestured to his carriage. "Allow me to take you to your destination."

"Very kind of you, but my carriage is on its way."

"It may be some time before it arrives."

Indeed it might. With an inward groan of resignation, she turned to the house. "Since you have called on me, let us go inside and have a proper visit while I wait."

She led the way into the house and deposited her package in a footman's hands. Up the stairs she led the duke, and into the drawing room.

She perched herself on a chair and hoped she appeared at least half as formidable as her grandmother.

The duke took a seat in the chair closest to hers and settled in comfortably. His hair had been styled since she last saw him on that hill. His now disheveled cropped locks brought more attention to his liquid dark eyes and to that sensual mouth and hard jaw.

"It is kind of you to receive me, Lady Clara."

"Since you saw fit to report to my family that I did not receive you previously, I now feel obligated to pretend I am amenable to this inexplicable desire of theirs to form a friendship with you."

"You are a very direct woman."

"You are a most persistent man."

"Persistence in man is a virtue, while directness in a woman—"

"Is a nuisance. Which begs the question of why you have bothered being so persistent with this nuisance of a woman."

"That is an excellent question. If you had seen me on my first call, by now you would have a full understanding of my intentions."

What an odd way to put it. Whatever his *intentions* were.

"Perhaps you will enlighten me now, and quickly, so I can resume my own plans—plans which you have interrupted."

He laughed quietly, as if at a private joke. "Your brother called you shrewish. I can see why."

Shrewish? Why, that spoiled, disloyal boy. "I prefer being called direct. As a gentleman, I am sure you prefer that word too."

"Of course. Allow me to be direct in turn, so you can be about your day's business." He leaned forward and set his arms on his knees. It brought his fine face quite close to her. "You know your grandmother's plan to have me marry Lady Emilia."

"I do."

"I have decided to decline the offer."

It was all she could do not to cheer with relief. Thank heavens someone in this sorry business was using some sense.

"I have decided that you will suit me, and the dowager's plan, much better."

A stillness rang in the chamber. It took a good long moment for her mind to absorb what he had said. Even then it sounded too bizarre to be accurate.

"Your sister is too young for me, and whatever settlement is offered with her, it will never be as good as a wife with her own property and income."

Good heavens.

She gathered her wits, but it took some serious groping through her stunned reaction. "Have you even met Emilia?"

"No, but it does not signify. I am quite sure that while she is lovely, she is not the bride for me."

"How can you say that when you have not even—"

"I know."

"You had better know differently, and quickly, because I am not available instead."

He sat back in his chair, not the least impressed by her definitive rejection. "It is understandable that you are surprised by my proposal. I am confident that you will come around, however."

Too agitated to sit, she stood and glared at the presumptuous idiot. Regrettably that brought him up too. Instead of what had been a satisfactory staring down, she now had to look far up at a face that hovered over her own.

"I heard no proposal. I heard an edict. I cannot imagine what gives you cause to think I would obey it. You are the last man I would marry, should I marry at all. Indeed, my father would turn over in his grave if I even considered the idea. Now, sir, I thank you for your call, but I must be about my day's business. Already I will be late."

She pivoted and strode out of the drawing room and down the stairs. She retrieved her package from the footman and headed outside. She sensed the duke on her heels the entire way.

Her hackney coach waited behind the duke's carriage.

He gazed hard at that hackney. "Why are you not using the family's equipage?"

"I chose not to." She descended the stone steps and aimed for her coach.

He walked alongside her. "You are going to a secret assignation, I assume. One that you prefer the family servants not know about. There is no other explanation for using a hackney instead of a family carriage."

She truly wanted to hit him with her package for saying that within hearing of the footman waiting to hand her into the coach.

She settled herself on the seat while the footman closed the door. The duke rested his forearm on the window's edge and waited while the servant walked away.

"I will not demand an explanation now," he said. "However, if you are going to meet a man, that liaison must end immediately, now that we are engaged."

She stuck her face to the window. "We. Are. *Not. Engaged*." She was almost yelling by the end of it, but the coach had rolled away by then, and only the air heard her.

A half hour later Clara stood at a library's desk in a house on Bedford Square. Spread out on the desk were stacks of papers and one blank sheet.

"I think we have enough for another issue of *Parnassus*, Althea," she said. "We can talk to the pressmen this afternoon about the schedule."

Althea bent her blond head over the stacks. She fingered one very small one. It consisted of the poems that their journal would publish. "You have included Mrs. Clark's sonnet, I see. I am glad."

Clara served as the anonymous publisher and benefactor of *Parnassus*. She had conceived the journal two years ago and begun building toward it at once. The first two issues had been fledgling efforts, but they garnered enough subscriptions to encourage her. Now, with her legacy, she could afford to attempt a regular schedule of publication.

Modeled on men's journals, *Parnassus* contained political news as well as reviews of theater performances and travel memoirs. She liked to fill it with information and facts but allowed a few sharp thinkers like Althea to write essays. Feminine interests were hardly ignored. Clara loved fashion herself, and *Parnassus* included a column devoted to it.

The journal's most distinctive feature was the mixture of writers. A viscountess and a baroness sometimes contributed, although the former used a pen name. However, Mrs. Clark was the widow of a merchant who now ran a millinery shop. Mrs. Clark had a gift for poetry that rang clear and honest and made no attempt to copy any other poet on earth.

Ladies of the ton, women of the City, mothers, sisters, and, yes, even bluestockings had subscribed. The secrecy of the project might have contributed to its success, she knew. The who and the where of *Parnassus* remained a tantalizing mystery.

Right now the where consisted of this house Clara had bought with her legacy, three months after her father's death. Memories of him had filled her when she signed the deeds, along with profound gratitude that he had arranged for her to have her own property and substantial income and not be beholden to Theo in any way. Theirs had been a rare bond. In truth, he had treated her like a son. He had taught her to ride and shoot and even said once that he regretted she could not inherit his estate and title. Theo would never forgive her for how she received the best of their father's love, she supposed.

She had mourned him deeply. Totally. The grief had undone her as nothing else ever had. She drowned in it to where she did not recognize herself. Finally, one day, she began to fight her way to the surface.

Parnassus had been her lifeline. Purchasing this house was her first clear step forward in her life. The journal's needs forced her to visit London periodically too. Until now those visits had been brief but now, at six months after his passing, she finally had resumed lengthier ones.

"The fashion article has not yet come in from Lady Grace," Althea mentioned.

Lady Grace Bidwell was the most recent addition to the contributors. The sister of an earl, she had never married. Clara felt a natural affinity for her, and Lady Grace had a clear eye when it came to fashion.

"I will write her a reminder, but not wait forever." Clara spoke with decisive firmness of the sort she had not long ago used on the Duke of Stratton, to little avail. That encounter kept invading her mind, and it soured her humor whenever it did. The more she thought about that proposal, the more outraged she became.

Althea turned her pretty blue eyes on Clara. A head shorter than Clara, and delicately boned, Althea had a presence that sometimes made Clara feel monstrous in comparison. Not that she was very tall herself, or stout. It was just that Althea was so exquisitely small. The widow of Captain Galbreath, an army officer, Althea lived with her brother, Sir Jonathan Polwarth, a baronet, and his wife. Althea had the life of a dependent relative now, the sort Clara's father had saved her from with that legacy.

"You are out of temper today," Althea said. "Is your brother annoying you again? Insisting you come back down to the country?"

"It is not that. Not entirely." Clara was not given to confidences, but she did want to share some of the recent, strange occurrences in her life. Not the proposal. No one would ever learn about that. "Both Theo and my grandmother have gotten the idea in their heads to end a long feud our family has had with that of the Duke of Stratton."

"I would think that is a good thing. Such long wars have little benefit."

"Grandmother never does things simply because they are good things, Althea. She has a mind like a poacher's trap, and her strategies would have put Napoleon to shame. She is determined, however, and Theo is as well. They even received him. My father always swore that Stratton would never darken his doorstep, but there he was."

Althea began stacking the articles, sliding clean sheets between each one as she did. "On your doorstep here in town, at Gifford House? I have heard he came up recently."

"Did you now?" It seemed a good way to avoid admitting he had indeed darkened her family's doorway here in town.

"There has been some talk about him. You would not have heard it because you were sequestered at Hickory Grange for so long after your father passed, and were not here when he returned from France."

Althea carried the big stack of papers over to another table and proceeded to wrap the whole thing in linen. Clara strolled in her wake.

"What sort of talk?"

Althea tied string around the thick package, finishing with a rustic bow. "Vague talk. The kind where you hear bits of things when you come upon people, but they stop talking once you are seen. Serious talk, from the looks of the dour faces. Whispered, secret talk. Mostly among those of our parents' generation."

"Surely those bits must have given you some idea of why he has garnered that kind of attention."

Althea shrugged. "I believe I heard my brother refer to him as dangerous. Something about duels in France."

"I heard about the duels. Theo told me. I think he fears if he does not sue for peace, Stratton will challenge him. What nonsense."

"I also interfered with some talk about him in a drawing room after a small dinner party. The hostess could not contain herself despite ending mid-sentence. She mouthed a final word of whatever she had been saying to her confidante."

"What word was that?"

"I am quite sure it was the word *revenge*. Now, if we are going to speak with the pressmen today, we should be on our way before it gets too late."

They donned their pelisses and bonnets. Clara envied Althea her celadon green and lemon yellow ensemble. She did not resent wearing mourning clothes. She would wear them forever if that would honor her father. She did miss ensembles with more color and style, however, and sometimes plotted incredible excesses at the shops once she could dress fashionably again.

With the manuscripts firmly tucked in her arms, Clara joined Althea while they walked to a hackney stand around the corner from the square. Her nose all but itched from the tantalizing information Althea had just fed her. Stratton might be high-handed, annoying, and arrogant, but he had just become interesting too, especially to the publisher of a journal.

Revenge? About what? It seemed a few in London knew, but it was not gossip for general consumption.

Once in the hackney and on their way to the printer's, Clara spoke her thoughts. "I find all of this provocative, Althea. If Stratton is bent on revenge, one wonders why and against whom. He is no ordinary man, after all. He is a duke. Who could have wronged a duke so badly that he seeks revenge? And to be considered dangerous . . . There is something very curious about all of this."

"I suppose I could ask a few questions, to see if I can gather more than bits."

"I will as well. Let us see what we can learn about this man. There may be a story for *Parnassus* in it."

She neglected to mention that more information might enable her to end Stratton's inexplicable and discourteous courtship too.

Chapter Four

Dust covered him. It rose from the pages when he turned them and settled on his coats like iron shavings on a magnet.

Adam forged on, reading the old newspapers, more interested in what was not reported than what was. An allusion here, an offhanded reference there, a name mentioned in passing—such were the pieces of evidence he sought, because he already knew there would be no outright discussion of the events he investigated.

He had come to the *Times* last, after turning other pages at the offices of other papers and journals. They all kept examples of their old publications somewhere. It might be in an airy library or a damp cellar, but with time and patience he had read every word published about the Duke of Stratton in the few years up to and through his father's death.

The death notices were the most useless, although a few in less respectable journals vaguely implied it might have been a suicide. The *Times* would never tread in that direction on a duke, so its notice extolled his father's accomplishments and taste. Reading it, one would never guess at the extreme provocations that had made a man take his own life.

Clues regarding the details and sources of those provocations were what he now sought. It had all been a very secretive business, so the bits he uncovered were all between the lines. No publisher would ever openly air those rumors. No man would speak about it except behind closed doors in the lowest voice.

And yet, words had been spoken, and they took to the air like pollen, so while no one made accusations, all had been known by the people in government who mattered.

He closed the tome of bound copies of the *Times*. He had hardly found the direct evidence he wanted, but he also found nothing to convince him he was wrong in his beliefs about how the tragedy had played out.

At the highest reaches of the government, questions had been raised about his father's loyalty. Things had been said to him by ministers and other lords. Someone had been collecting evidence. It went on a while, growing, perhaps a year or so. Isolated and friendless as the hounds closed in, he had taken his life so he might not face the kind of disgrace that stained a family's name for generations.

The final act and its reason were the only parts not under question, however.

I think Marwood is behind it all. That was what his father had written on the only note he left. Did he have proof of that? If so, he did not leave anything to indicate it. Was it an irrational conclusion, born of his state of mind and the long enmity between the families? Adam did not know. If his father thought Marwood was behind it all, however, then Marwood was at the top of Adam's list of men to investigate.

He left the *Times* building and made his way to his carriage. Deep in thought, he almost did not notice the woman across the street until something familiar about her pulled him out of his reverie.

She walked with a determined stride, as if on an important mission. He noticed the brilliance of her eyes, which implied so much about her. Intelligence. Spirit. Passion. Trouble. He did not mind the last quality. One rarely found the first three in a woman without the fourth. His time with her thus far had been brief, but none of it had been dull.

Although her reddish chestnut hair, visible as a frame to her face beneath the brim of her bonnet, looked stunning against the black of her ensemble, he suddenly wondered what she would look like wearing soft, pale green.

He pictured her thus while he crossed the street and approached her. As soon as she saw him, her expression fell. He wanted to laugh at the way she struggled to maintain a composure fitting for an earl's daughter. He imagined the impolite thoughts jumping into her mind.

"Lady Clara. What an unexpected delight to see you today."

"Yes. Delightful." She angled her head to the left, eyeing the path to freedom. "It is a day of errands for me."

"For me as well, although I am well done. What errand brings you here?"

She did not reply at once. He had asked an awkward question, it appeared.

"I am not on an errand here. I am simply walking down this street after attending to an errand elsewhere." She stepped to his side and scrutinized him with a frown. "Were you in an attic? You are covered in dust." Her hand went out and she brushed at his sleeve, producing a small cloud of dust.

He thought her gesture charming. "My valet will groan when he sees it."

"Hold still." Again her hand swept his coat. More clouds rose. She brushed him off like he was a child who had fallen in the dirt. Not that gently, however. Her hand slapped at his shoulders and chest.

"There. You are almost presentable. Now, I must be on my way."

"Will you be so ungenerous with your company? I have not seen you in almost two weeks. It was my fault, I know. I have not called on you. Due to all those errands, you see."

"Has it been that long? I had not noticed. In fact, I did not expect you to call at all. There was no reason to."

"We both know that is not true. However, here we are now. At least allow me to accompany you safely back to your carriage."

"That will not be necessary. I will be quite safe on my own."

"Please. I insist."

She stood silently, looking much like a little girl caught doing something naughty.

"Do you have your carriage here?" he asked.

"No." The answer came after a long pause. She bit her lower lip.

"A hackney again?" He glanced up and down the street. "Does he live near here? Your friend, I mean."

"There is no friend. Not the way you insinuate."

"Of course not."

"I am serious."

"Please understand that I am not shocked. I am half French, after all. I do not mind. I merely request that you end it." He lied smoothly. He did mind. Any man would once he set his sights on a woman.

"A request, is it?"

"I am being polite. A request for now. Eventually, of course, it will have to be a command."

Her eyes blazed. Hell, she was exciting when she was angry. Just as well, since he expected she would be angry often.

"You are deliberately provoking me, I think," she said.

"I promise to stop if you agree to a short visit to the park. We will keep the landau open so you will not worry about me imposing. Then I will bring you home."

"And if I refuse your offer?"

"I will probably follow you around, asking indiscreet questions about your mysterious doings in this area of town."

She heaved a sigh of exasperation. She removed a pocket watch from her reticule. "There will be hardly anyone at Hyde Park at this hour. Let's take a turn there, if we must. A very short visit, please. I have an appointment this afternoon."

"More mysterious doings? How intriguing you are." He offered his arm. She did not take it. Together they walked to his carriage.

The Duke of Stratton was becoming a serious inconvenience. Part of the joy of being an older woman known to be uninterested in marriage was that people tended not to notice what she did. Clara had enjoyed that freedom even before her father's death and now did so even more because she occupied Gifford House alone.

Stratton's curiosity about her complicated that. Now here she was, sitting in his carriage when she should have been visiting the decorator she had hired to make some changes at her house on Bedford Square. Since no one knew about the house, she could hardly have the duke trailing her there.

She did not care for how he maneuvered her into spending this time with him. She resented that he had won a little contest.

"Do you prefer town? You spend a good deal of time here," he said once they were seated across from each other and the coachman had opened the carriage to the air.

From anyone else she would think it small talk. From this man, she heard an intrusive question. "I like both town and the country. I spend time in both places. However, after all the months at Hickory Grange after my father's funeral, it was time to see some friends here and dip one foot into society again." Even as she said it, she worried that she gave him too much information.

"Your bluestocking friends?"

"Yes."

"What do you do when you are not talking letters with them?"

"If I told you, I would no longer be intriguing and mysterious."

It was a mistake to say that. She knew it as soon as she said it. His dark eyes settled on her, amused and too confident that he saw more than she wanted. That gaze unsettled her. She found it stark, almost naked, in its demand for her attention. It implied intimacies of the spirit that she did not want to have or acknowledge.

She hurried to brush her own provocation aside. "You will find my interests very boring and feminine. I visit drapers and feast my eyes on the fabrics I cannot wear now. I stroll through warehouses and covet silk cords and laces."

"Why not buy them now and store them until you can use them?"

"Because the anticipation is part of the fun. There is the danger it will build to a fever, however, and when I finally remove these black ensembles, I will be so reckless in my spending on a new wardrobe that Theo will have to bail me out of debt."

"Oh, I doubt that."

She knew then that this man had learned about the size of her inheritance. Had Theo told him? Perhaps he had only heard gossip, but that would be enough.

It entered her mind that his only reason to pursue her with that stupid proposal was her fortune. As if the Duke of Stratton needed that! Although, really, who knew if he did or did not? She had not investigated him the way he had obviously investigated her, although she intended to.

Still, a man after her fortune. How predictable. How commonplace. How disappointing.

Once they were in the park she asked her own questions, while she encouraged their stroll to leave the main path so they might not be seen together.

"Would you truly not mind if the woman you proposed to had a lover before you? You keep implying as much." She thought it a sophisticated and arch query and waited for him to avoid the meal once she set it squarely on a plate in front of him.

"You are what, twenty-four years in age? Only a fool would require innocence of a woman of that maturity."

"What a liberal outlook you have."

"I like to think so. I am only being a bit strict with you because I cannot risk my heir being the son of another man. I am sure you understand."

She looked over at him, hoping to see that little smile or anything that indicated his continued references to his proposal were now a private joke. Regrettably, he appeared most serious. She decided that objecting would only dignify the ridiculous notion, so she ignored it.

Since he had coerced her into spending this time with him, he could not object to some frank questions about his life and his family, especially if he really believed they would marry. Althea was charged with investigating this man, but every bit added to the pile would help.

"Why did you leave?" she asked while they strolled through a little copse of budding trees.

"It was time to come back."

"I did not mean why did you leave France. Why did you leave England?"

His mood altered in a snap, as if the question opened a door to the dark humor she sensed in him. "My mother did not want to remain here after my father's death, so I took her away and ensured she was settled in Paris."

"She wanted to go home, you mean. That is understandable."

"She had lived here for decades. This should have been her home, not a foreign land to escape. There were those who never welcomed her, however, or allowed her to make her place here."

"If she is happy in France now, that is what matters, isn't it?"

"I did not say she was happy. She did not want to return to France. She just did not want to remain *here*."

His sharp tone made her stop walking. "I am sorry if I misunderstood. I was careless in my response. Of course she could not be happy to leave her home of so many years." She swallowed the question that begged to be asked. *Why did she not want to remain here?*

They stood under one of the trees, in the tangle of linear shadows its branches made.

"Do you really know so little about my life?" he asked. "Did you never hear the talk about my mother? You were out before she left. Before my father died."

She did not have to search her memory long to remember some of the talk she had heard. Her grandmother's voice always dripped with disdain when she mentioned Stratton's *French* duchess. Grandmother was one of the people who suspected the worst of everything and everyone French during the war.

Others had sniffed when the Duchess of Stratton walked by at a ball, however. Clara had always assumed they envied her beauty and sought bad gossip out of spite. In truth she had not much cared what people said, however. The old war between her family and Stratton's had left her unsympathetic to whatever slights were visited on his mother.

"I will admit, now that you speak of it, that I do know something of what she endured," she admitted. "If that drove her away, it was not fair."

To her surprise he took her hand and raised it to a kiss. "That alone did not do it. However, it is good of you to see how unfair it was."

That kiss on her hand, brief though it was, created a bridge of intimacy. She felt that kiss all the way up her arm and down her body. His gaze captured hers before he kissed her hand yet again, slowly.

She did not pull her hand away. She did not avert her eyes, as she most definitely should. Instead she stared while that kiss and those dark eyes enlivened her whole body.

He drew her closer, closer, until she either had to step toward him or fall. She did a bit of both, stumbling awkwardly, and found herself in his arms.

He was going to kiss her. She was sure of it. That must not happen. Instead of pushing away, however, she could not move. His gaze paralyzed her and incited an unseemly excitement.

His arms embraced her. He looked down. Dazed, she closed her eyes and waited.

And waited.

And waited.

When nothing happened, she opened her eyes. Instantly the euphoria lifted, and she felt a fool. She tried to extricate herself from his embrace, but he did not allow it.

"Do you want me to kiss you?" he asked.

"Of course not. You are the last man I want kissing me, I assure you." She refused to look at him and continued trying to pull away.

"That is not true. Let us be honest with each other in this if nothing else." His head dipped and his lips hovered over hers.

Her breath caught. Heavens, but he was beautiful. And exciting. Even that darkness seduced. Thrills kept spiraling through her, begging to have excuses to become something more powerful.

"Part of the fun is the anticipation," he said quietly, imprisoning her with his gaze. "Although there is always the danger of it building to a fever." His lips brushed hers, ever so faintly, but enough to create a starburst of sensation.

It was a terrible tease. A provocative promise.

He released her and stepped back. She stood there speechless, and utterly defeated, shocked at how he had used her own words against her to imply they shared some sympathy on sensual matters.

"I must go." She turned on her heel and marched toward the main path. With each step, her indignation grew.

He walked alongside her, too contented by far.

"I can't believe you imposed on me like that," she said in her best *how-dare-you* tone.

"I imposed very little, especially given the circumstances. Indeed, had I made love to you up against one of the trees, I am not sure it would have been an imposition."

"If you think so, you have been in France too long."

She could not get to the carriage soon enough. She refused to look at him all the way to Gifford House. Once there, she barely suffered his insistence on handing her down. She steeled herself against the feel of his hand on hers, and the closeness of his body, and the way her whole being still wanted to react inappropriately.

She could not resist one last scold. Not only to remind him of proper behavior, but herself too. "Please remember in the future how a gentleman treats a lady, sir."

"I know how to treat a lady. You, however, are also my future bride. That changes everything."

She hurried to her door full of furious indignation. Once inside, she learned that this discomforting day would only get worse.

Theo, Emilia, and the dowager had come up from the country to join her.

Chapter Five

"Why are you so glum? You have not smiled since you entered the house." Clara posed the question to her sister after seeking her out in her bedchamber that night.

Dinner had proven a trial, with her grandmother issuing edicts regarding the days ahead, and Emilia and Theo nodding like schoolchildren. The dowager dismissed out of hand Clara's own objections to the demands the plans made on her time.

Emilia threw herself on her bed. "Grandmother wants me to meet Stratton. Since he is here in town, we followed him."

"You have not yet been introduced?"

"Theo keeps inviting him to visit, only to be put off." She pouted. "It is embarrassing to be thrown at him like this when it appears he would prefer to avoid me. Since I would like to avoid him too, I wish they would stop this pursuit of him. I realize he is a duke, but I found him rather frightening in appearance when he was on that terrace. Nor do I think it is fair that I am being offered to him like this before I ever have a Season."

Clara sat next to her and embraced her with one arm. "That does seem unfair." Emilia was lovely, and if given that Season, would have dozens of admirers hoping to win her hand. Clara had fond memories of her own first Season. She had not been looking for a husband, but she had loved all the planning and then all the social activities and balls. She had enjoyed the few stolen kisses that came her way too.

"Now I am here in town and have to sit everything out while all my friends go to balls," Emilia complained. "It is one thing to remain in mourning down in the country and miss out. It is another to all but hear all the fun through the windows while I sit in this house, wearing black."

"Perhaps we can convince Grandmother to allow you to attend a few smaller events. A garden party or two. And you can receive friends here. If you are allowed to meet with Stratton, why not other young men?"

Emilia's eyes lit with hope. "Do you think she will agree? Perhaps she will allow me to have a new dress or two made, not that I want more black dresses, but at least I will be going out to the shops then."

"I will try to convince her to permit something other than black for you at least. It has been past six months now. Other colors, simple and subdued to be sure, can be permitted for a girl, it seems to me."

Emilia threw her arms around Clara and kissed her cheek. "If you can obtain even that small reprieve, I will be so grateful."

"You write to your friends and let them know you are here and can both pay calls and receive. As for Stratton— you are not obligated to marry anyone if you do not want to. I hope you know that."

The joy left Emilia as quickly as it had emerged. "I have never been good at defying Grandmother. She frightens me even more than the duke does."

Of course she did. The dowager intimidated grown men. If not for Stratton's resistance, Emilia would be affianced already.

"Perhaps Stratton will never visit us here either," Emilia said wistfully.

Clara doubted that. Grandmother would not be put off now, no matter what stratagems the duke attempted. Unless he flatly refused to continue this peacemaking dance.

It would be best for all of them if he decided to do that.

"Are you going to tell me where we are going?" Langford asked the question while he and Adam walked their horses along Bond Street. "When you urged me to join you, I assumed you would explain why and where by now."

Adam had crossed Langford's path three blocks before. That had been no accident. Nor had been his neglect to mention their destination.

"I promised it would be diverting, and it will be."

"I must insist you reveal all. I do not think we are visiting some shop or heading toward a typical afternoon diversion."

Adam turned off Bond Street. "I will confess why I waylaid you, but you must first promise not to abandon me."

"What are you up to, Stratton?"

"I am calling on Marwood."

"*No*. That pup? Whatever for? I thought you were his sworn enemy, through inheritance."

"He thinks we should make amends and be friends. He has been insistent about it. He keeps inviting me to visit and followed me up to town to corner me. Yesterday he paid a call while I was out. So I wrote and finally agreed to return the honor."

Langford continued to pace his horse forward. At least he had not rejected this visit out of hand. "I suppose he is afraid you are going to challenge him over that ancestral slight. He has most likely been soiling his smallclothes since hearing you are back."

"I would never duel over insults fifty years old."

He got a sharp glance from Langford for that. "So you are agreeable to accepting his olive branch? My, that is *good* of you."

Adam ignored his suspicious tone. "Well, I have heard he has a lovely sister."

"You must mean Lady Emilia. She was a beautiful child, that is true, but no one has seen her in close to a year. I expect she is passing on this Season due to the earl's death. But, yes, it is anticipated that she has turned out more than well. Surely you do not intend to make amends to the point of courting her?"

"I rather thought you might want to."

Langford stopped his horse. "If that was meant as a joke, I am not laughing."

Adam grinned. "I am. Stop being so worried. One would think it were possible to sneak the nuptial noose on you without your knowing it."

"There are a few mothers who are giving that their best effort." He started his horse again. "Forgive me for lack of humor. I am feeling hounded. So we are calling on one of your family's enemies, with the main goal of ogling his sister."

"That sums it up neatly."

Langford shrugged. "Why didn't you say so?"

Their ride took them to the door of Marwood's town house on Portman Square. Adam waited until servants took their horses and they were at the door before speaking again.

"Ah, I forgot to mention it. His grandmother was with him when he called yesterday. I expect we will see her too."

Langford closed his eyes. He looked like a man praying for salvation. "I have assiduously avoided that harpy for almost a decade, Stratton. I may kill you for this."

"You would not have wanted me to face her alone, would you?"

"I would have sent you on your way and collected your remains after she was done with you. Hell, let us go in, and hope that she has fed on someone else already today."

"My lady."

Clara's maid Jocelyn whispered the address in a nervous tone.

"What is it?" Clara responded ever so calmly, although she wanted to express great displeasure. She had told Jocelyn she was to be left alone. Clearly and strongly told her that. Yet here the maid was, interrupting.

"A footman came to the door. He said your grandmother requires you in the library."

Clara set her head in her hands. She looked down at the surface of her writing desk. The printed pages of the journal, received from Althea yesterday, waited her proofing. They needed to be returned with corrections to the printer tomorrow.

She had hoped to be done by yesterday afternoon. However, ever since her family had taken residence here, there had been one interruption after another. Those from Emilia she did not mind. Those when her grandmother demanded her attendance did.

Not that Grandmamma required her for anything important. She merely wanted to talk and needed an audience. Clara had put some of that time to good use, at least. She had obtained agreement that Emilia should have a new dress or two and be allowed to pay calls.

Yesterday morning, unfortunately, they had engaged in a row when she refused her grandmother's edict that she join the dowager and Theo when they paid a call on Stratton in the afternoon. She had no trouble marshaling a list of reasons why she should not do that.

She had a meeting with Althea planned, for one thing. She thought they would look ridiculous if the entire family paid that call, for another. Finally, she did not want to encourage the duke to think she was in any way in agreement with this peace mission, let alone in his peculiar plan for achieving harmony between their families.

Not that she could explain any of that to her grandmother, so she had simply been defiant. She wondered how Grandmamma would make her pay for that.

"He conveyed that the countess was most stern on the matter, my lady. He said important guests have called, and she said you must come down."

"Important guests" could mean anyone whom Grandmamma deigned to receive.

She looked down at her simple dress. "I will change into my black bombazine with the jet beads, Jocelyn, if they are so damned important."

Jocelyn flushed at the curse and scurried to the dressing room. Clara followed, regretting the lapse. She really had to stop doing that.

Fifteen minutes later she entered the library and saw that the footman had not exaggerated. Even by Grandmamma's high standards their guests were important.

Stratton had returned yesterday's call. Nor was he alone. Another duke, Langford, accompanied him. Stratton, Langford, and Theo stood upon her arrival. During greetings, Emilia caught her eye and gave a desperate look.

"The dukes have been regaling us with descriptions of Lady Montclair's ball last night," her grandmother said, once they all sat again. "I daresay we are enjoying it more in the retelling than anyone did who was there."

"I should have liked to be there so I would know for sure," Emilia murmured.

Langford, a handsome man with brilliant blue eyes and dark curls that turned his cropped hair a little wild, regarded her with sympathy. "You did not miss too much, Lady Emilia. You will learn soon enough that balls are all much the same."

"My grandmother has agreed that even though our mourning has not ended, Emilia can be excused if she attends a few smaller events. Garden parties and such. That would be acceptable, don't you agree?" Clara deliberately did not so much as glance at her grandmother, since she had not yet raised this idea with her.

"I do not see why not. Let us know which she will attend, and Stratton and I will be sure to attend as well and speak with her there."

"How kind of you both." If two dukes spoke with Emilia at a party, no one would talk much about whether a girl in mourning should have come. "We will be sure to let you know. Won't we, Grandmamma?"

"Indeed."

Untold levels quaked beneath the surface gratitude of that one-word response. Clara heard disapproval of her boldness, and pending threats. Emilia, however, only beamed with delight that she would not be left out of absolutely everything.

Her sister looked beautiful today, but then she always did. The sun filtering in the windows made her blond hair all but spark with lights and also flattered her dewy complexion. Langford kept looking her way. Not that Langford would do for Emilia, any more than the other duke here might. Langford was known for a wildness that more than matched that of his rakish hair. Charming as sin, he would surely break the heart of any woman he married.

Clara tried not to see Stratton, but he sat just to the right of his friend and managed to invade her vision anyway. He barely looked at Emilia at all, something Grandmamma was sure to notice. Clara hoped that Grandmamma did not realize whom he looked at instead.

It was not as if he stared at her. Just often that dark gaze settled on her, to the point of making her self-conscious. She understood what Emilia meant about finding him frightening, only that word did not really fit the response he evoked. Rather, she found his attention forcing memories on her, of his standing too close, and almost kissing her, and saying things too intimate.

"The day is fair," her grandmother announced. "Clara, why don't you take your sister and the gentlemen to the garden, to enjoy the breeze and sun? Your brother and I will join you soon."

So it was that she led the way out the French windows to the terrace.

Adam arranged it that by the time they stepped onto the terrace, he stood beside Lady Clara and Langford accompanied Lady Emilia.

Langford could charm any woman of any age without trying. It was simply his nature. Some kings were born to rule, and Langford had been born to seduce.

He restrained himself to the extent he could because Lady Emilia was a young girl, but those blue eyes still pierced and that smile still cajoled. Lady Emilia became a flustered mess of giggles and blushes by the time they reached the gardens.

Lady Clara missed none of it. "Shrewd of you to bring him," she said to Adam. "Otherwise my grandmother might have interpreted your call as courting, and indicative of your agreement to her idea about a marriage."

"She would have been correct, of course, but only in error as to the lady. We will not explain that yet, however. It will be our secret for a while."

"I wish you would stop speaking like that, when you know it will be a secret forever because I will never accept. There is no reason for me to."

"There is good reason. Many reasons. It will be our secret while I show you what they are."

Up ahead, Langford must have told some joke because Emilia's laughter pealed through the air.

"I hope he does not get any ideas about her," Clara said, narrowing her eyes. "He will never do."

"He has never shown interest in young girls, so I would not worry."

"Are the two of you good friends?"

"We have been close friends since we were schoolboys." He laughed, quietly. "I forget how little you know about me sometimes."

"Your family did not exist in my family's view, so I never noticed you or with whom you were friends."

"Never noticed me? How wounding. Never? Not once?" He gave her a direct, teasing look.

She felt her face flush, because of course she had noticed him before he left for France, during her first seasons. Who could not? His handsome face and smoldering aura made him stand out. Once, at a ball, she sensed an odd calm in the ballroom, a spot of stillness. It had been him, acting like the center of a vortex around which the chaos of the assembly swirled.

He had seen her watching him, she suddenly remembered now. He had noticed her noticing. He had guessed,

she suspected, that she did not look upon him entirely as
an enemy in that unexpected moment.

He now dipped his head closer to hers. "I do not think
we did not exist for your family. I think we were much discussed. Not with you or by you, but your father and his
mother. Am I correct?"

His voice, breath, and closer proximity made her nervous. She checked to see that her sister had not gotten so
far ahead as to offer no sanctuary. "At times."

"Around Waterloo?" His voice softened. "Or in the
months after?"

Her mind swept back to that time, years ago, as if sent
there by a spell he cast. Conversations crowded her
memory all at once, like so many voices chattering in lay-
ered unison. She heard her father, so clearly that it pained
her, but his words were obscured by other voices talking
over and around him. Then she glimpsed him, sharply,
slamming his hand down on a writing table in the library.

"No," she lied. "Not around then. Not that I remember,
at least." She did not know why she refused to tell him. Perhaps because of the way he watched her expression. As if it
mattered to him how she responded. Mattered too much.

Up ahead, Langford stopped his stroll with Emilia. He
waited for them to catch up. Emilia appeared heady with
delight. She kept looking up at Langford like he mesmerized her.

"Oh, dear," Clara murmured.

"Do not worry. I will throw more appropriate men at
her," Stratton said. "Safe ones, who are not dangerous in
any way. She will quickly forget an afternoon's infatuation."

"Now, that was an odd call." Langford offered the opinion as he and Adam turned their horses onto Bond Street.

"How so?"

"*How so*, he asks innocently. You know how so. If I did not know better, I would say that you brought me so that you could throw me at that girl, despite your assurances. Well, I won't have it. And if the dowager is foolish enough to risk her granddaughter's virtue with me, she will have to put the girl in line behind the other girls whose mothers are also so careless."

"The intention was not to throw you at the girl but to avoid having me thrown at her. I had never met her before and did not want her family thinking a mere social call meant more than that."

"I am so happy that you found me convenient to your purpose. The next time, please give the honor to Brentworth."

"He would have frightened her to where she could not speak a word. Nor would he have been so careless as to allow me to risk his name being connected to hers."

"You are saying you chose me because I am an accommodating idiot. I do not want my name linked either. If it is, if Marwood starts rumors, I swear I will—"

"Here is what you should do. Call on them again in several days—"

"Do I look mad to you? We are talking about the Countess of Marwood. She who ruins women for fun and humiliates men as a game. I may survive this Season if I do battle only with the mothers now armed against me. I will surely fall if I must also watch my flank from this woman."

"I had forgotten how dramatic you are. Hear me out. Call again in several days, but do as I did. Bring another with you. Your brother, for example."

"Harry? He will bore the girl to death."

"She is very young. Calm, studious Harry will not overwhelm her, and she will have a friend in town. With time, who knows what might happen. He will have a clear field, after all."

Langford thought that over. "It might work. Did you take lessons in France in matchmaking?"

"I had lessons in all kinds of things. Now, I must stop here for a spell." He swung off his horse. "You are welcome to go on your way."

Langford looked down at the shop where Adam tied up his horse. "You are buying jewelry?"

"A small bauble."

Langford dismounted. "For whom?"

"For my lady fair. I will see her a few more times before gifting her with it, but it is time to choose something." He entered the shop, with Langford on his heels.

"Now I am confused, Stratton. You just advised that I throw my brother at her, and you all but ignored her today—" He stopped in his tracks. "Oh, hell. It isn't the girl at all, but the older one, isn't it? Tell me I am wrong, because it would be the worst match ever devised by hell."

Adam asked the clerk to bring out the pearl earbobs. Langford elbowed next to him at the counter. "If I am correct, pearls are the wrong choice. Pearls are modest, discreet, and conventional. That harridan begs for something bright and unexpected. Something that declares she bows to no man. Something that—"

"I am beginning to think you do not like her."

"No man does much, Stratton. The way she thumbs her nose at every suitor hardly encourages generosity in return." He gestured to the clerk to take away the tray of pearls. "Bring out your rubies instead, my good man. The bigger and more outré, the better."

Chapter Six

"I have decided that I have to move here." Clara shared the thought with Althea after they finished proofing the journal. It waited, all wrapped, for Althea to deliver it to the printer and arrange final printing.

"Are your relatives being a trial?"

"My grandmother thinks she can dictate my movements and command me to join her on any calls she chooses to make. My freedom in coming and going is over. I am reduced to sneaking away as I did today to meet you here. I half expect her to open my mail."

She gazed around the library of her house on Bedford Square where they talked. The house was not nearly as large as Gifford House, of course, but it would suit her. If she lived here she could more quickly finish her other plans for this abode.

Women lacked places to meet and relax, other than each other's homes. Men had their clubs, taverns, and coffee shops for that purpose. Why shouldn't women have refuges too? This house, with its dining room and library and drawing room, might serve as one, to a select group of friends. She would not even have to make many changes.

How nice it would be if a woman could leave her home and venture out, knowing that at her destination there would be friends and acquaintances with whom she could spend an hour or so, taking some coffee and cakes, or even, heaven forbid, a bit of sherry or wine. Clara thought she would love to have a women's club like that, so others probably would too.

"When do you plan to effect this move? It is a big step," Althea said.

"Tomorrow next. I have already informed my maid to start packing my trunks."

"Have you informed your brother and sister and, lest we leave her out, your grandmother?"

"Not yet."

"Do you intend to slip away at night and leave a note?"

"Of course not." It had crossed her mind. "Let us not dwell on the row that will ensue, but speak of other things. Have you learned anything regarding Stratton?"

Althea smiled smugly. "Perhaps."

"Are you going to tell me, or tease me?"

"I thought a little of the latter would be fair. It is very provocative news, and considering the guilt I suffered to get it, I ought to make you pay."

"Provocative, you say. I am all ears."

"I learned that there was a very vague rumor that the last duke did not perish in a hunting accident as was commonly believed. Rather, he turned his pistol on himself."

Clara stared at Althea. "Who told you this? It is a shocking thing to say if it is not true."

"I wormed it out of my great-aunt."

"The great-aunt who needs watching?"

"I tell myself I did not take advantage, but I think I did. She was visiting my brother, and we were left alone. I had just asked my brother what he knew about Stratton, when he was called away by his secretary. My aunt began sharing what *she* knew of Stratton, as if I had posed the question to her." She bit her lower lip. "I suppose I should have stopped her."

"Perhaps she confused him with someone else. Someone from many years ago."

"I do not think so, considering what else she said."

Clara leaned in, so she would not miss a word.

"She said *Of course, his loyalty had been impugned. What else could he do?*"

"*No.*"

Althea nodded. "Then my brother returned, and with one glare silenced her."

"I don't remember any rumors about his loyalty. Of course, no one would dare sharing such a thing openly if no official accusations had been made."

"She could also be wrong. Or, as you said, confused him with someone else."

Not for the first time, discussions of Stratton's family pulled memories out of Clara, deep ones about things to which she had never attached significance. Now, while she pondered this revelation, snips of images came to her from that time. She saw her father in his study, bent over the *Times* on his desk, squinting at a notice bound in a black border. She had only glanced to see what absorbed him because of his expression. It had not been one of sorrow or curiosity. Rather, a steely resolve had masked his face, which she thought odd considering he read a death notice of another peer.

"She also said it happened on a family property," Althea said. "She spoke like he had shown bad form in killing himself like that."

"How horrible." Clara felt sympathy for the duke now. It had been bad enough experiencing the passing of her own father. How much worse to go through that under these circumstances. "Small wonder that he left England so soon after. The current duke, I mean. If your aunt believed this, others did, I am sure. The whispers would have been unbearable during such grief."

"I think it just as likely he left due to that business about impugned loyalty, don't you? That sort of thing stains a family name, sometimes forever."

"Even if they are enemies to my family, I would prefer not to believe that part. However, it might explain those duels in France. Still, let us not assume your aunt was correct until we have similar information from others."

Althea stood and picked up the wrapped proof. "I should go now if I am to give this to the printer this afternoon. We need to plan how we will distribute the finished journal to the bookshops. Should I write to our ladies and arrange a meeting on that?"

"If you would. Monday would be a good time. I have a few family matters to address before then." Clara walked Althea to the door. "As for what you told me today, we must keep this to ourselves."

"Do you no longer want to learn all of it and publish an article?"

"If we do learn all of it, we will publish. Until then, however, this must be between the two of us alone. I do not want to do unintended harm by stirring up old tales."

Althea placed a little kiss on her cheek. "You have a good heart, Clara. You are being most sympathetic. Perhaps that old war no longer has the meaning it once did."

What a silly thing to say. Of course it did. She was not being sympathetic either. She was being responsible. Let the broadsides and gossip sheets smear a person's name with no evidence. Her journal was better than that.

Two days later, Adam and Brentworth spent the afternoon boxing. Their efforts completed, they washed and dressed.

Adam was tying his cravat when Langford entered the chamber so the three of them could partake of some ale in a tavern before riding home.

"Did you tell him?" Langford asked while he lounged against a wall, watching.

Adam ignored him.

"Tell me what?" Brentworth asked.

"He has already fixed his sights on a woman. He bought her jewels."

Brentworth turned his head to look at Adam. One of his eyebrows shot up. "The Season is still young. I doubt you have yet seen all the possibilities."

"This one is not at the balls and parties," Langford said. "This one is not among the young possibilities you speak of."

"Now you intrigue me," Brentworth said. "Who is it, Stratton?"

Adam donned his waistcoat and pulled on his frock coat.

"If you will not tell him, I will," Langford said. "For reasons only hell knows, he has decided to court Lady Clara Cheswick."

"Marwood's sister? Or, to be precise, Marwood's *older* sister? Did your brain take a blow while you were in France, Stratton? The younger one I hear is exquisite, but Lady Clara, even in her prime, had little to recommend her besides spirit."

"Too much spirit," Langford said.

"I like spirit," Adam said. "Men who fear it in women are sheep."

"Well, I suppose she is also pretty enough too," Brentworth conceded.

"Whatever that means," Langford said.

"And I hear she did inherit a nice fortune from her father," Brentworth added offhandedly.

"Stratton is the last man to need a fortune, nice or otherwise," Langford said. "Furthermore, don't you find his interest in a woman of that family, even one who is pretty enough and who possesses spirit and a nice fortune, highly suspicious?"

"I do indeed. What are you up to, Stratton?"

Finished with his coats, Adam faced them. "What do you think I am up to?"

"We are going to play that game, are we? Langford and I will put our minds to that question on the way to the tavern. I daresay we will know all within five minutes of making the effort."

Ten minutes later, seated in the tavern, Brentworth spoke again. "I have concluded there are three possible reasons for this peculiar courtship."

"As many as three? You do think fast."

"Stop it," Langford said sharply. "All that mystery may impress women and stupid men, but we know you. Remember that."

Adam drank his ale.

"Reason one," Brentworth announced. "Her nice fortune is nicer than we know and in some way enhances your own in ways we do not know."

Adam let him talk.

"Reason two—she is pretty enough in her own way. It is possible, I suppose, that her own way happens to appeal to you more than it does to me."

"Is that it, Stratton?" Langford asked, incredulous. "I don't know . . . her eyes are bright and provocative, true, but her mouth is too large and . . . I suppose some men might find her . . ." His words drifted away.

"Reason three." Brentworth leaned toward Adam,

across the table. "Pursuing her in some way helps your reason for returning. She is a means to an end."

Adam was tempted to congratulate Brentworth. The man had always had a very sharp mind, one that was willing to consider alternatives from which others, like Langford, might shrink. Right now Langford appeared embarrassed that Brentworth had implied Adam's interest in Lady Clara was at least two-thirds not romantic, nor even especially honorable.

Langford kept glancing from Adam to Brentworth and back again, as if he expected a row, or worse. His whole body tensed, ready to stop fisticuffs should they erupt.

"You have a very high opinion of me, I see," Adam said.

"Higher than I have of most men. However, in the end, you have a cause, and men with causes make choices for different reasons than do the rest of us."

"My cause does not require Lady Clara. I happen to find the lady intriguing and far from boring. She needs a bit of taming, true, but that is part of the fun. As for her eyes and mouth, Langford may find her lacking, but both features lure me into fantasies of untold pleasure. I daresay I would have plotted to have her no matter what her family."

"Ah, you are up to no good, it appears," Langford said. "I am relieved to hear it. That talk of lady fair had me thinking you intended marriage. If it is a seduction you plot, there is nothing to worry about."

"I most definitely plot a seduction." Which he did. She would never accept that proposal. He had known that while he made the offer. It allowed him to have an excuse to pursue her, however, and to have cause for further conversations and calls.

Langford all but rubbed his hands together. They now broached one of his favorite topics. A master of the sport himself, he never failed to offer excellent advice. He awaited such a request now.

Brentworth, always more skeptical and practical, peered critically again. "I hope you are not thinking to force her brother into a duel to protect her honor. It will not work. She is not a girl, and possibly not an innocent, and young Theo would never be so foolhardy."

"I have no interest in dueling with her brother, least of all over her honor. I am counting on him not much giving a damn about her."

"Good."

"Have you seen much progress?" Langford asked. "She is not known to suffer men's flatteries easily, or treat admirers with kindness."

"Things progress apace."

"What the hell does that mean? Speak clearly, man. Have you even kissed her yet? If not, those jewels are too optimistic."

"He is not going to tell you," Brentworth said impatiently. "He never has before with his conquests, and I doubt that has changed. Look at him, all amused and smug at our questions. Unless you get him foxed, little will be revealed."

Langford laughed. "Stratton, allow me to buy another round."

"Should I ever have something truly interesting to report, you will be the first to know. I would include Brentworth, but he is so above all of that now."

"I am not so much above it as glad for it. I feared you had serious intentions. After all, her own father did not think her suitable for a duke." Brentworth spoke in an off-hand manner, as if he shared common knowledge.

"What do you mean?" Adam asked.

Brentworth shrugged. "The old man idly broached the

notion with me about three years ago. I sensed that he felt a paternal obligation to try and match her up and saw me as a possibility, but nothing he said would encourage a man to form an attachment. It was a little like having someone try to sell you a horse but mention all the flaws in its form and temperament."

"Not that he needed to do that," Langford said. "She was not a new horse in the paddock, after all."

"Nor did my lack of enthusiasm for the notion bother him in the least. He seemed to understand and even agree."

"Perhaps that mother of his put him up to it, and having done his duty he was glad of the outcome," Adam said. "Lady Clara was his favorite, and they were very close."

"You would mention the dowager," Langford said. "What a way to ruin a nice day. You had better watch yourself with that one, Stratton. If she gets wind of your intentions, she may turn you from a stallion into a gelding."

"I do not think Lady Clara confides in her grandmother. She is too jealous of her independence to invite advice or interference. However, your warning is well taken. As for my intentions, the arrival of her family in London is a complication. I can hardly make progress in their drawing room with the dowager watching."

"You need to find ways to get her alone, you mean." Langford's eyes brightened. "Allow me to share the five best ways to do that, as gleaned from my experience."

Langford proceeded to wax eloquent about strategies. Adam was not too proud to pay attention. Even Brentworth listened.

Every man had a special talent, and only a fool would deny the one with which Langford had been gifted.

Chapter Seven

Clara methodically ate her meal and ignored the silence that had fallen in the dining room. She refused to acknowledge the center of that void of sound. Like the eye of a storm, her grandmother's quiet heralded the chaos to come.

"You *will not*." The deep, sharp command sliced through the peace. "You will remain here, where you belong. Where any unmarried woman belongs. With your family."

Clara paused eating, out of respect.

"Yes," Theo said. "I forbid it. It will bring scandal on this family."

"I am not a girl, Theo. Not a child. There are women who live on their own. It is comical for a grown woman to remain in her family home if she has the means to establish her own household." She spoke directly to her brother and aimed her gaze there too. "Nor can you forbid me. I am not dependent on you, nor am I your ward."

Thunder seemed to rumble across the table. Out of the corner of her eye Clara saw her grandmother straighten so severely she grew an inch.

"Why would it bring scandal?" Emilia asked. "I do not understand."

"As well you shouldn't," Grandmamma said. "Please leave us now, Emilia. I have much to say to your sister that is not appropriate to your hearing."

Emilia looked forlornly at her half-finished dinner. With a pout, she slid off her chair and left the dining room.

"You could have allowed her to eat first," Clara said.

"You could have announced your intentions elsewhere, but you did not. You did so here, now, and I will not permit your reckless notion to survive one more minute."

"I love you, Grandmamma, and respect you. However, I have made up my mind."

"Have you indeed! Am I and your brother and sister to be subjected to the whispers that will disparage our family because of such a move?"

"Whispers," Theo echoed, frowning. "We will be lucky if it is left at that."

"I cannot imagine why anyone would whisper." Clara lied. She knew all too well that people always whispered if given the chance. "What is the worst they could say? That we are estranged? Our behavior will prove the lie of that. That I am unruly? I daresay that has been said so often as to be boring."

Her grandmother glared at her so indignantly that those pale blue eyes almost turned the color of steel. "They will say your father was a fool to leave you a fortune, for one thing."

"A fool," Theo snapped, his deep frown revealing agreement on this point.

"Be quiet, Theo," Grandmamma ordered. "They will say that if you live thus, no man will ever marry you because living alone puts your virtue in question. Do not feign shock with me, young woman. You know as well as

I that when an unmarried woman leaves her family home, the question always is why she would need to? What does she want to do in her own home that she cannot do in her family's?"

"Perhaps she merely wants to live her life as she chooses, and not according to someone else's plans," Clara said. "That is my only reason. I am sure you know that. What others may ask or say does not signify. Now, I will move in two days. You can try to browbeat me into changing my mind, but I will not do so."

"I said I *forbid it*." Theo slammed his hand on the table the way Papa used to.

"Oh, Theo, please stop the histrionics," Clara said. "You have enough to concern you with your new duties. You do not need to look for trouble with me."

Her grandmother looked ready to explode. Within her fury there shook a good deal of confusion and shock. "Willful, reckless girl. If you do this, no one will receive you. No one will invite you to balls and parties. You will be alone in this abode to which you claim to escape. You will be an outcast, an—"

"Are you threatening me, Grandmamma? Listing the punishments you will yourself visit on me for disobeying your commands?" Clara barely kept her own temper in control. "*This* was why he left me that property, so I would not be under your thumb forever. Did you never realize that?" She stood. "As I explained, two days hence, I will leave. You are both invited to visit me if you so choose, or not, if you prefer to treat this as a hanging offense."

She maintained her composure until she was well out of the room. Her emotions swelled while she ran up the stairs, however. Finally in her apartment, she threw herself on her bed and gazed up at the blue draperies while doubts about her decision wracked her.

Was she being too bold? Reckless? She had not really minded living with them before, but now every assumption regarding her expected behavior had become an irritation. While Papa was alive, he served as a shield. If Grandmamma started a campaign to find her a husband, and none of the men appealed to her, he would let his mother know that he did not care if she married, ever. That would end it, at least for a while.

In so many ways he did battle for her, on matters big and small. How she missed him now. The grief was no longer new, but the ache still turned raw when she thought about him, especially when she felt alone like this. She wished she could go to him and have him soothe her unhappiness. He would probably suggest they ride out, to the park or beyond, and leave her grandmother's overwhelming interference far behind.

People would question why she wanted to leave? She found that hard to believe. Everyone knew her grandmother. Everyone had seen the force of her will and the ways society allowed her free rein rather than risk being the object of her social machinations. A bulwark, Stratton had called her. That word hardly sufficed. Few men could stand up to the dowager's power. Almost no women dared try.

Would she use that influence against her own granddaughter now? Clara worried she would.

"Are you sleeping?" Emilia's quiet voice came from the doorway.

Clara sat up. "No. I am just contemplating my future."

Emilia came and sat on the bed. "I understand why you want to do this. I would go with you if I could. I do not hate Grandmamma, or even dislike her, but she can be like the most strict governess ever imagined, and one never outgrows her the way one does a real governess. Perhaps that is why girls marry. To get away from their mothers and grandmothers."

"Don't you dare marry for that reason. Promise me. Take the time to choose carefully, even if it means suffering her meddling."

"She frightens me sometimes. I am not as strong as you are."

"She frightened me too, when I was your age. A lot. She still does sometimes. I am not as brave as I appear, Emilia. With time, however, I learned not to bow so quickly, that is all."

Emilia traced the pattern on the coverlet beneath them. "Two days, you said. I suppose you will not be coming with me to the dressmaker on Friday now."

Clara slid her arm around Emilia's shoulders. "Of course I will be with you. We will have a grand time. And I reminded Grandmamma about your attending some small parties yesterday, and she was agreeable, so I think you will not miss out on everything."

Emilia's expression lightened. "How good of you to do so before you made that announcement at dinner today."

"It is called strategy, Emilia. I like to think I have a knack for it."

"She may change her mind now, though."

"I do not think so. You see, if you attend those parties, she will have to as well. I believe she is itching to do so."

Emilia rested her head on Clara's shoulder. "Thank you. I don't need a grand ball every night, but a few small parties would be nice."

Clara was sure her grandmother would be glad to chaperone Emilia to a party or two. If she remained out of society for a whole year, society might forget her power, after all.

* * *

Adam handed his card to the servant at the house on Park Lane. Without a pause the man turned and led the way into the soaring expanses of the mansion built by the last Duke of Brentworth.

The current one greeted him when he entered the library. As big as a ballroom, the chamber rose over thirty feet to accommodate a gallery level that wrapped around the sides. Fruitwood bookcases covered every wall, filled with volumes collected over the centuries.

"You look quite small in here," Adam said. "I suppose that means any man would."

Brentworth stretched out his legs, finding some comfort for his height in the upholstered chair where he lounged. "It begs for another twenty bodies, doesn't it? Perhaps I will start a lending library so it fills up."

"It will be the best one in London, if you do. There is talk of starting a university here in town. You can offer free use to the students too."

"A splendid idea. I will consider it. Now perhaps you will tell me what brings you here. I am glad for the company, but I suspect there is a reason for it."

Adam had debated how to raise the reason. He had considered for days whether to even broach the subject with Brentworth. Their conversation in the tavern had decided the matter for him, but that did not make it any easier.

"I am sorry I was not here when you inherited," he said. Langford had received his inheritance first of the three of them. Then Adam. Brentworth was last, a mere two years ago. "Your father was ill for a long time, I know."

"You heard much while in France. Yes, it was a long time. A difficult time. He spent most of it here." He waved his hand, gesturing to the magnificent library. "Reading. Receiving callers. He and I had many long talks, so some good memories came out of it. And he passed peacefully. Compared to you, I was blessed, I suppose."

Adam had no idea if that was true. He had witnessed no long decline. Nor had there been long talks. Had there been, he wondered what might have been said. Confessions? Regrets? Final lessons on responsibility? A good deal of his anger after his father's death had been with his father himself. To end things abruptly before it was time had struck him as very selfish.

"Did he say anything about my father?" There was no good way to ask, so he just set it out there.

"I have been waiting for that question. I had begun to think you would never ask it."

"I did not think you had anything to say until recently."

"What changed your mind?"

"Our conversation at the tavern. Your surprise and interest in my pursuit of Lady Clara was different from Langford's. More complicated."

"I wondered if I had prodded your attention without intending to. Well, damnation to being right about that." Brentworth stood. He ran his fingers through his hair, then shook his head. "I would do you no favors in satisfying your curiosity. Nothing good will come of it."

"I still ask that you tell me what you know."

Not a happy man, Brentworth aimed for the door. "I need fresh air. I am going to the garden. Follow if you insist on interrogating me."

It was not an invitation, but Adam followed.

Out on the garden terrace, Brentworth finally halted his determined stride. He assumed the stern, uncompromising expression that made ingénues fear him.

"He was ill. Very ill. I must emphasize that. At such a

time, things are said that are old memories, and perhaps not accurate to the facts."

"I understand that. What did he say?"

Brentworth speared him with a glare. "You have no idea? I find that unlikely."

"I know what I know. I need to find out what others knew and said, and why. Put yourself in my place, and you will understand why."

Brentworth's expression softened. He looked away. His gaze drifted over the perfectly tended garden that covered over two acres. It was a rare indulgence in London, spread on property that if developed into another house would bring in thousands. The last duke had been a man of educated, refined taste, as evidenced in that library and this garden, and an art collection among the finest in England.

"He felt some guilt over your father's death. Shadows of cowardice haunted him, that he had not objected to the rumors or at least demanded a fair investigation. He was already sick then, of course, but—"

"He of all of them could not be blamed."

"Yes. Well, he told me that he believed if there had been a real and fair investigation, it would be learned that your father never provided support to Napoleon when he left Elba. Had never helped his new army. Those were his words, Stratton. I was astonished. Those of our generation had heard rumblings about disloyalty, but this was specific, and I gather known only among some of the older peers."

The older ones, which meant the most powerful ones. The ones in government. The ones who could ruin a man with a raised eyebrow. Adam was astonished too. He had speculated on what the accusations of disloyalty meant, but he had never expected them to be so damning.

"Who accused him of doing this? What proof did they offer?"

"He did not say, and I did not press him. At least as to who made the accusations. He did say that the Earl of Marwood kept stoking the fire, however. He assumed it was because of that old animosity between your families. So you can see why I found your interest in Lady Clara either peculiar, or . . ." His speech drifted off.

He did not need to complete the sentence. Adam knew the rest. Either peculiar or an act of revenge. A small way to even a big score.

Was that all it was? He did not know for certain himself, but he did not think so. There were better ways to take revenge than that. He'd spent years itemizing them. Nor did he feign desire for Lady Clara. He had wanted her since that day on the hill.

He wasn't even sure yet that Lady Clara's father had been at the heart of those rumors. Even this new evidence that he encouraged them did not prove he had been.

All the same, he could not deny that more than desire had initiated his pursuit of her. Remaining in her attention allowed him a chance to learn what she knew, if anything, about the matters he now discussed with his friend. And, yes, seducing her would also partially settle the score for the late earl's old sins, and perhaps more recent ones, he had to admit. He could not deny there would be some satisfaction in that even if he enjoyed a more significant kind too.

If that made him a scoundrel the way Brentworth thought, so be it. It was past time for the son to fulfill his obligations to the father, no matter what that father may have done.

"Do you have any theories about how the supposed disloyalty took place?" he asked Brentworth, since he needed to clarify the accusations if he were to ever finish this.

His friend shook his head, but his expression reflected deep consideration. "I have never put my mind to it. However, if I now do—money, I assume. Money sent to France to finance the new army. Not to Napoleon directly, would be my guess. That would be both difficult and risky. However, to his supporters. It would not have been hard to get it to them."

"I have combed through the ledgers of the estate and found no large disbursement of money at that time."

Brentworth shot him a hard look. "So you went looking for it? I think my revelations today are not news to you, then."

"They confirm conclusions I had drawn. He could not be disloyal in his person, nor was he in his words. What was left but money?"

"Not a lot, I suppose." Brentworth gave his shoulder a firm grasp. "I am sorry I had so little for you. Perhaps as you go forward, you should not focus on what was said back then, but why it would be said. The rumor lived for a reason, even though not true."

Adam accepted the advice as sound. Of course, both he and Brentworth knew the biggest reason the rumors had thrived. She lived in France now, while her son tried to clear her husband's good name.

Chapter Eight

Clara's arms rebelled at the weight of the chair. Across the upholstered cushions, her maid Jocelyn's face reddened from the strain.

"Could this not wait until you hire some strong men?" Jocelyn asked in a strangled voice.

They inched along, finally dropping the chair at the spot Clara had chosen. Jocelyn took out her handkerchief and blotted at her face, then reached over and did the same to Clara's. "You will look a fright by the time you leave to meet your sister."

"I am impatient to see if my ideas about this chamber will work, and that chair kept interfering with how I wanted to see the space. I begin to think that I will have enough room for an extra divan. Once we move this other chair, that is." She walked over to the second chair and bent to lift it.

"I am a lady's maid, ma'am. We do not move furniture."

"Until I hire more servants, you are a house servant, Jocelyn. If you could cook us dinner last night, you can help me with this now. It is not a chore I was born for either."

"It is too heavy for us. Please wait until you have a man or two to do it."

That might be a week hence. Notices had been placed for a few servants, but it would take time to receive responses and complete inquiries.

Clara had made good on her intention to move out of Gifford House. Yesterday morning the servants had piled her trunks onto the town coach and she had been driven away. No one bid her farewell. The dowager and Theo remained in their apartments, and even Emilia was forbidden to come down.

Clara had not minded one bit. A brief spell of nostalgia fell on her spirits as she rolled off, mostly due to fond memories of time spent in the house with her father. Once the carriage moved through the town, however, joy and excitement took hold.

She and Jocelyn had spent the ride to Bedford Square debating which servants to hire. A cook and coachman for certain, and a housekeeper and chambermaid. Jocelyn insisted a manservant would be necessary too, to serve as butler and footman, but Clara was not so sure. While of good size for her purposes, this house was not some grand town house in Mayfair. Nor did she want a male presence there all the time, interfering with the feminine goals of her new home. She had no space to house a manservant, anyway. The coachman would have to take lodgings nearby.

With four bedchambers above and four more in the attic for servants, this household could never grow very large. The bedchambers were unlike what she had known at Gifford House. She had no apartment here. No sitting room and little private library. No huge dressing room and separate wardrobe. Here she used just one chamber and an attached dressing room, where she also stored her garments.

This library was of good size, however, as was the dining

room. There was no drawing room as such, but instead a nice sitting room that also served duty for breakfasts.

Well, she was only one woman. How much space did she need? And the public rooms would do nicely for her other plans.

Jocelyn finally approached the chair. With a heavy groan she pretended to try and lift her side, only to let it fall at once from her grasp. "I fear I used all my strength on the last one."

Clara was about to scold her when a knock sounded on the front door. "Go and see who that is, please, while you recover from your sudden weakness."

"Ladies' maids do not answer the door, ma'am."

"Oh, for goodness sake." Clara marched out of the library to tend to the door herself.

She grasped the latch, expecting to find a neighbor or soliciting tradesman. Instead she opened the door on the Duke of Stratton.

"Oh. You." The lack of welcome slipped out before she could catch it. She blamed that on her surprise to find him on her doorstep. And on her dismay at the way a beam of joy shot through her unexpectedly. "How did you find me?"

"Langford, his brother, and I called on your family, only to learn from your brother that you no longer resided there." He gazed up the façade. "I have always thought Bedford Square attractively designed, with houses most fitting for its size and scale. It is a good distance from Mayfair, however."

"You explained how you learned I was not at Gifford House. You did not explain how you discovered I was *here* instead."

"If you invite me in instead of expecting me to converse across the threshold, I will tell you."

She held the door wide. "Of course. Please, come in."

He did so, proving at once that the more modest scale of houses on Bedford Square made men like Stratton appear all the bigger. He so dominated the small reception hall, and her, that she led the way to the library mostly to give herself more space. She found it empty. Jocelyn had taken the opportunity to disappear.

He took in his surroundings, as if assessing whether they would do. For him or her, she could not tell. She did not sit because she did not want him to stay. She had things to do, and his arrival promised nothing but trouble. She almost never felt nervous, but increasingly this man caused a cautious jumpiness inside her. Unfortunate memories of allowing his embrace affected even the simplest conversation between them.

"Are you going to explain now? How you found me?"

"Many coachmen are not opposed to receiving gratuities in return for their helpfulness."

"In other words, you bribed my brother's servant."

"I suspect your brother would have told me for free, but I did not want to create trouble between the two of you." He once more surveyed the chamber. "It is a handsome library."

"Thank you. I like it. I have some changes to make and was attempting to do so when you arrived. Actually, you can help."

"I would be happy to do so."

She pointed to the second chair, then the new spot where she wanted it to go. "I need that moved to there. My maid and I managed the first one, but she rebelled at lifting the second."

"She showed more sense than you did. You should not be lifting furniture." With two strides he faced the chair. He moved it right where she told him.

She should thank him, and be more polite. Only he had accompanied his help with a scold, and she thought that negated her obligations. Only it didn't. She wished she could pretend he did not fluster her. Only he did. Enough that she had some trouble maintaining her cool disdain and thinking clearly enough to find a way to get him out the door.

"Thank you."

He acknowledged that with a bare nod before pacing the length of the library and gazing out the back French windows. "You bought this, I assume."

"Why do you think so?"

"The furniture is too fine for a house that you let. No one would risk these drapes to the care of tenants. They are not utilitarian but speak of the taste of a woman denied the indulgence of her wardrobe for a while."

His interpretation of the drapes proved very accurate. She had relished the chance to choose the fabric and trim and consult on the style.

"The furnishings also mean that you have owned it a while too, even if you only now have taken residence."

"I do not know why you are wasting your superb talents of perception on me and my humble abode, Duke."

"I am wondering why you bought this house if you did not intend to live in it. It is idle curiosity on my part, nothing more."

Not too idle, from the look he gave her.

She really shouldn't. Truly she ought not. But—"You have found me out. I needed a secret place to meet my lover."

"Ah. Well, we cannot have that now." He walked back through the room, his attention all on her. "I will have to post a guard at the door to discourage such visits. Should no lover arrive, I am left with the conclusion you spoke of the future, and of me."

He stood too close now, looking down in a way that did

not bode well for her composure. She was determined, however, not to make a fool out of herself the way she had in the park. "That is a shocking thing for you to say. It is bad enough for you to make assumptions regarding a marriage. It is far worse to imply what you just did."

"If you would prefer marriage to a love affair, the offer still stands. However, if you are set against it, as you claim, I will accommodate your desire."

She never found herself speechless, but she did now because she could not conjure up a good response. How had she allowed him to trap her between two options that consisted of the same thing, only one was honorable and one not? It did not help that his eyes all but glowed when he added that *accommodate your desire* part. She could not ignore the double entendre, nor the way an unhelpful thrill streaked through her body.

He appeared amused at her predicament. "This house will be convenient in either case."

"It would not be appropriate for you to call on me here with any frequency, if that is what you mean." She stammered it out. She felt as though a cloud had entered her head.

He reached out and softly stroked her lips. Only then did she realize they were trembling. She was being an idiot again but could not stop, especially since that feathery touch felt very nice and made her face and neck tingle.

"I will be very discreet. There will be no scandal. However, I like the idea of visiting you here, where the dowager and your brother cannot interfere."

Interfere with what? She had no idea if she said it or thought it.

"With this." He bent until his lips met hers.

That kiss stunned her in the best way. Marvelous little sensations multiplied while vague observations floated in her dulled mind. She marveled at how surprisingly soft his lips were, and how he did not merely press her mouth but made impish nips and movements that increased the enchantment. She noted when he took her head in his hands and held her to his exploration. She enjoyed too much when those hands dropped and embraced her until she pressed his body and felt the tension in him. Then she was accepting kisses to her neck and chest and caresses down her body.

He intends to seduce me. She did not know how that thought emerged, but it was in her head while Stratton lured her deeper with pleasure. Stratton. *The Duke of Stratton.* Some of the cloud dispersed while that name fixated in her mind.

Just then, when a modicum of rationality tried to stake a claim, he escalated his tactics and slid his tongue into her mouth.

She liked it. She did not lie to herself about that. It stirred her deeply and hinted at intimacies to come. However, it also startled her enough that her mind actually found itself. *The Duke of Stratton is trying to seduce me.*

She turned her head. She pressed against his hold, hard. She stumbled out of his embrace and turned away to compose herself.

She heard his breathing, and her own, and knew she had permitted too much to occur. This man had been impossible already. She did not think he would get any better now.

"You should go," she said.

"No."

No? Rather suddenly she felt very much herself again. She turned to face him.

A mistake that. He smoldered there, his gaze on her, his jaw and mouth hard. He looked dangerous and sensual and too handsome to bear.

Too much passed between them in the silence. That she

had lost ground and he had gained it, that she might hate his family but she did not dislike him nearly enough, and that something had started here that he at least intended to finish.

"You *must* go," she said firmly.

"Why?"

Oh, he was bold. "Because I must too. I am to meet my sister at a dressmaker's, and I need to start out." She brushed past him and walked to the door. She stepped into the reception hall and called up the stairs to Jocelyn to bring down her pelisse.

"At least you do not live here all alone," he said, following her out.

"Of course not. There will be more servants soon. The notices have been published. I expect to hire an army. In a week I daresay I will be tripping over them."

"I assume that means you do not yet have a coachman. I have my carriage here. I will take you to your sister."

She had planned to hire a hackney. "I will permit that because I am late. However, if you so much as try to touch me, I will stab you with a hatpin."

Jocelyn came down and handed her the pelisse. She donned it, tied on her bonnet, and allowed the duke to escort her to his carriage. Only because it was more convenient, she told herself. It had nothing to do with the sensual haze that still threatened to descend on her.

"This color should be unexceptionable," Clara said, tapping a fashion plate in a consulting room at Madame Tissot's shop. "It is not nearly as dark as the other gray. More dove colored, but still subdued."

"Not too boring and old, you mean." Emilia's excitement about shopping for a few new dresses had been almost ruined by the commands she carried to the shop from their grandmother. Dark purple or gray had been the decree. Emilia blurted it out as soon as Clara entered the shop and had almost burst into tears too.

"I am sure Grandmamma does not want you to look like an old woman," Clara said. "We will find a lovely fabric similar to this in color. It is almost silver. Perhaps we can find one that even has a tint of lavender in it too. I am sure that Madame Tissot will have some ideas."

"I should order a good muslin as well. Does that have to be gray too?"

"I don't see why you cannot wear white, or cream, in a muslin. It is hardly the color of festivity, and you are still a girl."

"I am so glad that Grandmamma did not come. And that you did. Now if we could just get *him* to leave." She angled her head toward the door, beyond which one would find the reception chamber.

Clara glanced in that direction even though she could not see through the door. She knew to whom Emilia referred. Stratton had insisted upon waiting, to bring her back when she and Emilia were finished.

Emilia pondered three plates, unable to decide on that muslin dress's design. "I don't want to look too much a child, but I fear Grandmamma will never allow me to wear this one here unless it is remade." She pointed to a dress with a neckline that showed rather more of the chest than a girl in mourning might reveal.

"One of the new fashionable high necks should take care of that," Clara said. She gazed at her own set of plates, none of which had been painted white. One, however, showed a color much like that of a pale, muted hydrangea. "Look here at this, Emilia. The color is mostly blue, with a tint of purple. I would want the color on this other design here, but wonder if it would pass as still respectable for the daughter of man buried just over six months ago."

"I am hopeless and cannot help you. Perhaps he could."
She again angled her head toward the door.

"What would he know about it?"

"He would know what his mother did, wouldn't he?
And if dukes do not raise eyebrows, why should anyone
else?" Emilia said. "Not that you care much about that."

She did not care about eyebrows, but she did care about
being seen as not respecting her father. On impulse she
stood and opened the door.

Stratton had made himself comfortable in the reception
salon. Legs extended, boots and arms crossed, his lowered
lids shielded his eyes from the feminine frippery that surrounded him. Clara could not tell if he napped or not until
she saw the smallest gleams beneath those lids.

He straightened and stood. "You are finished?"

"Hardly. You really should go about your day. This
could take some time still."

"I do not mind. Furthermore, as afternoon passes into
evening, you should not be crossing town alone even in a
hackney."

If this man knew how often she did things alone in town
at all hours he would probably become more of a nuisance.
"If you are going to be here, you may as well help. Both
Emilia and I could use a gentleman's opinion about a few
things." She held the door wide.

He followed her back into the chamber. He took it all in
with one of his sweeping gazes before giving her a quizzical look.

"This is the dress that Emilia wants," Clara said, pushing the plate toward him on the table surface. "If it is in
cream muslin and she wears a fichu, do you think it would
be objectionable? It has been over six months, so—"

"There will be no gloss or shine to the fabric, and no
more embellishment than perhaps this raised embroidery
here. You can see it is most discreet," Emilia rushed to say.

"I cannot imagine anyone would object. You are a young innocent. I was surprised to see you in black when Langford and I called. White seems more appropriate to me."

Emilia's face lit. "Oh, I am so glad you think so." She jumped up and went looking for Madame Tissot, so as to be measured.

He turned his attention on Clara. "Are you also allowed to step out of black now?"

"Perhaps a bit. My grandmother wants us to only consider deep purple or grays. I was thinking, however, that this color might do just as well." She tapped the hydrangea. "Although I suppose it has some rose in it, and that would never do."

"I do not see rose. I see a bluish purple."

"I do too. And it will not be this deep a hue, but paler."

He took the plate. "Is this the dress?"

"Goodness no. That is far too—" *Fun*, she almost said. *Fashionable*. "This one here is the style."

He gave a little shrug. "I prefer the other, but I understand the problem. This should be attractive on you too. Where will you wear it?"

"Emilia and I are going to accept a few invitations to quiet, small gatherings. Garden parties and such. Perhaps a dinner party given by family friends. She is missing what should have been her first Season and feels it sharply now that she is in town and all her friends are telling her about the balls."

"So you will be her chaperone."

"I suppose so, if we can escape my grandmother's company."

"Who will be your chaperone in turn?"

She laughed. "I am too old for a chaperone. Perhaps you forget how ancient I am."

His gaze raked her from head to hip. "I would like to see you in something besides black, I know that much."

I don't wear black now when I am at home and not planning to go out. Call on me on such a day and—She caught the thought up short, astonished with herself for even contemplating such a thing. "Perhaps we will both attend one of those quiet events and you will."

"I will have to make sure that we do."

One of Madame Tissot's seamstresses entered then and invited Clara to follow her so she too could be measured. As she left, she looked back and saw Stratton reaching down and flipping through the fashion plates.

Before finishing with the dressmaker, Clara ordered several other dresses on impulse. Her conversation with Stratton reminded her that she would have opportunities to use a larger wardrobe in the weeks ahead. None of the women who would visit her house for meetings about *Parnassus* would be shocked if she added some color. Althea had been urging her to do so for weeks now.

She also promised to pay Madame Tissot a premium fee if the entire order was given priority in the queue. Madame proved more than happy to arrange that for a mere extra 30 percent. The seamstresses would be put to work immediately, and two of the dresses should be ready within the week.

Two men waited in the reception salon when she and Emilia emerged from the back chambers. Theo's lead coachman sat there, chatting with the duke.

"How kind of the duke to help you pass the time, Simmons," Clara said while both men shot to their feet. "But then the two of you have met before and had other conversation, haven't you?"

Simmons, a stocky man with a fringe of graying hair around a bald crown, shrank back at her tone. She gave him a severe look to let him know she did not appreciate that he had traded her whereabouts for this duke's coin.

The coachman became all business, gathering up Emilia and escorting her down the stairs. Clara and the duke followed and watched Emilia roll away.

They had stayed at the dressmaker long enough that dusk was gathering. Clara gazed at the duke's carriage. Her better sense urged some caution.

"I think I will hire a hackney after all. You really should not have stayed, especially since it was all for naught."

"Are you afraid of my company because of that kiss, Lady Clara?"

"Perhaps a little."

"That is probably wise, although I do not think you frighten easily. I certainly do not think you allow fear to govern your choices and actions. Nor do I believe it is *me* that you fear, even a little."

Oh, the look he gave her. So aware. So knowing. He might as well have said *You fear yourself with me, which is different.*

What a conceited, impossible man. How had she forgotten that? Right now, standing beside the street, it seemed incomprehensible to her that she had allowed those kisses in her library earlier today. Her sympathy regarding his father had probably turned her judgment, and now he used it against her. His reasons might still be obscure, but not the intentions.

Afraid of herself? Hardly. Afraid of him? Not at all. She was not some awestruck child, too inexperienced to see what this man was about. She had fought off her share of seductions in her day, and they had been more artful than his lack of subtlety. She had enjoyed her share of kisses without turning into a fool too.

She strode to his carriage. "Directly to my home, please. No detours and no delays, if you do not mind."

Lady Clara could not be enjoying this carriage ride much. She sat so stiffly that she swayed hard from left to right with the jostling of the equipage on the uneven pavement. She had not moved in any way since settling into the cushion across from him.

He half expected her to pull out that hatpin and hold it at the ready. He did not doubt that she would use it.

Picturing that led to other images. "Your brother said your father taught you to ride and shoot," he said. "It sounds like you were very close to him. Were you his favorite?"

Her stern expression softened at once, so much that he almost regretted the question.

"I suspect I was. No, that isn't fair. I know I was. He loved all of us, however, even if Theo may think—I came from one part of my father's life, and Theo and Emilia from a later part, that is all. At least I think it is."

"Did he indulge you all the more after that first part ended?"

"He did not indulge me. What a word to use. We enjoyed each other's company. We fit each other like favorite garments."

Indulge was exactly the right word, from everything he had seen and heard. The late earl treated this daughter like a son. He had allowed her to remain unmarried and had provided the means for her to be independent.

He had probably confided in her.

"Women in your situation sometimes think it unfair that they cannot inherit," he said.

"I did not think that, although once he told me that he did. I think he really meant that he regretted I had not been a son. He frankly told me as much, and it did not hurt me. Men such as he marry to sire heirs, not daughters. He felt that obligation deeply, as all peers do."

"And so he remarried?"

"I suppose that was one reason for it."

The main reason, most likely. Adam pictured the late earl. He could see him with very young Lady Clara, explaining to a child why he was taking another wife, telling her that she would not be displaced and be at the mercy of a stranger in their home. He did not like the earl and had good reasons to be both suspicious and angry about the man, but the ways he had cared for this daughter suggested he had not been all bad.

"Did you know that this idea that our families make peace was his?"

That amused her. "I am very sure it was not."

"Your grandmother said as much, that first day when I visited. Your father gave her instructions on what to do."

Her brow puckered. "That makes no sense. If he wanted such a peace, he could have seen to it himself."

"Perhaps he thought a new generation meant a new, clean page. He may have assumed that I would have cause never to trust him or listen to such a plan if it came from his lips. I find it odd that he did not tell you his thinking on this, since you were so close to him."

She pondered that, not happily. "He barely mentioned your family at all in my presence, as I have said."

"Not even to your grandmother? If they plotted this together, you might have overheard them."

She frowned all the more. "And yet I did not," she murmured, as if in her mind she found that odd too.

"When will your new wardrobe be ready?" He changed

the subject lest he give in to the impulse to kiss that frown away.

She pulled her thoughts away from wherever his questions had sent them. "I told them to see to my sister first."

"So you are condemned to black another month? That is unfair."

"If I merely wanted some color, I could wear what is in my wardrobe. I left fair-weather garments in London and have now moved them to Bedford Square."

"Do you have a riding habit among them?"

"I do, but I did not bring my horse to town and should not borrow one of my brother's now. Nor would I wear bright blue in the park where anyone could see me."

He saw her in that bright blue, flushed from galloping into the breeze. "I have a horse that you can borrow."

Her eyes lit for an instant before she subdued her excitement. "I do not think it would be appropriate for me to use your horse."

"Is there a rule of propriety about that? Similar to how often a woman dances with a man who is not her intended?"

A smile tried to break. She bit it back. At least the frown was gone.

"Hear my plan, and refuse if you choose. On Sunday I will bring a horse to your house," he said. "You can wear the bright blue because we will be out of town before anyone is up and about. Instead of the park, we will ride in the country. I will have my cook prepare a basket."

She just looked at him.

"You know that you miss riding," he said. "Nor will we have to weave among the fashionable set on a park's path. We can ride hard if we choose."

She visibly wavered.

The carriage stopped just then. They had arrived on Bedford Square.

He helped her alight from the carriage.

"I will call at ten on Sunday," he said.

She did not say anything. Since she was not a woman who held her tongue when in disagreement, he decided that meant she consented.

Chapter Nine

Clara went to bed on Saturday with a little prayer that it would rain in the morning. When she woke to a gloriously beautiful day, however, she greeted the weather with more enthusiasm than she expected. She blamed that on how long it had been since she had enjoyed a good ride. Any equestrienne would want to be in a saddle on such a day.

Jocelyn helped her dress and only raised one eyebrow when Clara called for the blue riding habit. Clara decided one eyebrow was allowed when the woman had been her maid for close to ten years and now performed multiple duties with only a few complaints about ladies' maids not doing that kind of thing.

Jocelyn helped her dress, then fixed her hair and set a small hat on her crown. She anchored it with two hatpins, then prepared her reticule.

By ten o'clock she was ready, standing by the library window to see if Stratton would show. She had not actually accepted his invitation. He might have concluded coming here with an extra horse in tow would be pointless.

Promptly at ten o'clock she spied him turning his white horse into the square. A beautiful chestnut horse paced behind him.

Jocelyn even did door duty when the knock sounded. She brought Stratton into the library, where Clara still feasted her eyes on that magnificent chestnut. It was a gelding, and his lean lines suggested Arabian blood.

"I was not sure you would come. I never responded to your invitation."

"I assumed that while you could resist my company, you would not forgo that of a good horse."

"You were correct." She gathered up the train of her habit. "On such a fair day, to deny myself would be a sin."

"We can't have that. Sins of omission are the worst kind. All of the guilt and none of the fun."

"No sins at all are the best kind." She trusted he heard what she was saying. *There will be no sinning of any kind today.*

It wasn't that she did not trust him. She simply did not want to spend the day explaining how those kisses had been an error and that she only agreed to this ride because he had lured her with a fine horse and a finer day.

She noticed when she passed Jocelyn that both of her eyebrows were up now.

Stratton helped her into the saddle. "His name is Galahad. He is not accustomed to a sidesaddle, but I am sure you can handle him. He may require a firm hand, however." He patted the chestnut's neck, then mounted himself.

She and Galahad became acquainted while they made their way south to the river. The horse resisted restraint and did need a firm hand. It pleased her that Stratton had brought Galahad and not some boring, safe horse with little spirit left.

Very few people were on the streets at this hour on a Sunday. The pealing church bells sounded loud in the quiet town, as did their horses' hooves. They moved through a London rarely seen.

Once they crossed the Vauxhall Bridge, the countryside beckoned. The road alongside the river stretched open and free. No clutter of carts and wagons jammed it on Sunday morning. She gave Galahad permission to canter, then pushed him to a gallop.

They charged down the road with Stratton close behind. She raised her face to the wind and sun and enjoyed how the horse beneath her stretched to go faster. It had been weeks since she had a good, fast ride.

Some wagons meandered near a crossroad up ahead, and she pulled her reins to bring Galahad back to a walk. Stratton's horse fell in next to hers.

"That was glorious," she said. "I must try and bring my own horse Thunder up to town and stable him near Bedford Square. Then I can ride out every Sunday morning."

"What would interfere? It seems a simple plan to me."

"Theo may claim Thunder is not mine but his. Which, legally speaking, is true."

"Surely he would not be so churlish as to refuse you the horse you have ridden for years."

"Oh, I can handle Theo. If my grandmother tells him to refuse me, however, he will probably obey her."

"She is nothing if not a redoubtable woman."

"What a kind word you choose. My brother is trying to be his own man, but it is hard when faced with such formidability."

"Yet you are not cowed."

"I will confess that when I defy her, I still tremble after all these years. However, I have trembled so long that I no longer capitulate. It took a long time to find the courage. In a few years, I expect my brother will too."

"Or not. I did not joke that day we met when I referred to her influence. She still has the power to have people shunned. Perhaps you can defy her because you do not care about such things too much. Your brother, however, probably does."

Was that where her courage came from? A decision that she would not be ruled by the kinds of social whips that Grandmamma used? Those whips had cracked loudly at that dinner when she announced she would move elsewhere.

What if Grandmamma made good on her threats? Clara did not think herself a slave to society, but she would not like it if she was never received again or the invitations ceased arriving.

"Let us ride to Richmond Hill," Stratton suggested, pointing to the good mail road heading southwest. "The prospects are very fine, and we can share the contents of this basket while we enjoy them."

Richmond Hill was a popular spot, but the day was still too early to have attracted others to its heights. They galloped again, to cross the miles, and rode to the hill's crest almost an hour later.

Stratton plucked her off her saddle. "We will have company soon on such a day. Let us go beyond those trees there, so perhaps we can enjoy the view of the Thames without children running to and fro in front of us."

They led their horses out of the sun and through the cool shade of the trees until they emerged onto a strip of high grass near the edge of the hill's crest. Stratton tied their horses to a sturdy sapling, then lifted a basket off his saddle.

Clara admired the view stretching below her. The terrace walk meandered a short way down the hill, from which visitors could admire the views. A few pleasure boats had ventured onto the Thames, which curved below. One empty barge slowly made its way toward London.

When she turned her attention back to Stratton, she saw that he had laid a thick blanket on the ground. It billowed here and there atop the heavy grass and looked much like a feather mattress recently aired and fluffed.

She looked at that blanket, and him, and the wine emerging from the basket. She noticed how those trees shielded them from eyes as well as noisy children. Not that any of either currently existed up here. Other than the birds' songs and her own breathing, she could not hear a sound.

She and the duke were thoroughly alone.

He watched her take in their surroundings and isolation. The trick was to keep her from marching to her horse immediately.

He eased the cork out of the wine and poured some into the two crystal glasses. He held one out to her. "There is good well water too, if you want some."

After a considered pause, she walked back to him and took the wine. "What else is in that basket?"

He sat and poked through it. "Cooked fowl, cheese, bread, cakes and strawberries. And this." He held up a nosegay of small crocuses and one yellow narcissus.

She took it and sniffed deeply, then sat, arranging herself so she faced the view, not him. "I am only staying awhile because it is lovely and peaceful up here. However, if we do not have company soon, we will have to leave, so do not unpack that food."

"I will be happy for even ten minutes. Because of the peace, as you said." And because he could look at her while she watched the river. She was lovely in any ensemble, even black, but this bright blue habit enlivened her beauty. The color matched her eyes, and its contrast with her chestnut hair made her appearance extremely vivid.

"I think a painter would be glad to have you for a subject right now, Lady Clara."

Those blue eyes turned to him. "Why?"

"The colors and lighting enhance your natural beauty, and you in turn improve on that of nature. It would be a fine composition without any artistic license."

She blushed and returned her gaze to the river. He sensed that the flattery confused her, as if she were not accustomed to compliments and did not know how to react.

"Before, when we spoke of my grandmother, I thought it sounded like you had been one of her victims," she said. "Were you?"

"I was not. She does not turn her power on men, least of all men who will be dukes."

"Was it your mother, then? I know Grandmother did not like anything or anyone French, but that was not unusual during the war. I know she said things on occasion, but I do not believe her words were given much weight."

He debated whether to avoid this conversation. She gave him such an earnest look, however, that he found himself explaining. "The words that you heard are not what mattered, but others spoken long before. The dowager did not approve of my father's marriage. It was not her business or concern, but back then she saw herself as the arbiter of society. And so when my mother first took residence in town, the dowager let it be known that this French duchess should not be accepted. Society fell in line because it was easier to do so than to fall out with your grandmother over a stranger. The campaign was most effective, and also very cruel."

She hung her head and closed her eyes. "How difficult

it must have been for your mother. She would have had no friends to rely on here. No circle where she felt welcome."

"It made her very unhappy, that is true. It also did nothing to encourage our fathers to be more friendly." Her empathy, as it had in the park, touched him. It was good of her to appreciate how hard those years had been for a woman whom she had never met. "Then, after some years of this, the dowager suddenly lifted her heavy hand. Perhaps she grew bored with the game. Invitations came after that, although with the war, very few women would claim her as a close friend."

"I am relieved to hear that the worst ended, however. I do not understand why your mother being French should have caused so much grief either. She was not the only French émigré living in England."

"She was not of the aristocracy. That was probably part of it."

"Please do not tell me she was the sister of a revolutionary."

"Her father was a scientist and not political at all. But they were of the intellectual bourgeois, and that class was associated with the trouble. So I suppose there were always those who wondered about her sympathies."

She frowned. "After hearing this story, I am all the more confused as to why you agreed to meet with my family, let alone entertained a plan to bury the sword through a marriage. I would think you would much prefer to see my grandmother miserable and worried than contented."

Her gaze sharpened on the view, then she swung it directly on him. "I am not part of your own plot, am I?"

"What plot could that possibly be?"

"Do not dissemble. The plan was for you to marry Emilia, but instead you turn your wiles on me. That alone would make my grandmother apoplectic and could be a revenge for what she did to your mother."

"I do not seek revenge for my mother. Nor can I imagine why my proposal to you rather than your sister would matter to your grandmother. The same goal is achieved with either of you, isn't it?"

He reached over and toyed with a tendril of hair dangling below her hat's brim. A flush rose up her neck to her face. But she did not push his hand away.

"My most notable quality is my fortune, I assume."

"A good fortune has a way of outshining even the finest character and most entrancing eyes. I, however, have no need of another fortune. That is *my* most notable quality. As for you, besides your eyes and alluring mouth, your reckless spirit and self-possession find favor with me. Indeed, I admire all those traits that probably make your family despair and call you a shrew."

"I intend to scold Theo for that. It was most disloyal."

"He made you sound interesting, not unappealing the way he intended. I would no more want to have a docile woman than you would want to ride the quiet mare the groom tried to send today, instead of Galahad." He spied a hatpin and plucked it out. Then another. He stabbed both into the ground beyond the blanket. "I have deprived you of your weapons."

"I keep one on my reticule."

That reticule rested out of her reach. He removed her hat and cast it in that direction.

He cupped her neck's nape and eased her toward him. "Believe me when I say that I have desired you since that day you upbraided me as a trespasser. It is convenient that you desire me too."

* * *

How had she gotten here, on her back, with the duke all but covering her? That thought pierced Clara's thoughts when the possessive kisses left her mouth and new ones pressed her neck and chest.

Soft hair brushed her face. Masculine weight filled her arms. Rivulets of sensation ran though her body with increasing frequency. She opened her eyes a slit to the bright blue sky above, then looked down to where kisses now circled her breasts. He made her wish the fabric of her habit did not shield her from the full effects of what he did. Astonishment at her reaction had long ago turned to desire for more.

He awoke amazing pleasure in her. Dangerous pleasure. She did not heed any cautions her mind tried to present. She wanted more of this, enough to store for months or years, enough to sustain her memories on days when she did not feel very young anymore.

It is convenient that you desire me too. Oh, yes, yes. She did now. That was the name for the edge within the pleasure, for the more that she hoped he would dare, for the urgency in her blood.

She moved her hand over his shoulders, feeling his form, then down his back. His strength beneath her palm excited her even more. Those kisses burned right through her garments now, tantalizing her until she arched toward him.

His caress smoothed up her body until it closed on her breast. She thought she might die from the delicious torture he created then. He touched her as if he knew just how to drive her further into madness.

Soon she could not control herself or her reactions. She imagined him tearing off her clothes and covering her completely and filling the need that pulsed and called now, that chanted shocking urges in her head.

He did nothing like that. To her furious disappointment,

he even stopped the best caresses and soon removed his hand from her breast. She wanted to scream.

"You are too arousing to bear," he murmured before kissing her neck gently. "Your passion inflames my own all the more. However"—he kissed again—"we are no longer entirely alone."

She heard them then. There were others on the hill. Not many, and not too close, but—she comprehended what might have been seen on this blanket soon, if Stratton had not kept his senses better than she had.

She sat bolt upright, then scrambled to stand. She snatched up her hat. Stratton handed her the hatpins so she could fasten it to her crown.

By the time she was done, he had the basket and blanket packed away. He looked at the shrubbery, then strode to her, took her head firmly in his hands, and claimed a final, fierce kiss. And she loved it, every second of it, but—heaven help her, what had she done?

Stratton untied the horses. The world became too real. She found it awkward to still be with him, and worse yet to have him lift her onto her saddle.

She avoided any further intimacy on their way back to town. She rode briskly, galloping when she could. She did not want conversation with him. Casual chatting would be impossible. What could she say after what had happened?

To her shock, he reached over and grabbed Galahad's bridle while they paced toward the bridge. He held the horse firmly.

"You are embarrassed. Do not be."

"I am not embarrassed. I am . . . dismayed." It seemed the best word for the confusion of emotions inside her. "I should not have—We should not have—"

"I want you and you want me. Of course we should have."

"I do not want—" She caught the lie before she finished. Oh, such a lie. Even now with all her suspicions revived, she wanted him. Just looking at him made her body betray her in a hundred ways. *Do not be a coward*, she scolded herself. *Do not pretend. He already knows the truth*.

"I *should* not want you," she said firmly.

She yanked the reins and freed Galahad from his hold. She trotted across the bridge and made her way to Bedford Square. Along the way the rest of her sensual haze lifted, leaving the world very crisp indeed.

Her thoughts did not leave the man riding alongside her. Only instead of her body making her sigh with pleasure, her mind now insisted on lining up the many reasons she should not want him. Not only the old animosities made him a kind of forbidden fruit. Other considerations forced themselves into her mind more starkly than in the past.

He might have returned for revenge, the on-dit said. Against whom? For what reason? She thought about how Grandmamma wanted to make peace with him, and how Theo was afraid. Was it possible they thought the danger came not from that old argument, but from something more recent? Did Stratton want revenge against *them*?

She wanted to reject that idea because it changed why he pursued her. It turned those kisses into something very unromantic and calculating. There were all kinds of revenge, after all. All kinds of ways to conquer the enemy. Not all of them required pistols or swords.

She glanced over at him. He appeared very handsome on his steed. Very confident too. As if he assumed he was winning some contest. If so, she was the prize. One of them was not plagued by doubts about the meaning of what happened on that hill.

You want me and I want you. She could not disagree with that. But an act could be motivated by desire and also by other far less honorable things.

Once at Bedford Square, she slid off her saddle, not caring how clumsy she looked. She took the reins and pressed them into Stratton's hands.

"Thank you. However, I cannot do this again. I cannot do that again. Please do not call on me in the future."

Chapter Ten

Clara's decree that he not call again irritated Adam profoundly for two days. Not only was his desire frustrated, but also his conviction that he was making progress in his quest for the whole truth about his father.

On the third morning after their ride, he hit upon a way to share her company again. He arranged to meet with Langford and Brentworth later that day.

The bottle of port that they all shared was half-finished before Adam proposed to Langford that he host a garden party at his house. They sat in the card room at White's, losing money to each other on this rainy evening, making the lamest of wagers on ridiculous things.

"Here I thought you wanted us to get together in the spirit of friendship, and instead you had ulterior motives. May I say, as directly as is polite, that if you have need of a garden party, you must host it yourself, Stratton."

"He can't," Brentworth said after tipping his glass to his lips. "If he hosts it, he cannot spend all his time flirting with Lady Clara."

"I have no ulterior motive," Adam said. "Nor did I even suggest he invite Lady Clara."

"Not yet. It was coming soon, though," Brentworth said.

"Self-interest was the furthest thing from my mind. Indeed, the idea came to me because Langford keeps complaining about being hounded by those mothers. If he hosts a party and does not invite the two young ladies in question, it should put all the talk to rest."

"Talk? What talk?" Langford sat up straight, suddenly alert.

"Oh. You have not heard. What a faux pas on my part to refer to it."

"Do not castigate yourself, Stratton. He was bound to come upon it eventually," Brentworth said.

"Come upon what? Speak plainly, one of you."

"There is talk that Miss Hermione Galsworthy expects a proposal before the Season is out," Adam said. "Very soon, actually. It is said—"

"Her mother is only stirring gossip in the vain hope that I will rise to the bait. These women are relentless. Well, I won't have it. I will—"

"It is said," Brentworth repeated, "that at the Fulton ball you kissed her. Behind a potted palm, no less. Really, Langford, if you are going to misbehave, try to find more discretion."

Langford blanched. He drank a long swallow of port.

"Well, did you kiss her?" Adam asked. "If you are going to allow the enemy to compromise you like that, I will have to reconsider the respect I give your advice on strategy."

"I did *not* kiss her . . . She . . . kissed me."

Brentworth leaned in and made a show of being perplexed. "How ever did that happen? She is half as tall as you. Did she climb up on a chair, grab you by the ears, and plant a big kiss on you? Pretend to have a cinder in her eye, then steal a kiss when you bent to check?"

Langford scowled at him.

"You can see the brilliance of my idea," Adam said.

"Have that little garden party, but do not invite her or that other one whose mother is probably plotting how to thoroughly compromise you now that the stakes have risen and time is of the essence."

Langford narrowed his eyes on Adam. "Perhaps I will. I should also leave Marwood and his family off the guest list, so no one misunderstands my interest in his sister."

"I care not if you invite Marwood. As for his younger sister, your brother Harry will want her to be there, I am sure. He seemed quite taken by Lady Emilia when we all called at Marwood's house that day. Since she will need a chaperone, you can also invite her grandmother—"

"*No.*"

"Or her older sister."

Brentworth grinned. "Nicely done, Stratton."

"Langford may be the prince of seductions, but I pride myself on being a king at extricating myself from their consequences."

"That is better than Brentworth, who has become the emperor of having no fun."

"Why do you say things like that? You know very well that it isn't true," Brentworth said.

Langford gave Adam a man-to-man look. "There was a fine party late last summer. Brentworth here deigned to attend. Only once he arrived he made us all promise not to encourage gossip about it later."

"I did not think in these unsettled times that it would benefit the realm to have every drawing room and coffee shop abuzz about lords chasing naked Cyprians in the forests of the Lake Country during a game of satyrs and nymphs."

"The gossip is half the fun. If you did not approve, you should not have come and enjoyed yourself so much."

"It was not a matter of approval, but of discretion. I

know that word is not in your vocabulary, but it is worth learning."

"Discretion be damned."

"So you always have said. Since your indiscreet behavior is not saving you from those mothers, and indeed is being used against you, your reputation does you neither credit nor benefit. I, on the other hand, am amazingly free of such feminine tactics. Which of us has managed this more wisely, do you think?"

"He scares them," Langford said to Adam. "The face he wears while he suffers their blandishments has even the most ambitious mother shrinking away. He is called the Most Ducal Duke now. It is not intended as a compliment."

"If it keeps schoolgirls from throwing themselves at me at balls, I'll live with the title." Brentworth shook his head. "*A potted palm?* What did you think was going to happen when the little flirt lured you there?"

Langford flushed again. "Well, I have no intention of hosting a garden party. I would be made a laughingstock. They are for old ladies to host."

"Since Langford here is too stubborn to see the salvation that your plan offers, I will do it, Stratton, and save him in spite of himself," Brentworth said. "My garden is far nicer anyway."

"I have a very fine garden," Langford said.

"Brentworth's is better," Adam said. "You will come, however, and pay a lot of attention to the girls invited, so no one concludes you indeed have formed a tendre for Hermione Galsworthy."

"I will come, as long as you understand that I will not attend on Marwood's younger sister," Langford said. "Let my brother Harry flirt with her, if he even knows how."

"I do not want you to attend on any of Marwood's sisters," Adam said pointedly.

"A week hence, then," Brentworth said. "There will be no potted palms, Stratton, but the garden is replete with obscuring shrubbery suited to your purposes. I trust you will make good use of it. Discreetly."

"I told you that my plan was not for my sake, but Langford's."

"Ah. Of course. Forgive me, I forgot that part."

"I still say you need a footman," Jocelyn muttered into Clara's ear while setting down the refreshment tray.

Clara ignored her. In three days a housekeeper would take over duties such as serving tea and coffee to guests and answering the door. Another woman would clean. A third would cook. Her household was expanding in a satisfactory manner as far as she was concerned.

The one hole in the list remained the coachman and groom. She would attend to them, then buy a carriage and pair. Perhaps she would purchase a riding horse as well. She had so enjoyed galloping along on Galahad.

Her thoughts quickly moved from the galloping to other activities in which she had indulged that day, as they had too often since parting from Stratton. She would not mind so much if those memories engendered revulsion or at least self-castigation. Unfortunately instead she found herself well flushed and aroused before she summoned a more appropriate reaction and also reminded herself that he may well have ulterior motives.

That brief romantic lapse had been enjoyable, but she hoped Stratton did not misunderstand or attach any special meaning to it. If he did, she would have to remind him of her views about marriage. A few kisses and caresses were harmless enough, but she would not allow any man to own her, which was what marriage meant.

She locked those thoughts away now lest one of her guests comment on her color. Fortunately they busied themselves accepting cups of tea or coffee from Jocelyn and nabbing little cakes with their fingertips.

"The printing will be finished tomorrow and the subscribers' copies will go in the mail by week's end," Althea said. "Clara met with our delivery women on Monday, and each will come by and receive the copies she will bring to the bookshops to which she attends."

Lady Farnsworth, black-haired and steely-eyed, balanced her cup and saucer in one hand while perusing a proof of the journal with another. "It is certainly the most impressive volume so far. I think the order of the entries gives it a certain gravitas without appearing so weighty as to bore one silly."

Lady Farnsworth's own essay came first in that order. She was one of their contributors who used her real name, and a political report by the widow of a baron did lend gravitas to the journal. As politically minded as any man, Lady Farnsworth might not be received by the finest ladies, who disliked her growing eccentricity, but it was said the smartest men welcomed her company. As to her social standing, she had long ago become outspoken in her opinions on what she called the tribal oddities of the ton. Well into the autumn of her life, she had ceased caring who liked her.

Clara and Althea had decided Lady Farnsworth's reports alone would give the journal credibility and had been delighted when their invitation to write for *Parnassus* had been accepted. At least they might stifle any criticism that a journal full of apparently anonymous writers might well be the work of only one person.

"I am more impressed by how well the printer engraved the drawings I had made," Lady Grace said. She wiped her delicate fingers on a linen, lest the sugar in the cakes mar her impeccably designed silk ensemble. Lady Grace always wore garments that made Clara envious, and her tall, willowy form enhanced those fashions perfectly. Add her delicate face, very dark hair, and a rosebud mouth, and other women might be excused for hating her. "He will include those pages correctly, I hope."

"We have seen the first copies off the press, and he has handled it expertly," Clara said. Those pages had cost a pretty penny. She could not deny that an essay on fashion was much enhanced by drawings of those fashions. If *Parnassus* ever had to pay its own way, however, that might be a luxury it could not afford.

"It all appears in order," Lady Farnsworth said, setting the proof aside. "You have outdone yourself. I daresay we should be toasting with something more celebratory than coffee."

"I have no ratafia, regrettably."

"What *do* you have?"

Althea gave Clara an impish smile. "Yes, what do you have? Surely there is something here for medicinal purposes."

"I suppose there may be some sherry. Jocelyn, see if you can find the sherry and four glasses."

Jocelyn had no trouble finding it since it lived in a nearby cupboard where it might be removed easily, illness or not. Indeed, Clara kept some glasses right there with it.

Lady Farnsworth took the decanter and poured herself a full glass before passing it back to Jocelyn. The maid did the honors for the rest of them.

"Oh, look, you published another one of Mrs. Clark's poems. I am so glad," Lady Grace said. She still reviewed her own proof, spread on her lap. "Oh, my, this one is rather pointedly satirical." She read while she sipped. Little laughs punctuated her concentration. "Is her name really Mrs. Clark?"

"It is."

"There are thousands of Mrs. Clarks in London, so she might as well use it," Lady Farnsworth said. "A name like that is as good as being anonymous." *Unlike my name, which is known far and wide and takes courage to use*, she might as well have added, since her comment included that implication.

"Will we do another volume before the Season is out?" Lady Grace asked. "I ask so that I know whether to make notes as I attend the parties."

"I would like to try and publish every other month, if we can manage it," Clara said. "Now that I am living here, I can bring in some help more easily, so it does not all fall to Althea and me."

Lady Farnsworth's eyebrows arched high. "You are living here?" Not much surprised Lady Farnsworth, but from her tone this had.

"I moved here last week."

"Is that wise? I mean, a woman alone . . ."

"I am not alone and will be less alone as the servants I hired start coming."

"Your grandmother cannot have approved, not that she approves of much anyway." Lady Farnsworth never hid her dislike of Clara's grandmother. The two of them were of the same generation, and Clara surmised there had been some unpleasantness between them in years past.

Lady Grace giggled. "I think it is safe to say she did not. I am correct, am I not, Clara? But our Clara is courageous, and I say brava! If my brother were not so malleable, I would be tempted to do the same." She set down her glass. "I must take my leave now. I look forward to receiving my copy, Clara. You and Althea have a fine journal there, and it will be all the talk."

She stood. Lady Farnsworth unburdened herself of her refreshments and stood as well. "That will not be all that is the talk," she murmured.

Once Clara saw them out, she returned to find Althea flipping through one of the proofs.

"We outdid ourselves, if I do say so, Clara. However, every two months may be too ambitious."

"We will not know until we try."

"We will need more contributors, however. If you publish that frequently, it cannot always be the same names and voices."

"Then I will find new ones." She spoke confidently, not sure how she would do that. "It is difficult to expand the subscriptions unless there is a regular publishing schedule, so if I am serious about this I need to consider what it will be."

"Quarterly would be acceptable."

Clara trusted Althea's judgment. That her friend now advised more cautious growth meant it was a path to be taken seriously.

Althea reached for one of the cakes. "Lady Grace is so funny. She grabbed one of these right away, but we had to listen to her say *oh, I shouldn't* three times while she ate it. I wish women would not do that. Either enjoy the sin or don't commit it, I say. And having embraced the sin, do not fret later about how it might make you stout."

"Sin freely or not at all, you mean."

"Exactly. Perhaps I will write my next essay about that. It is a viewpoint women need to hear."

Clara wondered if Althea would only discuss eating cakes in that essay. Knowing Althea, probably not. Other sins would come into her argument. Althea was nothing if not logical and consistent.

"Is that how you live, Althea? Do you sin freely?"

"The evidence is that I do not sin at all. You did not see me devouring your cakes today."

"I am not talking about cakes."

Althea turned her whole body in Clara's direction. "What are you asking me?"

Althea was probably Clara's closest friend now, but she found she could not say what she meant.

"Are you asking me if I have had affairs, Clara?"

"Of course not. That would be rude and bold."

"But you would not mind if I confided in you, correct?"

"Please do not. I should never have blurted that." She leaned forward and grasped the sherry decanter. "Rather suddenly this looks appealing."

"Do not apologize. You are curious. As am I. I wonder why this topic is of interest to you now."

Clara drank rather more of the sherry than was normal for her. It gave her something to do while she found a way out of this conversation.

"Have you contemplated taking a lover?" Althea asked. "Is that the real reason you moved here, or at least one of them?"

"I have no need of a lover. At least not now. I simply wondered if as women mature, they find their views on such matters changing."

"Most definitely. If yours are changing, you are not unusual. We are not girls anymore."

So there it was. She was not unusual to find herself indifferent to the rules with which she was terrorized as a girl. Not unusual to be fascinated by pleasures long denied her. She supposed part of the change was that she now had much less to lose.

"Of course," Althea continued, "your situation is not quite the same as mine. I am a widow. You are not. That does make a difference. I am sure that you understand that."

"Too well. No one would raise her eyebrows on hearing *you* had set up *your* own household, I am sure."

"I doubt eyebrows would rise more than a fraction if I took a lover, as you wondered. You, on the other hand . . ." Althea reached over to give her hand a gentle squeeze. "It is the curse of the unmarried woman, I suppose. All those notions about virtue and innocence hang on such women forever. Even Lady Farnsworth, who prides herself on her liberality, would not approve if you took up with some man. Nor would he escape unscathed after taking advantage of you."

I cannot claim he took advantage. I would like to, but I cannot.

Jocelyn came in to take away the tray. Before reaching for it, she removed a letter from her apron pocket and handed it to Clara.

Althea had risen to prepare to leave, but she halted when she spied the letter. "It looks important. Superior paper and a very fine hand. And postpaid."

Clara opened it so she could satisfy both of their curiosities. "This is odd. I barely know him." She handed the letter over to Althea. "The Duke of Brentworth has invited me to a party next week. A garden party."

"He is said to have the finest in town. Garden, I mean. What is this here about your sister?"

"He cannot invite her directly since she is not out, but he has included her in my invitation. If I tell her, she will insist on going, so I will have to as well."

"Your grandmother could chaperone if he invited your whole family."

"I will find out if Brentworth invited my entire family. Nothing I have heard about the man suggested he would voluntarily suffer Grandmamma's presumptions, but he may have invited her all the same."

"If not, you must do the duty, for your sister's sake."

"If I must force myself, I suppose I can manage it."

Althea laughed and gave her a kiss good-bye. Clara read the invitation again and wondered if Madame Tissot would have one of her new dresses finished in time.

Chapter Eleven

Adam was delayed from attending Brentworth's garden party by the arrival of a letter in the afternoon post. Upon seeing the handwriting, he sent his valet away while he read it.

His mother's hand showed as steady as ever, but her words proved less comforting.

My dear son,

Your last letter troubled me. Your questions indicate that you are persisting in your intention to learn about your father's death. I had thought, incorrectly it appears, that your years here had dulled your anger. I had also thought that upon returning to England you would conclude it best to allow his spirit to rest in peace.

I was unaware of the rumors of which you have now informed me, that he gave aid to Napoleon's last army. Certainly no one whispered them to me. Nor did he confide in me, but he would have never wanted me to share the extreme distress such rumors would bring him. Although you have now given me the likely reason for the death he chose,

*I find that it only fills me with disquiet and regret,
so I am not thanking you.*

*As to your query about what kind of support he
might be thought to have given France, if not
money, I have no answer. That you ask implies that
you believe he may indeed have done this, and that
pains me deeply. I trust you know in your heart that
he was not that kind of man. Nor, other than me, did
he have any special sympathies for my people, so he
had no reason to betray his home.*

*As for the Earl of Marwood, that sorry war had
been waged for years before I married. Such men
normally draw their sabers over honor, a woman, or
land. I never attempted to learn what initially
caused it. It was so far in the past that it had
nothing to do with me, and learning that history
would not end the acrimony.*

*Spring has come to Paris, and as always it
alternates between glorious mornings and
afternoon rain. I hope to see you soon. When
England starts to bore you, as soon it must, I look
forward to your visit or, hopefully, your renewed
residence here. I have ensured that your own house
is kept in good repair, and I always tell certain
inquisitive ladies that you will be back soon.*

He had assumed he could learn something from her. He
would have never written to her about any of these questions otherwise. Instead he had distressed her to no good
purpose.

Her gentle scolds were nothing new. Her desire that he
leave the past alone was not either. For five years she had
convinced him that the prudent path was the forward one.
Whenever he would grow restless about his unfulfilled

duty to his father's name, a visit to her would soothe the turmoil trying to take hold of him again.

You should marry. Give the title an heir and give me grandchildren, and find happiness. He always thought she knew more than she said and kept it from him lest it only feed the dark turbulence that might one day get him killed. Now, when he had at least half the truth in his hands, she insisted she knew nothing at all.

He submitted to his valet's final ministrations in a dull mood and dallied with other mail before setting off on his horse for Brentworth's house.

Perhaps it was the sun that improved his spirits, or the gaiety of the small crowd milling about the large garden. Certainly the sight of Lady Clara did not hurt. She sat with her sister and Langford's brother Harry on a bench in the center of the formal plantings nearest the house. Her sister wore the white muslin that they had ordered at the dressmaker's that day. Since most of the girls also wore white, only the simplicity of the garment marked her as different.

Lady Clara also wore a dress commissioned that day. Although decorated by simple embroidery so subdued as to be almost invisible, its color made all the difference. In the clear light of day, that hydrangea hue appeared more vibrant than it had in the shop.

He walked to them. She had said not to call. She had not said not to speak to her. Not that he would have obeyed such a command anyway.

Harry noticed him first and hailed him with a happy greeting. Harry looked much like his older brother, only still rangy in the way of young men about twenty years in age. He also wore spectacles, the result of too much reading by candlelight over the years. Adam assumed that long after he and Langford were forgotten, some esoteric history tome written by Harry would live on in the libraries of the world.

"It is a fine day, is it not, Stratton?" Harry appeared drunk with delight. Since Lady Emilia did not look bored, things must be going well between them.

"Yes, very fine."

"Most fine," Lady Emilia said with a big smile.

"Indeed it is fine," Lady Clara said without even a small one.

He availed himself of an open spot on the bench next to Lady Clara. She inched her rump closer to her sister and farther from him.

"You ladies are more beautiful than the blooms," Adam said. "That color is very becoming, Lady Clara."

"I thought it would do, under the circumstances."

"I am sure you look forward to the day when you wear a variety of colors again. Blue, for example. Bright blue, to set off your lovely eyes and contrast with your hair."

"She has such a garment," Emilia said. "He might be describing your blue riding habit, Clara. It does flatter her, sir. No one could fail to admire her when she wears that habit and sits atop a fine horse."

"I am sure," Adam said.

Clara sucked in her cheeks.

Harry's mood had dampened a bit upon Adam's addition to their group. Now he brightened, as if struck by divine inspiration. "I spied a bed of tulips when I entered. Would you favor me with your company while I go take a look at it, Lady Emilia?"

Emilia turned hopeful eyes on her sister. Clara gave Harry a critical glance, then another over her shoulder. "I suppose a short stroll through the plantings would do no harm. Remember what I told you on our way here, Emilia.

We do not want Grandmother scolding me for being an inept chaperone."

Emilia walked off with Harry before she finished. She took advantage of the additional space to scoot farther away from Adam.

"What are you doing here?" she asked.

"Brentworth is one of my best friends. If you had not spent your first Seasons ignoring my existence, you would know that."

"It entered my mind that he might be. Did you put him up to this? He does not entertain here often. I think the last time I was at this house was three years ago, before he inherited."

"No one puts Brentworth up to anything. He decided on his own to do this." Officially true, if not completely so. "Perhaps he has decided to entertain more and thought this small gathering would be a good start."

"It came at a convenient time. It is a good start for Emilia too." She looked over her shoulder again, to find her sister in the garden.

"Are you obligated to sit here the whole time?" he asked. "Is there some rule unknown to me that you cannot enjoy the sun and blooms if you are in mourning?"

"Of course not. It is just . . ." She looked around the garden and bit her lower lip. "I feel a little strange. I know all these people and yet feel removed from them all in a new way. As if they do not matter. As if I do not matter to them either."

He knew that strangeness well. "You have been separated from them longer than you realize. Your father's passing changes things too. We are all put in columns by others and get moved around as time goes by."

"So I was previously in the Marwood daughter column, and now I am in the Marwood sister one?"

"Something like that."

"This one is not as prestigious. I am now less interesting."

"Perhaps less useful is a better way to put it."

"My, you are cynical sometimes. I suppose that four years ago I was in the *ingénue on the marriage market* column, but that has changed now too. I am now in the *spinster on the shelf* column."

"I would say you were in the *mature woman who knows her own mind and self* column."

"That is generous of you. However we title it, I rather like this place."

He gestured to the other guests. "I think they know that. It is perhaps another reason that you feel a strangeness with them."

She stood. "If I am so comfortable with my mind and self, I should not allow others to make me feel strange. I think that I will be sociable for a spell."

He watched her walk off and greet two ladies chatting nearby. He could tell that before anything more was said, those ladies expressed sympathy for her loss. That would probably happen with each person she met, since most would not have been at her father's funeral in the country. He did not expect her to be sociable for too long.

He sought out Brentworth. He found him on the terrace, suffering a political harangue from the Viscount Weberly. Flushed and loud, the older man made pronouncement after pronouncement about the need to crush rebellions as they emerged and not wait for the niceties of legal action. Brentworth just listened, but when he saw Adam he used that as an excuse to extricate himself.

"I thought Weberly would never cease," he said, steering Adam farther away and in the direction of the punch. "I long ago learned that it was a waste of breath to try to explain to minds like his that while it may be expedient to imprison demonstrators without trials, it was neither legal nor English."

Weberly was not alone in advocating the government act in ways contrary to law and tradition. Fear motivated him and others. The French revolt still cast a long shadow, revived whenever unrest rumbled through the country. Since it roared at times now, Weberly and his ilk grew increasingly fevered in demanding action that would ensure their necks remained safe.

Brentworth procured two cups of refreshment from a footman manning the punch bowls. He handed one to Adam. "You will like this. It is a West Indian potion with a fair amount of rum. That other bowl's content is sweet, typical, and lacking any fortification."

"I am sure the ladies appreciate the choice."

"You would think so. Several of them, however, have availed themselves of that which we drink, several times over. I am keeping my eye on one of them, lest she pass out cold before the afternoon is over."

"Where is Langford?" Adam used the question as an excuse to cast his gaze around the garden until he spied Lady Clara.

"Out there somewhere, taking your advice rather too seriously to flirt with all the young girls."

"He was born to flirt, and they are so appreciative that he cannot stop himself."

"He had better make sure one of them does not drag him behind a shrubbery, or there might be hell to pay. Are these girls getting bolder, or am I getting older?"

"A bit of both, I think."

"Speaking of flirting, where is your lady fair?"

"Over there beside the fountain, talking with Hollsworth and his wife."

"Shouldn't you be there too?"

"All in good time."

"I suppose that first you need to assess the terrain before mounting an assault."

"There will be no assault. I am a gentleman."

"Call it what you will. As for the terrain, there is a delightful folly in the far northern corner, amidst that grove of fruit trees. A little temple to the goddess Diana. It is very cool back there, even on warm days, so it is unlikely to draw many of my guests."

Adam eyed the fruit orchard in question. "I remember it, now that you remind me. The statue of the goddess is far nicer than one expects in a garden."

"It is ancient Roman. I should probably move it to the gallery."

"Lady Clara is a cultured woman. She probably would want to see it in its current location before you do."

"Do you think so? Regrettably, I have all these guests to attend to and cannot direct her there. Perhaps you will tell her about it for me."

"I will try to remember to do that, assuming she and I have cause to talk again." He set down his glass, then headed down the terrace, toward the fountain.

Clara extracted herself from a lengthy discussion regarding the new fashion for very high necklines and spied the Earl of Hollsworth standing near the fountain. His countess smiled amiably in her direction, so she joined them.

Hollsworth stood very straight despite his advancing years. Thin white hair rose in wisps from his head. Thick spectacles caused his eyes to appear very small. He smiled a greeting while the diminutive, gray-haired countess welcomed her.

Hollsworth had been a friend of her grandfather and later her father. A quiet man, he observed more than contributed at social gatherings. Her father had told her once that Hollsworth's retiring demeanor meant people often spoke without realizing he listened. Her father considered him one of the most well-informed peers as a result.

Lady Hollsworth gave Clara's dress a thorough examination. "Well done. I am so glad to see that you and your sister have ventured out and chosen to put aside full mourning. Young women should not have an entire year removed from their budding lives, and I find it odd that such a custom is becoming fashionable. Don't you agree, Charles?"

Lord Hollsworth just smiled and nodded.

Clara devoted her attention to the countess, flattering her own fashionable ensemble. She had just finished when the earl straightened even more, enough that it drew his wife's attention.

"Oh, dear," she murmured, looking past Clara. She glanced askance at her husband, whose face turned to stone. "Surely he is not coming here."

Clara looked over her shoulder. The *he* in question was Stratton, who appeared to be walking in their direction.

"He is an old friend of Brentworth," she said, even though the duke's presence did not need explanation.

The earl's jaw shifted. The countess peered up at him, concerned. "Why don't you go admire the plantings, Charles."

With a stiff nod, the earl walked away.

"Forgive us. However, my husband does not choose to converse with Stratton. Nor would he want to cut him directly. You can see the conundrum."

"I see it clearly. I am not sure I understand, however."

The countess kept her gaze on the garden between them and the house. Clara moved so she could see it too.

Stratton took his time in his stroll, pausing to greet other guests, but remained on a line that would end with them.

"He came back for reason. Notice how the men all greet him too heartily but grow sober as soon as he passes. He has come to find someone to blame for his father's rash act, I assume. My husband would like to avoid a discussion with him about all of that," Lady Hollsworth said.

"Lord Hollsworth cannot be worried that the duke will challenge *him*. Stratton is not without basic decency and would never dare to do such a thing with a man of senior years, especially after a simple conversation."

Lady Hollsworth's eyebrows rose. "I am sure many think so, but one never knows. Also, you are an odd choice to be his defender. Several times over. I expected you to follow my husband so as to avoid being a party to the meeting about to occur."

"My grandmother has decided we should make an effort to end that old argument. Since no one seems to remember what caused it, I suppose she is correct."

"This gets more curious by the second. Is the dowager not feeling well these days? She is not a woman to develop a faulty memory for any other reason." Since Stratton was almost upon them, she fixed a smile on her face as he approached. "Let your grandmother suffer his inquisition about those jewels, if she has decided to make peace. My husband does not want to find himself parrying Stratton's questions."

"What jewels?"

"Stratton! How kind of you to seek out an old woman." Lady Hollsworth greeted him and made a curtsy.

He exuded charm that should put any woman at ease. "I could not pass on the chance to speak with you."

"You had only to call, and the chance would have been yours sooner."

"I will take that as an invitation. And Lord Hollsworth?" he asked. "He is well?"

"Most well. He was just here a short while ago but sought the refuge of the flower gardens when Lady Clara and I began chatting about dress fashions."

"I am sorry to have missed him. Perhaps I will cross his path later."

"He would be most agreeable if you did, I know." She made a display of rising on her toes and searching. "I should find him, I suppose. Clara, you and I will talk again soon, I hope. Call on me."

She strolled away, leaving Clara with the duke.

"That was a little rude of her," Clara said.

"I counted on her leaving, so you and I could be alone."

"I do not think that will last long with all these people here."

"I am sure it will. No one here is seeking conversation with *me*."

He knew the reactions that followed him as he walked by.

"You cannot like how the men treat you with caution. It is as if they refuse to accept you as one of them."

"With my station, they must accept me. I knew it would take some time for my absence to be forgotten or my return to be understood. Let us take a turn, if you are in the mood for it. Then some of the other guests can sit on these benches around the fountain, which I do not think they will do if I remain in this spot."

The benches had indeed emptied once he arrived. Clara agreed to a turn through the gardens.

She still could not understand how blasé he remained about the social slights. "Do you know why men like Hollsworth avoid you?"

He bent his head to sniff the blooms on a lilac bush. "Some worry I will take offense at something they say. If they do not dishonor me, offense would be impossible. Yet it concerns them."

"Hollsworth certainly knows that even if he insulted you outright you would never challenge an old man. I said as much to the countess. She said he wants to avoid a conversation with you."

He merely strolled on.

"Do you not mind that they all consider you dangerous?" She gestured broadly with her arm toward the rest of the garden.

"Do you as well? That would indeed wound me. I don't care too much about the others."

"I have not decided yet." She lied. She did consider him dangerous. To her. It had nothing to do with duels or the past or any of the reasons everyone else treated him with caution. Even now, strolling along these garden paths, she was not her normal self. His proximity flustered her. Looking at him threatened to leave her tongue-tied.

Their path took them along the edge of an orchard abloom with flowers. "There is a folly in there," he said. "A tiny domed Roman temple to the goddess Diana. The statue is antique."

The fruit trees had not yet fully leafed. Sunlight dappled the paths beneath the branches. She thought she spied the dome. Joining Stratton when he ventured into the orchard did not concern her. They would probably come upon other guests among these apple trees.

The air cooled despite the splashes of sunlight. The folly stood in the far corner, near where the stone walls met. The marble goddess wore an animal skin and carried a quiver of arrows on her back. She bent to lace the sandal on a foot propped on a tree stump, against which her bow lay.

Clara mounted the three steps that circled the structure

and passed through the arcade that held up the dome and framed the statue. "It is very realistic. The different textures have been depicted so accurately one thinks they will not feel like stone." She ran her fingertips across the animal skin.

"It is probably early Roman. Brentworth's father was a well-traveled man, with a keen eye for quality in art."

She paced around the statue. He came into the folly, only he looked at her, not the goddess.

"You did not bring me here to admire this statue, did you?" she asked.

"I brought you here because you demanded I not call at your house."

She turned to find him right behind her. Her heart rose, blocking her breath. Suddenly the orchard did not appear thin and open but instead dense and obscure. She could barely hear the sounds of the party in the open garden.

He lifted her chin with his fingers. "Had you not been so strict, I could have done this there." He kissed her, softly at first but then more passionately. Sensations cascaded through her, so that she did not want to be at all strict right now.

He broke the kiss but kept his hand on her face. "I cannot allow you to spurn me, Clara. To deny this. I do not think you really want to either."

She had been very sure of herself after their ride. Her mind had been most clear. Right now she could not remember what her thinking had been.

He spoke the truth, though. She did not really want to deny how alive she became when he kissed her. Considerations of his motivations ceased to matter then. She did not want to reject the pleasure or the flusters. She should, but she did not. She savored the way just seeing him excited her. She had dwelled within the memories of what happened on that hill for long spells ever since they last parted.

He kissed her again, and embraced her. The warmth of his body both comforted and entranced her. So good. Too good.

"If you repeat your command that I not call on you, I will have to pursue you into orchards and gardens all summer," he murmured into her ear. "Discretion may become nigh impossible."

Within her heady delight she vaguely noted that he had not stood down. He had warned her that first day that he never did.

Still, she should repeat her command. She should not do anything to encourage him. She should remember why these kisses were not only wrong but disloyal. Once this soulful intimacy ended, she surely would again care about all of that—

Sounds penetrated the silence around them. A giggle, and a man's laugh. Not far away. Nearby, on the path.

Stratton abruptly released her and stepped out of the temple, leaving her alone with the goddess.

A beam of sunlight illuminated a white dress and blond head among the apple blossoms. With another giggle, Emilia stepped into the little clearing with the temple. Her companion's face fell when he saw Stratton.

"Harry, how good of you to show Lady Emilia the way to this treasure," Stratton said. "Her sister tried to find her before venturing here herself." He pointed at Clara.

Harry saw Clara. So did Emilia. They both flushed.

Clara scolded herself while she fought to maintain her composure. In allowing the duke to once more bedazzle her, she had neglected her duty. Emilia was going to receive a very strong lecture on not being so stupid as to allow a man to get her alone like this.

"Come and see the statue," she said. "It is impressive."

Visibly relieved, Harry accompanied Emilia into the folly. They all admired the goddess together, then all walked back through the orchard and into the sunny garden.

Clara decided she and Emilia should take their leave. She dragged Emilia to Brentworth so they could thank their host. While they left, she saw Stratton near the benches, watching someone. Her gaze followed the line of his, directly to the Earl of Hollsworth.

Social niceties completed, she and Emilia settled into Theo's coach for the ride to their respective homes.

"Did you have a good afternoon and enjoy yourself?" Clara asked, pointedly, as the necessary social lessons lined up in her mind.

"My afternoon was not *nearly* as enjoyable as *yours,* I think." Emilia shot a meaningful look across the carriage cabin.

It was Clara's turn to flush. She swallowed the long lecture she had intended to give her sister.

Chapter Twelve

Clara and Althea stood side by side in Clara's library on Friday morning. On a long table, fresh copies of their journal waited in stacks. The printer would mail the ones to subscribers, but these had to be delivered to book shops, and the women who did that, friends of Mrs. Clark, would arrive at noon.

Clara admired the thick booklets. The ones being mailed had no covers, but these sported ones of heavy blue stock with a nicely engraved title. They would look beautiful in the shops.

Althea called out a number, and Clara took that number of copies and moved them to the end of the table. Althea followed and placed a paper with a shop's name on that group.

So far, half of the journals had been assigned to their shops.

The chore had taken longer than expected because Clara had been describing the garden party. Not the part about being kissed again, of course.

"Then Lady Hollsworth said, as clearly as you hear me

now, *Let your grandmother answer his questions about those jewels.* I asked her what she meant, but by then Stratton was upon us, so she never answered."

"How intriguing. It is a wonder you did not tell the duke to go away so you could receive your response."

"I try not to be rude, Althea."

Althea checked her paper. "Ackermann's. Fifteen."

Clara counted out fifteen copies and moved them to the other end of the table. "Have you learned anything of interest?"

"I keep hearing the same things. Talk of those duels. Concern he will challenge people here. There is an assumption among some people that he will have to, in order to cleanse the family name of whatever besmirched it. Some of the older women believe honor means he cannot allow things to stand as they have been."

"Times have changed. Families no longer wear the sins of their ancestors like marks on their foreheads. To suggest as much is very old-fashioned."

"It is not a typical sin, however, is it? The rumors had to do with treason."

"There was no public accusation, Althea. No trial."

"Do not become vexed with *me*. I am merely saying—"

"I know what you are saying. Nor am I vexed with you. I am annoyed by all of these vague whispers from people who do not seem to know anything for certain."

"Someone knows more. However, the story is over, so whoever it is will not now raise the question again. Especially with the duke back in England."

Yes, someone knew. Probably several someones. Like Hollsworth.

Had her father known too?

Jocelyn entered the library with the morning mail. Clara

paused counting books while she flipped through the few letters. One made her freeze. She tore it open and read it.

"Oh, no. Of all the days to choose—" She looked frantically at the table, laden with copies of the journal.

"What is it?" Althea asked.

Clara waved the letter. "My grandmother has something important to tell me and intends to come here right after noon, before she makes her calls."

"Here? Oh, dear. The women—"

"Will be arriving just when she does. Entering, and carrying out stacks of these journals." She strode to the library door and called for Jocelyn. "Can you finish this on your own, Althea? I will make every effort to return before noon, but I must go to my brother's house before my grandmother leaves to come to mine."

Jocelyn arrived and Clara sent her for her pelisse and bonnet. She looked down on her dress. It was part of the wardrobe left here after last summer, and not black or even subdued blue or purple. Upon waking from discomforting sensual dreams, she had impulsively put on a red dress.

No one would see her except family. The family in question would not approve, however.

"I will take care of everything here," Althea said. "You are not to worry. I have my list and will be done in a quarter hour."

Jocelyn brought in a bonnet and pelisse. Black ones. Red and black. She would look like a harlequin. "Jocelyn, please help Althea finish counting out the booklets. I must leave at once."

She hurried to the door, to go hire a hackney for the long ride to Mayfair.

Almost an hour later she entered Gifford House, only to learn her grandmother had not come down yet. Praying that she would not be drawn and quartered for the presumption, she went up to her grandmother's apartment.

She paused outside the door. She never intruded here. She had not since she was ten years old and had snuck in to explore her grandmother's dressing table. Fascinated by the jewelry and paints, she had tried them on, admiring herself in the looking glass. Even now she could see her reflection, then the shock of seeing her grandmother right behind her.

She had paid dearly for putting on that necklace and rouge. Her grandmother had whipped her with a switch while forcing her to gaze at her sins in the looking glass the whole time. Then she had ordered her imprisoned with only bread and water to eat for a week. Her father had been away and did not return and grant a reprieve for two more days.

She could not look at this door and not see herself in that looking glass while a cane stung her bare bottom.

Taking a deep breath and putting the image of herself all painted and bedecked out of her mind, she ventured inside.

She found her grandmother just as her maid was about to fit on her wig. Hair mashed under a net cap and body ensconced in an undressing gown with layers of lace, her grandmother did not notice her until the maid touched her shoulder and pointed to the door.

Those large, pale eyes gave a scathing glare, then turned back to the looking glass. "Take care of me, Margaret, so that I can talk to my intruding granddaughter."

Margaret fitted the wig, tweaked a few gray curls, and stood back.

"Now go and get Theo. Tell him I need him here."

Margaret scurried out of the dressing room.

"Clara, did you wear that dress to provoke me? It is hideous at any time, but especially now."

Clara sat on a divan near the fireplace. "I received your

note. I thought it better to hear this sooner rather than later."

Her grandmother turned on her chair. "Later was not much later. You could have waited until I dressed, at least. Or until you had reconsidered your own garments."

"My apologies. It sounded very important, so I came at once."

Her grandmother turned to the looking glass once more and pinched her cheeks until two pink splotches formed. *Don't pretend you do not paint. We both know you do. You whipped me once for discovering that.*

"You did not want me seeing that house of yours, is what you really mean."

Theo rushed in then. He noticed Clara, averted his eyes from Grandmamma's dishabille, and sat in a chair. "I hope this will not take long. I was on my way out to ride in the park."

"Not long at all. I wanted you here, however, when I explained matters to your sister."

"What matters?" Clara asked. A funny little worry branched through her. She doubted these matters would please her, considering her grandmother's tone.

"I have heard about Brentworth's party. Several of my friends wrote to me. I am pleased to say that their opinions of Emilia's behavior were unexceptionable."

"I tried to be a good chaperone." At least this was not about Harry.

"They also wrote that Stratton was there."

"Yes, I believe he was."

"Believe he was, do you? The way I read it, he spent over an hour in your company."

It seemed as though the dressing room had grown smaller. "Not an hour, I am sure."

"At least an hour, two of my friends reported. Of equal interest is that he spent no time at all with Emilia."

"That is not true. I was present when he and she chatted."

"So he chatted with her for a minute at most. It is clear, Theo, that we made some inaccurate assumptions about the duke and will have to correct our strategy."

"It does appear so," Theo agreed.

"Do not blame Emilia if he was not agreeable to your last one," Clara said. "Expecting him to marry someone from our family was a flawed strategy from the start. I told you that."

Her grandmother stood. In a swish of lace she moved until she sat beside Clara on the divan. "A flawed strategy?" She chortled into the lace at her neck. "Not in principle, it appears. He may have found Emilia lacking, true. However, it appears he finds *you* interesting. I am not a rigid woman. If success means substituting sisters, so be it."

Theo appeared confused. "Stratton wants *her*?"

"It seems he went out of his way to have her company at that party."

Theo came close to laughing. "Hell, that is rich."

"Your language, Theo. As for the duke's preference, there is no accounting for taste."

"I am sorry, Grandmother. It is just that Emilia is so perfect, and Clara is . . ." He shrugged, then cast out an arm in Clara's direction, as if to say *well, that is what she is*.

"She is not the wife I would advise for a duke, but since he did not listen to me on the subject, we will accommodate his peculiar decision."

Theo shook his head. "I don't see the match making him friendly to us. Within six months of the wedding he will be sure he was hoodwinked and be out for blood for sure."

"Should I leave so that the two of you can discuss me

forthrightly? I would not want my presence to interfere," Clara said sharply.

Her grandmother patted her hand. "We have vexed her, Theo. Calm yourself, dear."

"I am quite calm, thank you. However, I regret to tell you that you have completely misjudged the duke's interest. He finds it amusing to goad me, nothing more."

"That is just a boy pulling the hair of a girl he likes," her grandmother said.

"I do not like having my hair pulled. You seem to have forgotten that no matter what the duke prefers, I will not be marrying him or anyone else."

Theo groaned. "Not this again."

"Yes, this again. And again. And again. I fail to understand why you persist in thinking my decision is some passing fancy, when I have held firm to it all these years."

"Decisions can be changed, as this one must be." Her grandmother patted her hand again. "For the family's sake, for your brother's sake, for my sake, you will marry him."

So agitated that she feared she would scream, Clara stood. How dare they interfere at this late stage of her life? *Because Papa is gone and not here to stop them.*

"If this is the important news, I have heard it. I will go now. I encourage you to find some other solution to whatever threat you think the duke presents. Theo, if you keep your wits and do not insult him or his family, he will never challenge you, so all of this plotting is unnecessary anyway."

"If he proposes and you refuse, you will be the one insulting him," Theo snapped.

"I am leaving. I refuse to listen to more of this madness."

"You will not leave. You will stay right here while we plan how you reel him in now that he has been hooked," Grandmamma said.

"Good heavens, Stratton isn't some dumb fish. There will be no reeling. Good day to you."

She got as far as the staircase before the shaking started. She did not know if it resulted from her anger and shock or from the inexplicable desire to laugh.

Halfway down the stairs the last impulse disappeared in a blink. What if Stratton told Theo and her grandmother that he had already proposed? They would be relentless in coercing her to agree. She would have to move to Brazil to save her sanity.

"I am always happy to watch the auctions, but are we here for a reason, Stratton?" Langford asked.

"I intend to buy a horse. What other reason would bring me here?"

They stood in the yard at Tattersalls, along with twenty other men, while horse after horse came out for inspection and bidding. Thus far none had been good enough. Certainly not the bay currently on the block, even if the auctioneer had touted the mare as suitable for a woman.

"You intend to buy today? The five horses in your stable here in town won't do? The twenty you have in the country need a new friend?"

"It is not for me. It is a gift."

"*Ahhhhh*. For your lady, you mean."

"She needs a horse. A very good horse. She is as fine an equestrienne as you will find. She rides better than you do, even though she is stuck on a sidesaddle."

"No woman rides better than I do."

"Once I get her this horse, you can race her and we will see about that."

"You are giving her a lot of gifts. Is it appropriate? First that ruby necklace, now a horse." Langford peered at him. "You *did* give her the ruby necklace, I assume."

"Not yet. That is for later."

"How much later? It has been weeks."

"I am waiting for the right moment."

"Which has not come yet, apparently." Langford grinned. "Methinks the grand seduction is not unfolding as you intended. No, no, there is no need to explain. I am not the kind of man who presses a friend for such intimate details. Perhaps you should have taken notes when I gave my lesson, however."

Adam would not mind thrashing Langford. Had he not wanted another opinion on the horse he chose, he just might have.

"Does she know you are buying her a horse?"

"No."

"A surprise, then. Does her brother's stable have room for another horse?"

"I don't know."

"Shouldn't you find out before you buy one?"

"Stop being so damned practical." That was better than telling Langford that Lady Clara had moved from her family home and now would arrange her own stabling.

Movements near the auctioneer claimed Adam's attention. The bay had been knocked down and grooms led her away. A man led out the next horse. The gelding had deep chestnut coloring, almost black. It stepped high and resisted the hold on its bridle.

"Now that is a damned fine animal," Langford said.

Adam thought so too. He walked over to get a close look, with Langford in his wake.

They gave the horse a thorough examination. Langford checked teeth while Adam lifted legs and hooves. Others also crowded around, but the auctioneer's practiced eye must have spotted the gentlemen likely to bid high because he hovered near Adam.

"Three years old," the man repeated, having just announced that information. "A real beauty. Spirited enough to race. A riding horse, to be sure. Not fit for a carriage, although he can be trained for one."

"How does he take a saddle?"

"He tolerates one well enough. A gentleman like you should have no problem. I would be lying if I did not admit that I would not put a weak rider on him. Has his own mind, he does, and needs a firm hand."

"He sounds just like the rider I have in mind. They may suit each other."

"Then here is hoping you win him. I expect the bidding to go high."

Adam retreated. Langford joined him. "So that is the one? Are you sure? If he throws her, you will feel very guilty."

"She won't get thrown."

"If you say so." Langford did not sound convinced.

Fifteen minutes later Adam arranged payment for the horse and its delivery to his own stable.

"We are not bringing it to her now?" Langford asked while they walked away.

"*We* are never bringing it to her. I am alone. Another day."

"Pity. I wanted to see it. If she loves horses so much, she will probably fall at your feet in capitulation when she receives this one."

Adam pictured that and laughed, although in his mind's eye the capitulating Lady Clara refused to totally surrender.

He was not sure he would want her to.

Chapter Thirteen

Clara woke early Monday morning. The servants she had hired would begin today, and she needed to explain their duties and her expectations. She doubted she would be done by evening.

She dressed and went down to the morning room to have some breakfast. A full sideboard greeted her. Unlike Jocelyn's spare offerings, today there was enough food to feed ten people. She tried some of the eggs. Hot eggs, unlike the lukewarm ones Jocelyn managed.

A woman entered while she ate and placed the mail next to her plate, then retreated. Not Jocelyn. It had looked like one of the women she had considered for the housekeeper position. Presumably it was the one she had hired.

She got up and went looking for the woman. She found her in close conversation with a girl near the stairs down to the kitchen. Upon seeing her, both curtsied. The girl scurried down the stairs.

"I see you are already here, Mrs. Finley. I had hoped to greet you when you arrived."

"Your maid let me in, and I set to it right off. I hope you do not mind."

"Not at all. The cook is here too, I noticed. Could you

tell her that in the future she need not make so much food. I live alone and do not have a big appetite in the mornings. Also tell her that it all tasted wonderful, and the coffee was excellent."

"Yes, milady."

"Could you let me know when Mr. Brady, the coachman, arrives?"

"He is below right now, milady, awaiting your call. Brought a groom like you asked, he said."

She asked Mrs. Finley to send the coachman and groom up to the library. A half hour later all was resolved. The groom was hired, and Mr. Brady was sent out to investigate carriages and a pair for sale so she might have a reason for his employment.

Mrs. Finley ventured into the library as the two men left. "Will you be wanting to direct the cook on meals and such, or should I handle it?"

"I think I will leave it in your capable hands. Tomorrow we will sit down and draw up a reasonable account for you."

"Will there be anything else now, milady?"

"One more thing. Please, sit."

Mrs. Finley settled her stout figure on one of the chairs. Clara had hired her in part because she was a mature woman who came with good references. Mostly, however, Mrs. Finley had reminded her of a housekeeper in her father's employ years ago.

Right now, dressed in a simple gray dress and a large white cap that covered most of her brown hair, Mrs. Finley looked worried. Clara thanked her for taking the household in hand so quickly and neatly, then broached the real topic she wanted to discuss.

Having all these servants posed a risk to some of the journal's contributors. They would no longer visit an empty house used only for meetings. They would now come to a full household in which the journal's activities were visible to curious eyes. A woman who wrote under an assumed name would not like the servants of London aware of her identity.

"When I met with each of you, I was very clear that anyone who works here must be discreet in the extreme. I want to emphasize that once again and ask that you in turn speak with the others about it. I cannot have the servants gossiping to their friends about this house. At times important people visit, even outside calling hours, and their comings and goings are not to be mentioned outside this property. Any lack of discretion will be worse than thievery in my view. I am that serious about this."

"Yes, milady."

"I regret that I must charge you with enforcing this rule. If you suspect any of the others of being disloyal, you must inform me."

"Yes, milady. You are not to concern yourself. I will make sure lips are buttoned when they leave this house."

It was the best she could do. She hoped it was enough. One slip and she would have to find another home for the journal. That would be inconvenient.

Her busy morning had taken only an hour and a half, thanks to Mrs. Finley. She went up to her chamber and spent the rest of the morning with Jocelyn, going through the wardrobe to find dresses appropriate to half mourning. Having made their appearances at Brentworth's party, Emilia and she had begun receiving invitations to other events. She looked forward to playing chaperone at a few more.

At half past one, while writing letters, a rap on her door brought Jocelyn out of the dressing room to open it.

Mrs. Finley stood on the threshold, flushed and a little breathless.

"My apologies, milady, but a gentleman has called." She handed Jocelyn a card. "A most distinguished gentleman. One of those important people you spoke of this morning. I've put him in the library."

Jocelyn closed the door and handed Clara the card with a bland expression, but her eyes sparkled.

The card belonged to the Duke of Stratton.

Without either of them saying a word, Jocelyn came over to fuss with her hair, then gave her dress a critical frown before nodding.

As presentable as she could manage, Clara went down to the library. She found Stratton perusing the mostly empty bookcases. At the moment he was at the one that held the published copies of *Parnassus*. She trusted he had not removed any of them for a closer inspection, but if he had he would just assume she subscribed.

He turned on hearing her step. Her heart rose on fluttering wings at the smile he gave her. "You need more books."

"The decorator recommended a shop where I can buy them by the yard. I thought it would be more fun to choose each one myself. It will take more time, but in a few years I will probably have most of the shelves full."

He came to her, bowed over her hand, and kissed it. "You neglected to repeat your command that I not visit, so here I am. Are you angry with me?"

She could not say what she should say. He would know she lied. Worse, he would know her for a coward and a woman who did not know her own mind. "I am not angry. I am glad that you called."

"Come with me," he said, still holding her hand and coaxing her to the doorway. "I must test my luck and hope this does not anger you either."

She followed him to the front entry. He opened it to reveal his horse tied out in front. Another horse stood beside it. A wonderful horse, as fine as Galahad and similar in build but darker in color. Almost black. It wore a sidesaddle.

Stratton went down and gave the horse's neck a firm stroke. "You can name him what you like. I have already arranged for his board and care at a stable in the nearby mews."

She stepped down and joined him to stand where the horse could see her and she him. "He is beautiful. I do not understand, however."

"He is yours. I found him for you. Women do not go to the auctions, so to get the best I had to do it. Do you like him?"

"I adore him." Oh, what a horse. He had gorgeous lines and an imperial gleam in his eyes. She petted his nose. The horse eyed her, taking her measure just as she took his. "What do I owe you for him?"

"Nothing. He is a gift, of course." Stratton sounded vaguely exasperated but appeared delighted with her reaction to the animal.

A gift. A very valuable one. To accept would be compromising. To refuse outright would be insulting. "I must insist on buying him. I will do so when my trust next pays out."

"You are a stubborn woman. I went to great trouble to give you a gift, and now you are turning me into little more than your horsemonger."

"I appreciate the trouble. I do. I could have never found him myself. He is a wonderful surprise. However, I cannot accept a gift this valuable."

He sighed with annoyance. "I will have my steward

inform your trustee of the amount. I am not going to take your money outright or willingly agree to this."

"Thank you. I must give him the perfect name and will put my mind to it."

"If you change into a habit, we can go for a ride in the park before it gets too crowded. You can contemplate his name while you ride him."

Her better sense said she should decline this ride. Her excitement over the horse silenced that voice in two seconds. "Come inside and wait while I dress properly. Only a short ride, however. I have many household duties today."

Twenty minutes later she sat in the saddle. The horse immediately tested her when they set out. He tried to trot before her signal. She reined him in firmly.

Stratton missed none of it. "The auctioneer warned he needed a firm hand. He is spirited, and as you just saw, somewhat rebellious."

"I can manage him."

"I knew you could. The two of you have much in common and will find common ground quickly."

"Are you comparing me to a horse?"

"Only in the best way."

"I suppose I do not mind too much. It could have been something else. Like a fish."

They made their way to the Strand and rode its length, maneuvering through the crush of carriages. She kept her attention on her horse, to ensure that the common ground they found was that which she chose.

When they reached Mayfair, Stratton guided them onto the residential streets so they would not parade down Bond or Piccadilly. Finally they entered Hyde Park.

"Have you chosen a name yet?" he asked.

"He is opinionated, moody, and persistent. Perhaps I should call him Duke."

"I don't know any dukes with those qualities."

"Don't you? I do. The park is fairly empty, it is so early. Shall I give him his head? The poor thing is in agony at this pace."

"Absolutely. I will follow."

She brought her horse to a gallop quickly and aimed for the western area of the park. A few other riders exercised their mounts there, charging to and fro. She found a perfect rhythm and enjoyed the speed as much as her horse did.

She pulled up and Stratton did beside her. "I have decided. Duke it will be. There is real nobility in him."

"Duke it is, although when I am with you it may not be clear whom you address."

"I will call you Stratton."

"I would prefer it be Adam."

It seemed a small thing, but she knew it was not. She doubted anyone except his mother called him Adam. This invitation to informality implied a continued and growing intimacy.

She debated her answer. While she did, a horseman rode toward them, hailing Stratton. She squinted to see who it might be and recognized the horse, the coat, and the blond hair. Theo closed in fast.

What bad luck.

Theo reined in his horse and favored her with a huge smile. He all but glowed. Even while he greeted Stratton, his delight was all for her. She had not seen her brother this happy in months.

Very bad luck.

"What a fine mount you have there, Clara. One of yours, Stratton?"

"He is mine," Clara said. "I just got him. I did not want to impose on your generosity all the time."

"I would not have minded, although it would have been inconvenient for you to cross town for my stable." Theo glanced slyly at Stratton to see what, if any, reaction that evoked. Since the duke did not appear the slightest bit confused, Theo must have concluded Stratton knew where she lived now. His blue eyes sparkled with satisfaction.

Damnable, hellish luck.

"I must return to my friends," Theo said. "I will leave the two of you to entertain each other." He pivoted his horse and rode back whence he had come.

"You are not pleased he saw us," Stratton said.

"Not at all."

"You will have to tell them sometime."

"There is nothing to tell."

"Of course there is. Will the whole world know that before you do?" He turned his horse. "Let us go this way."

This way led into the depths of the park, far from the bridle and walking paths. No one would see them here and grin knowingly the way Theo had done.

No one will see us here. She looked over at Stratton, thinking she should object. Only she did not want to. She hoped he was up to no good. A tightness in her breathing said as much. A disgraceful anticipation claimed her. She might be standing on a precipice, preparing to jump, hoping she would fly and not fall.

He dismounted on an isolated patch of grass and tied his horse. He plucked her down from Duke and tied him as well. Together they sat on the grass.

"I would appreciate it if you did not tell anyone you tried to give me Duke as a gift," she said. "It could be misunderstood as other than a gesture of friendship."

"Probably so, since I am not in the habit of giving mere friends horses. I am also unlikely to kiss them senseless, or caress their bodies, or—"

"You know what I mean. I also think we could just all decide that whatever caused the break between our families is over and done and no longer important. So much anger when no one even knows what happened is ridiculous."

"I know what happened."

She turned in surprise. "You do? Lady Hollsworth said it was probably honor, a woman, or land."

"It was land. My father explained it all to me. Your father probably did the same with Theo, although I doubt he and I heard the same stories."

She waited. He watched the horizon, his fine profile tempting her to reach out and trace its line. Maybe she would let him remain silent and just spend the next half hour looking at him.

Only she was curious. If this man was in her life now, she wanted to know why he had not been before.

"Are you going to tell me?"

He seemed to think about that. "It started with our grandfathers. There was a tract of land in the county that they disputed. An inheritance on your grandfather's part, but my grandfather had an earlier claim."

"Or said he did."

She received a sharp look for that.

"I am just reminding us both that there are two sides here. Two stories. Please, go on."

"It went into the courts, and as such things happen, nothing was resolved during their lifetimes. The lawyers got fat, the rents went into escrow, and nothing progressed."

"Is it still like that?"

He shook his head. "Your father found a solution. While my father was in France, courting and marrying my mother, your father went to the courts again. He revived the dormant case and pressed for a judgment. Our solicitor was caught off guard by the fast movement. It was all done within one week. Needless to say, your father received the benefit of that judgment."

"I do not care for how you said all of this. Not for your choice of words, nor your tone. You have implied that my father was dishonorable."

"More that he was very shrewd."

"I am sure it was a coincidence that the courts addressed this right then."

"Clara, there are no coincidences in Chancery. The timing and the speed spoke of someone with strong influence pushing this forward."

"I still think that—oh!"

He pulled her toward him and into an embrace. "Hush," he murmured before kissing her.

She allowed those kisses to vanquish her indignation. They removed any thoughts of old family wars from her mind. She could be very happy, she thought, being kissed for hours in the sweet breeze.

That was not to be, however. He checked his building passion. For a long, quiet spell they sat there, entwined, not speaking. She ached, and wondered if he did too.

"Is it your intention to always live alone?" he asked.

"Yes."

"Why?"

"Can you believe that no one has asked me that before? I am not sure I have even asked myself." She did now, so she could try to answer. "My father remarried when I was a child. Since his new wife was not my mother, I may have noticed things I otherwise would not. The way she obeyed and deferred. The assumptions he made about his power over her and her property. I did not especially like her, but I still thought it unfair. I had more freedom than she did. I even had more of the real him than she did. He never taught her to shoot or took her hunting. Her place in his life was a very small one, it seemed to me."

"There are some couples who share more affection than you are describing."

"I do not know if they lacked affection. Perhaps they loved each other deeply. It made no difference. So I decided one day, when I heard her petitioning to visit a friend, like a child might beg a governess, and heard him deny her that small freedom—for no good reason, it seemed to me—I decided I would not live like that if I had the choice. And I did have the choice. Of all the privileges of my station, that has been the greatest one."

He gently stroked her cheek with his fingertips. "Was it also your intention to live like a nun? To deny yourself physical love? It is a part of your nature as surely as your ability to think and to know emotion."

"I never intended that. You are not the first man to kiss me. I have not lived like a nun."

He leaned forward and kissed her. "That is good to know."

Again those yearnings flowed, enough that she kissed him back with more aggression than she had used before. He turned hard and demanding in response.

"This will never do," he murmured between kisses that belied his words. "If we keep doing this in places like this, inevitably we will be seen."

She found the strength to press him away and create a gap between their bodies. His arms remained around her, however.

He was right. They risked too much with these games. She risked everything.

"Come with me to my house," he said. "It is only a few streets away."

She wanted to agree to go. Every inch of her body did.

But those streets were the most dangerous streets in her world. Dozens of people who lived on those streets knew her. Hundreds. She could not ride down one of them without being recognized. Nor could he. To then risk being seen entering his property, his home . . .

"That will never do either," she said. "You know it will not."

"In a few minutes I may know it. Right now I want you so badly I do not give a damn who sees what."

She had to laugh at that, ruefully. "I am not allowed to not give a damn."

He released her from his embrace but kept one arm around her. "I will find a way. When I do I intend to take my time, after the hell I am going through."

Take his time?

He noticed her puzzlement. He crooked his arm around her neck and eased her head next to his. "Kissing you. Touching you. All of you. Your neck." He kissed her neck. "Your breasts." His hand skimmed over her breast, creating a jolt of pleasure. "Your thighs." He caressed her thigh from knee to hip.

He did not stop talking. He told her, in shocking detail, what else he would do. It was the kind of thing decent men never said to decent women. At least she did not think so. She would have stopped him except his words mesmerized her, and her simmering arousal threatened to become a conflagration.

A deep silence heavy with sensual power followed his scandalous description.

"We should ride back," she said.

"I can probably do so in another ten minutes."

It took her a moment to understand what he meant. Then she blushed hotly. He laughed.

Society had arrived at the park by the time they rode

back to the gate. People were busy with each other, and being seen, so she did not notice too many people paying attention to them.

"I can ride home on my own," she said. "Tell me which stable you arranged for me to use."

"I will not hear of it. I will escort you there."

She would have preferred he not do that. Now that she was riding again and no longer in his embrace, she could not rid herself of the feeling that she had been scandalous today. Deliciously so. Not because of the kisses but rather for having heard what he said, and how he said it, and allowing those faint touches and sensual provocations.

At her house, he helped her dismount, then took her horse's reins. "I will bring him to the stable. It is Cooper's place, in the western mews."

"Thank you."

He bent to give her a kiss before returning to his saddle and leading Duke away. She watched him until he turned off the square.

Before entering her house, she looked up the façade as if something invisible called for her attention. She caught a flash of a white cap at a window before it disappeared. Jocelyn had been watching them. Or else Mrs. Finley had.

Chapter Fourteen

Clara sat at her library table with paper, ink, and pen. She tried to plan the next edition of *Parnassus*.

It was not going well. Her mind dwelled elsewhere, not on the mix of essays and articles that might appeal to women readers.

While she ate her dinner, a few hard truths had presented themselves. They demanded attention and contemplation, and since she could not remove them from her mind, she faced them squarely now.

First, Theo had seen her with Stratton and drawn conclusions that were not warranted. She would be lucky not to find her grandmother placing an engagement announcement in the papers before the week was out.

Second, while the two of them had not attracted much attention, they had been seen together. After spending time with each other at Brentworth's party, rumors were bound to start.

Third, she had learned the history of their families' old feud, and in telling it Stratton had blamed her father far more than his. She thought that ungallant. If he had not kissed her, she would have pointed out how unfair his interpretation had been. Only he had, and once more caused her to forget too quickly why she was not supposed to like him or to accept his company and how those rumors of his seeking revenge might be true and might even touch on her family.

Four—she sighed heavily when she admitted this—unless her astonishment led her to misunderstand, or unless Stratton spoke in poetic euphemisms, she had all but given him permission to do things to her that she had never realized men did to any women, least of all women like her.

Finally—she sighed again, at her lack of good sense—she might have also allowed him to think she was agreeable to an affair. Which she was not. A kiss now and then was one thing. An affair would be too delicious—no, not delicious! Where had that word come from? Rash and dangerous, that was what it would be.

She repeated those two words again in her mind. She focused on them. She pictured herself explaining that to him. Except he looked magnificent in her imagination, that little smile forming while she disabused him of that entire notion. Then he interrupted her with a kiss, and a hundred sparkles of excitement enlivened her in that fantasy. And in reality too, where she sat on the chair.

She got hold of herself and forced her attention again to her blank paper. She picked up her pen and dipped it, determined to do more this evening than swoon over the Duke of Stratton. She had allowed too much familiarity, and look where it had brought her. To secretly relishing just how dangerous a man could be.

Adam prowled his house, pacing through its immense chambers and halls. His banyan billowed behind him.

He had unbuttoned it because its warmth smothered him. He felt no night chill, even with many of the windows open. Rather the opposite. A discomfort like a fever tormented him.

The heat burned in his head more than his body. Erotic images and impulses lodged there. Nothing had dispelled them. Not reading. Not burying himself in estate accounts. Not itemizing what he had and had not learned about the intrigue surrounding his father's death.

Immersing himself in those details had been a desperate, futile attempt to break Clara's hold on him. Everything indicated her father had added fuel to the fire of those rumors and possibly started them himself. The dowager may well have urged him on. Her current belated efforts to forge a peace all but said so.

He still cared about that, furiously so, but thinking about Clara kept interfering with the righteous anger he had carried back from France. Her blind loyalty to her father, seen again just this afternoon, mattered now, even if it had not at first. When he first decided to pursue her, it had been an impulse born of lust and revenge, an oblique way to prod old enemies by taking possession of that family's most privileged and prized daughter. Now he envisioned her hurt if he discovered things that impugned the late earl.

Duty, duty. He chanted that word in his mind when he found himself making excuses for not doing what he needed to do, all because of a woman. He could not ignore that the more he knew her, the more she weakened his resolve. Who would care if he let history lie buried? Not his mother.

His strides took him to the gallery outside the ballroom. Moonlight streamed in the long windows on one side of the long hall, giving form to the benches and plants and framed images. He walked down its length beneath the gazes of ancestors until he came to his father's portrait. He had not sought out that painting, but he stopped when he saw it.

He and his father did not look much alike. Adam took after his mother more. His father had been thoroughly English, with a long, full face and intelligent eyes. He wore a white wig in the portrait, and a vague smile. He had looked nothing like that the last time Adam saw him, and it was that last view that remained vivid in his memory now. Perhaps if his father had known what a pistol ball to the temple did to a body, he would have chosen another way.

Duty, duty. He could not turn back, of course. Acknowledging his duty did not banish thoughts about Clara or even cause him to weigh his choices rationally. He strode on, pacing through the night, fighting a battle that he knew a man almost never won, against the urge to possess a woman he desired.

Not for the first time that night Clara broke out of sleep and into wakefulness. She twisted in her bed, pulling the sheet and coverlet this way and that, turning on her side. While she thumped her pillows, her eyes opened for a moment. Yellow and silver light pooled on her bedclothes. Fully awake now, she looked at her window. The drapes were drawn back, and light from both the moon and the square's streetlamps filtered in like fairy dust.

She thought she had seen Jocelyn close the drapes. Apparently not. Annoyed by her maid's carelessness, she hopped out of bed and padded over to do it herself.

"Do not. With no lamp, I will not be able to see you if you do that."

Her hand clutched the drapery while her body froze in shock. She pivoted. Stratton sat in a chair across her chamber, as relaxed as if he owned the house. In fact, it appeared he had been sitting there some time, from the way his legs stretched out and the manner in which he rested his head on one bent arm's hand.

"What—How did you get up here?"

"Your housekeeper let me in. I knocked, she arrived at the door in dishabille, and with one look she turned and brought me up. She was good enough to point to your door before continuing to the next level."

"What bizarre behavior."

"She seemed to think you expected me." He drew in his legs and leaned forward while he shrugged off his frock coat.

"She just started today. I will have to explain to her in the strongest terms that—" Bits of her conversation with Mrs. Finley that morning interrupted her thoughts. The bits about discretion and important people visiting, even at unusual hours. No one was more important than a duke. Nothing required discretion more than an unmarried woman's affair with a man.

The duke now unbuttoned his waistcoat. Panic thumped in her heart.

"The housekeeper made a mistake. The household—my maid—"

"Your maid saw me too. I looked up the stairwell while she was peering down."

"Oh, dear heaven."

"Neither she nor the housekeeper seemed shocked by my arrival. Only you do." He removed the waistcoat and set it on top of the frock coat on the chair by her writing desk. "Do you want me to leave, Clara? If you do, say so

now, before I finish undressing. It will be very annoying if
you become a coward after I am naked."

Naked.

He waited. She stared. How hard could it be to say *yes,
I do want you to leave?* Very hard, it turned out. Because
most of her did not want him to leave, and the rest was not
sure.

He bent and removed his boots. He stood. "You look
lovely in the moonlight. Ethereal. All silvers and grays."

She looked down at herself. Unless she was mistaken,
that light made her thin lawn nightdress transparent. She
did not know if she appeared ethereal, but she suspected
she looked almost naked herself.

She resisted the impulse to pull the drape around her.
She did not care for the way he used that word *coward,* as
if sending him away showed a lack of character instead of
admirable restraint. A respectable woman deciding to
remain respectable was not a coward. She was careful and
sensible and—and—She sighed, because the excitement
singing through her refused to hear the old, predictable
lessons about good sense and every other boring word ever
used to discourage pleasure.

All the same, she would have to stand her ground,
almost naked though she was, and do what she must. To
have him in her own bedchamber, her own bed, was
beyond dangerous. It was insanely reckless.

She looked up to explain that to him, confident that he
would understand like the gentleman he was. Just as she
did, he pulled off his shirt, and suddenly she forgot what
she intended to say.

Clara just looked at him, her eyes wide with excitement
and fear. It had occurred to him, when she woke and he

saw her shock at his presence, to give her one kiss and retreat. Except she did look lovely and would look more beautiful once he removed that cap. Nor did she scream or order him to leave. Instead she watched him, so obviously of two minds that he guessed the debate in her mind.

It was the cap that told him for certain that she did not feign surprise at seeing him. A woman anticipating a man's arrival in her bedchamber would never wear that. The fool of a new housekeeper had drawn conclusions that Clara herself had not. He had been delighted by the mistake before he knew it to be one. The idea that she expected him, welcomed him, and made arrangements to receive him banished any indecision. He had almost taken the stairs three at a time.

He went over to her and took her into his arms. "You have not spoken. I am here because of a comedy of errors, but it must still be your choice if I stay."

She placed her palms flat on his chest, then laid her cheek on the skin between them. The fine lawn on her bed dress offered little barrier to the feel of her body beneath his hands and arms. Her soft, sweet warmth entered him and soothed the restless discontent he had lived with tonight.

"You must be gone before five."

"I will be gone well before."

"You must tell no one. You must swear it. And you must promise to die before you tell my family."

"Die?"

She looked up into his eyes. A spark of the Clara he so admired shone brightly amid others that reflected her enchantment. He could feel her arousal. But she had not abandoned herself. "Yes, die. They are not to know."

"I so swear." He would probably swear to anything right now.

She stretched up and wrapped her arms around his

neck. She gave him a small kiss. "Then I have decided I will not be a coward, as you put it so ungenerously."

"That was my hunger for you trying to tip the balance in my favor."

"I know. It worked."

He plucked off the cap. Her hair tumbled down. He stretched his fingers through it and held her head to a kiss that had waited hours to be released. The ferocity of his desire burst hot and hard. It threatened to conquer him. He had to force control so he did not ravish her then and there.

He unbuttoned the top of her nightdress until it gapped enough that he could ease it down her shoulders and arms. She huddled against him to hide her nakedness. He pushed the dress over her hips, then lifted her in his arms and carried her to the bed.

She pulled the bedclothes up as soon as he laid her down. He settled next to her. "Are you cold?"

She shook her head.

He eased the bedclothes away. "Then don't do that. I want to see you."

She closed her eyes as he peeled away her shield. He left her like that while he stood and removed the rest of his garments. The sight of her lying there had his mind burning.

"It is said the French are very good at this," she said.

"I am half English."

"Perhaps you should speak French, so as to call on that half."

"I do not think I will be speaking much. My mouth will be too busy."

He rejoined her and braced on one arm while he caressed her neck and down her chest between her breasts. Already their tips rose hard and high.

Her own hand stroked his arm. She looked up at him.

"Do you really intend to do all those things you spoke of this afternoon?"

"Not all of them tonight." He would not have the patience.

"That was very bad of you. Very scandalous."

"And yet you did nothing to stop me. Not one gasp. Not one word."

"I was too shocked."

"It looked to me like you were fascinated." And aroused. Definitely aroused. He would never have gone so far if not for that. He palmed both tips lightly.

She gasped. "Oh! That feels even better without clothing."

He made sure she learned just how much better. He caressed her breasts until she moaned with pleasure, then lowered his head and used his tongue and mouth.

Wildness claimed her so quickly she must not have fought it at all. Her passion inflamed his own. Erotic images plagued him, but he kept enough sense to know this was not the night for them.

He stroked to her legs, then pressed his hand up between her thighs. Joyful shock rang out in her cries. He explored her moist softness while he continued arousing her with teeth and tongue. Lost to the sensations, she parted her legs more and told him with her begging sighs that she wanted more when his caresses increased her pleasure.

Raw hunger broke free in him. Nothing less than thrusting inside her would satisfy that need now. He gritted his teeth and stroked the places that would force her to her release if she permitted it. He heard her climb in her cries and felt it in her body's movements. He also felt her fear. He pressed his mouth to her ear and told her to let go. She did, embracing that oblivion with a scream.

He moved to take her. Her arms rose to clutch him. He

leashed enough sense to go slow at first and learned that was a damned good thing. He held himself back so he did not hurt her further while desire howled in him. He silenced that primitive voice long enough to know the calmer pleasure of the feel of her encasing him. He stroked long and slow while he could, but eventually the need for completion defeated him. Release came like a cataclysm. It pitched him into dark silence where no other senses existed and where utter peace waited.

Having experience with many women, Adam knew better than to fall asleep the way his whole body encouraged. Instead, as he emerged back into the world, he rolled off Clara and pulled her into his arm by his side.

It behooved him to say something as soon as his mind would cooperate. Experience gained him nothing there, however. This was a first time for her, which made it his first time too, in a manner of speaking.

Clara was ready to talk even if he was not. For reasons he never understood, women turned chatty at such times. She was no exception.

"That was very nice," she said. "It did not hurt nearly as much as I expected."

"That is good to know." The nice part pleased him. The not hurting part relieved him. It seemed to him he might have hurt her, now that a few memories infiltrated his mind.

She rose up on her elbow and looked at him. "I know gentlemen are supposed to feel guilty when they have been with innocents, but I trust you do not."

"I do not feel guilty at all, since I intend that we will marry."

"See? There is that guilt, even if you deny it. Well, I absolve you."

"Clara, I already proposed. Remember?"

"You did not really propose. You did not mean it. It was an easy, safe proposal because you made it to a woman who never intended to marry. I am only saying that I do not want you now making it serious out of guilt."

"It is not guilt. Although, considering what just happened, there really is no choice now."

"Of course there is. Do not pretend that honor now requires it. You knew I was a virgin yet did not restrain yourself. More to the point, you knew I was a virgin who would not marry you even after we did this."

He would not insult her by saying he had known nothing of the sort. The odds had been about even on the virginity question. She was the kind of woman who might have taken a lover out of curiosity if nothing else.

She may have just done that with him.

"So we are agreed. No guilt, and also no obligations," she said.

He agreed to nothing. There was time enough to argue about it another day.

That topic finished to her satisfaction, she nestled in beside him again. "I know why you really left England. I know about your father."

He had barely put his mind back together, and this turn in subject took him aback. "What do you know?"

"How he died. You must have been very sad."

"I was more angry than sad. At him. At his reasons."

"I know about those too. The reasons. It all sounds most unfair to me."

"What do you know?" he repeated, carefully.

"Bits and pieces only. About the rumors. I heard some jewels played a role."

He made great efforts to keep his tone casual and not pointed. "Who told you that?"

"Lady Hollsworth, at the garden party."

It had been a mistake not to force a conversation with Hollsworth. A mistake to put it off.

"I know nothing about any jewels. I think she misspoke," he said.

"Perhaps."

Nothing more came for several minutes. He dared allow himself to begin falling asleep.

"I have thought since I first met you that you carried a darkness in you," she said, pulling him awake again. "Something that made you brood. Just now, while we were together in pleasure, I was spared even the slightest touch of grief for the first time in six months. It seemed to me that perhaps the darkness lifted in you too, for a while. If so, I am glad."

It had lifted, in ways it never had in France no matter whose bed he shared. That she had noticed impressed him. That she was glad for it touched him.

She required no confirmation that she was correct. Having said her piece, she was done. She nestled beside him, silent in her contentment, not even demanding more conversation.

Chapter Fifteen

"Milady, milady!" Mrs. Finley's frantic call penetrated the door of the bedchamber.

Clara bolted up in her bed, still half-asleep. Her nakedness slapped her awake. While she grabbed her bedclothes around her, trying to cover every inch of skin up to her neck, her gaze bolted around her chamber, seeking evidence of her visitor.

None could be seen. He was gone, probably hours ago while she slept, just as he promised. The only evidence of last night was *her*.

Jocelyn hurried to open the door. Mrs. Finley gasped out words between heavy breaths. "The countess. The earl. Here. Their carriage." She stopped and inhaled deeply. "The house is not ready. There is not enough breakfast. I will run and tell the cook to do something." She turned and hurried off.

Jocelyn ran to the window overlooking the street. "They are at the door."

"What can they be thinking, coming at this hour?"

"It is almost ten o'clock."

"Help me to get washed and dressed so I can receive

them. No, first run down to Mrs. Finley and say she is to
most definitely put them in the morning room with breakfast, and if my grandmother refuses, then in the library. I
will be down soon."

Jocelyn ran off. Clara found her nightdress among the
tangled sheet and coverlet and pulled it on. Was it her
imagination that the whole bed carried a scent this morning? She sniffed, then flushed. There was no mistaking
what had happened here.

She rushed to the dressing room. Hot water already
waited and she began to use it, not waiting for Jocelyn.

Jocelyn returned and grabbed a towel. "They may be
coming up here. Mrs. Finley is holding her ground, but the
dowager is staring her down and I do not think it is a fair
match."

Why, of all the—"Do something with my hair, quickly."

"I cannot manage more than a knot now."

"Then make a knot. But first close the door to my bedchamber. Bolt it. If my grandmother so much as takes a
step in that direction, you are to throw yourself against the
boards and refuse to move no matter what she threatens."

The knot was barely done when they heard voices on
the stairs. Jocelyn ran to the wardrobe, grabbed an undressing gown, and threw it across the chamber to Clara.
Clara drew it on and buttoned it with shaking hands.

"My good woman, you will move, or my son will move
you," the dowager threatened darkly, her voice booming
right outside the dressing room door.

"I am telling you she was still abed and instructed me
to ask you to wait until she dressed, milady."

"I do not wait on my grandchildren. Rather the opposite.
Can you believe your sister's boldness, Theo? She intrudes
on my chambers while I dress, but I am not to do the same,
it appears. We will have none of that. Stand aside, I say."

"Go and invite them in through this door, Jocelyn, before Mrs. Finley is cast down the stairs." Clara did not like her grandmother's tone. Not at all.

Jocelyn opened the door and stood aside. Grandmamma sailed into the room with a rumpled and yawning Theo in her wake.

Any sternness left her grandmother once she set eyes on Clara. A happy smile stretched her face. She came over and bestowed a rare kiss on Clara's crown. "No, do not get up. Tell your maid to continue if she was about to do something with that terrible hair. A knot? I would be the first to say you are due for a new style, but that is not it."

"Good morning, Grandmamma. Theo."

Theo grunted. As soon as their grandmother sat, he threw himself onto a small divan and stretched out his legs. Grandmamma whacked those legs with her parasol. "Show some respect, Theo. We are not at some tavern. Forgive him, Clara. I seem to have had him woken not long after he returned from a night of doing who knows what." The way she skewered Theo with a glare suggested one who knew what, or at least suspected.

Clara was not above seeking an alliance for what she thought would be an unpleasant conversation. "He is young, Grandmamma. You cannot expect him to behave like a fifty-year-old man."

Theo sent her a glance of gratitude.

"Fortunately he also lacks the discretion of one, or I might have never learned how your courtship with Stratton progresses apace. Well done, Clara. Well done, indeed."

Clara glared at Theo. He shrugged, helplessly.

"What did Theo say?"

"In his delight and relief at seeing your rendezvous with Stratton in the park, he told me all about it." She leaned forward. "And I do mean all, Clara. *All*."

"Yes, we rode in the park together. I did not think you would want me to cut him. Nor is rendezvous an accurate way to describe it."

"You do not have to dissemble with me, dear. I know about accidental meetings that are not true rendezvous." She gave a big wink.

Clara dared not respond. She could not be sure what Theo had seen or not seen. She had assumed that after he spoke with them, he busied himself with his friends. But what if, on seeing them ride toward privacy, he had followed? What if he had seen more than riding and talking? What if he had seen *all*?

She peered at her brother, hoping to discern just how bad her situation might be. Unfortunately, he had dozed off.

"Let him sleep," her grandmother said. "Now, tell me. Has Stratton given you any valuable gifts?"

Only a very fine horse and a night to remember for the rest of my life. "What do you mean, valuable? Like a nice lace handkerchief?"

"Oh, my, no. You are so very green. With your advancing years, I often forget that. Valuable like expensive jewelry."

"He has given me no jewelry of any value."

"How unfortunate. I had rather hoped . . . After what Theo told me . . ."

"What exactly did Theo tell you? And was he drunk when doing the telling?"

"If he was drunk, it was from happiness. He all but danced with delight when he returned from that ride. The duke is clearly in love, he said. The man could not take his eyes off you, he said. The two of you rode away to where you might find some *privacy*, he said." She lowered her chin and looked up meaningfully on that part.

Clara feared she might blush and give it all away. "If he had followed us, he would have found us having an argument. A rather loud one on a subject not for the ears of the entire ton. Although the duke and I have a friendship of sorts, it is not in any way romantic. Considering our two families, how could it be?"

Grandmamma did not care for that. She pursed her lips and contemplated this unfortunate news. "He has no need for a friendship with you of any kind, Clara. If he seeks your company, his intentions are rather more than friendship. You must tell me if he gives you, or attempts to give you, any fine jewelry. It implies things when a man does that. For a woman of your breeding, it is a declaration and all but ensures that a proposal will be forthcoming very soon, if not immediately."

Clara wondered what it implied for a woman not of her breeding. Intentions not honorable, most likely.

Her grandmother once more whacked Theo's legs with her parasol. "We will take our leave so that you can dress. Do see about a new style for your hair. And tell your maid to tidy up." She speared the nightdress with the tip of her parasol and held it aloft to wave like a flag. She began to speak but stopped. She peered at that nightdress. She sniffed. "Goodness, find a new laundress too. What did yours use on this garment? Fish water?"

"I will be sure to find a better one."

The nightdress fluttered close to Theo before Grandmamma dropped it. Theo stared at the garment on the floor, then frowned. He turned to Clara with a quizzical expression.

Clara looked right back and feigned obliviousness to his curiosity. That scent now seemed to fill the dressing room.

"You should also replace that housekeeper and your maid." Her grandmother continued intoning opinions while she stood. "And do not get any pets. I cannot abide women who live alone and keep menageries."

"And here I was thinking to buy a parrot from South America. I thought I would bring him over so you could teach him to talk. Then I would have the joy of your lessons all the time."

"Be careful, Clara. I am not too old to recognize sarcasm, and you walk a fine line these days with me. Come along, Theo. And remember, Clara, any gift of value, any gift at all for that matter, tell me at once. No, tell me about *anything* that happens with him. I do not want you mishandling this opportunity. You will need my advice."

She sailed out. Theo glanced once more at the nightdress before following. "Do try not to ruin it, Clara. It isn't as if any other man would take you on now," he said in parting.

Jocelyn entered after they passed, and closed the door. "That sounded jolly."

Clara thought Theo's last words sounded ominous. As if he knew. Or guessed. She glared at that nightdress. Grandmamma might have forgotten that scent, but as a young man recently come into his fortune, Theo might be very familiar with it these days.

"Help me dress, Jocelyn." She thought about that blank paper still waiting for her in the library. She would try to make some progress on it today. It would be hard. Already her thoughts floated back to the night before, and her heart to the emotions discovered within that intimacy.

Adam finished his letter to Clara and gave it to the butler to post. He also gave instructions to the man to send to the servants at one of his properties.

Correspondence finished, he called for his horse and

rode to the City. He swallowed a temptation to call on a house in Bedford Square and continued straight away to a building near Lincoln's Inn. There he presented himself at the chambers of Claudius Leland, his solicitor.

Mr. Leland had inherited his duties to the Duke of Stratton a year prior to Adam's inheritance. Letters from Mr. Leland had arrived with regularity in Paris, long missives containing many details about the estate. With Adam gone, the solicitor had taken it upon himself to demand reports from every property and even visited the main ones each quarter. True, he had missed how the steward at Drewsbarrow had stolen several thousand pounds, but the thief had been very clever with the accounts, and Adam did not hold that sorry event against the solicitor.

Now Mr. Leland peered at him through spectacles. He was not a young man, but his thin hair remained red and his coloring still healthy. They sat in two chairs by a nice fireplace. Bookcases covered the walls, most of them filled with ledgers and portfolios. One deep shelf held scrolls. Although the hour was early, Leland offered some sherry. Then he waited to hear the reason for the visit.

"I am curious about any estate jewelry," Adam said.

"Your forefathers accumulated some fine pieces over the generations. Most are not of styles to be fashionable today, but the stones and metals are of very high value. For the most part, they are left with the bank. One would not have such valuables in one's home any more than a prudent man keeps thousands of banknotes on hand."

"And the estate owns them? How does that work?"

Mr. Leland crossed his legs. He looked like a man happy to explain his particular expertise to anyone, especially a new young duke whom he still needed to impress. "Officially they belong to each duke in turn. There is no way to entail such things. Traditions of inheritance do form, however. For example, it is customary in families for someone, usually a trusted solicitor, to explain to a new duchess that while she can wear the jewels, and while any gift given directly to her by her husband becomes her personal property, the family jewels are not hers in a legal sense and remain with the estate."

"So my father or grandfather could have given any of these valuables to whomever they chose. Or sold some of them."

"As can you now, of course. Do you have an interest in doing so?"

"I am more interested in learning how someone would know if I did."

"Ah. We now have a conversation that we have thus far been denied. No one would know if you did, except you, me, and the next duke. An inventory is taken of all of the property when there is a death of its owner. One was done by me after your father passed. Another inventory of the valuable property is done every ten years thereafter. If there is a lack of concordance between the two, it is my duty to inquire as to why."

"I expect that at times something goes missing with no explanation."

"It is my duty to find it, even if that means ascertaining there has been a theft or careless loss. Sometimes with my patrons I already know something has been sold because it is in the accounts. More commonly my patrons inform me when personal property of such value is disbursed so that I can make a note and not wonder how it happened."

"Yet the first inventory that you made was after my father passed."

"That is true, but I have all the records. They were moved here when I had the honor of taking over for my predecessor. Would you like to see the last inventory?"

"I would."

Leland hopped up and, head back, perused those shelves. Reaching up, he grasped a thick, large ledger. It almost toppled him over as he brought it down. He set it on a desk with a loud thump.

"Now, let us see . . ." He opened it, thumbed to a page close to the back, and turned the heavy pages. He flipped more, then stood back. "The section regarding the jewels is right there."

Adam bent to the page. Line after line described jewelry in some detail. "And the inventory before this?"

Leland set a paper in the current page, then searched for the prior one. "It is not as complete, of course. Not every bridle in the stables, so to speak. Only the cream in the pitcher." He found the inventory, paged through, and gestured. "There. 1811."

Adam scanned down the list. It matched the most recent one. "And the 1801 inventory, if you don't mind."

Leland looked troubled now. He found the inventory.

Adam immediately saw a disparity. "This set here is not in the later two."

Leland peered at the page. "Gold filigree with pearls and sapphires, diadem and necklace." He flipped to the later inventories. "It appears it is not. I assume that your father explained its absence before 1811, or at the time that inventory was made by my predecessor."

"Or an error was made."

"We do not make errors, Your Grace."

The set had been removed from the list, that was certain. "Do we know what it looked like? I might stumble upon it in a cupboard someday."

"Of course we do." Leland returned to the bookcase. This time he used a ladder to access a higher shelf and removed a box labeled *Stratton*. He brought it to the table. "Drawings are made. They prove useful in many situations."

The box included dated drawings of silver services and paintings as well as jewelry. Adam recognized much of the property. After some digging he uncovered the drawing of the missing jewelry.

The simple description did not do it justice. The necklace alone held at least thirty pearls and five good-sized sapphires. The gold had been worked like filigree but with much thicker wires than the word implied. The diadem was even richer. "Heavy," he said. "One wonders if any duchess wore it."

"Perhaps a very sturdy one." Leland chuckled at his little joke.

"I would like to take this with me."

"It is yours, of course. Perhaps you will find the jewelry someday, tucked away in a good, safe spot that was then forgotten. I cannot tell you how often that happens. One would think someone handling such valuables would remember what they did with them."

Adam folded the drawing and tucked it in his coat. His father had shown him all the good, safe spots in the family properties. He would check them. He did not think these were the jewels that Clara said Lady Hollsworth spoke of, however. These had gone missing far too early. Since no others had disappeared, most likely Lady Hollsworth spoke in error or repeated some unfounded rumor.

Not money, and not jewels. How else could a man give aid to the enemy while remaining in England?

Two days later Clara was discovering that keeping an affair a secret from absolutely everyone required an extraordinary level of subterfuge. One that she came to believe she could not manage.

It began simply enough, with an invitation from Stratton

to accompany him to the Epsom Derby Stakes. They would go down in his carriage, he proposed, and stay at one of his properties not far from the downs. In her initial excitement, she wrote back and agreed.

Then the planning started. How to explain her absence from the house? The new servants would accept whatever she said, but Jocelyn would find any excuse suspect.

Worse, how to explain her presence at the race with Stratton as her escort? And how would she explain her lodging when someone asked, as someone was sure to do?

Not everyone would be there, but a good portion of the ton would make the short journey. Most of the young men would attend for certain. That meant Theo would probably see her. He would have his suspicions confirmed. If he told their grandmother that she and Stratton had . . . were . . . Suffice to say there would be the devil to pay.

It entered her mind while she weighed what lies might work and whether she would be willing to use them, that the duke did not care much if everyone assumed the worst of them. Hadn't he again mentioned that they would marry? As if he were actually serious about that? Perhaps he counted on pending scandal changing her mind about her answer.

She would not pretend she had not pictured marriage to him a few times during the last few days. She blamed it on the latent influence of their intimacy. However, whatever optimistic fantasies she conjured would quickly be dashed by realities she could not escape.

It would mean no control of her income. No independence. She could no longer subsidize *Parnassus* and it would cease publication. It would be sad to have to tell Althea and the others that the adventure was over. She would hardly be a person anymore, truth be told. With a few words she would have to become a woman she did not know.

She decided there was no way to go to the Derby Stakes with Stratton. That saddened her to a surprising degree, and not only because of her disappointment in not seeing the race. In order to dispel the melancholy, she decided to visit some of the bookshops to see if copies of *Parnassus* were selling.

Her coachman had helped her purchase a modest coach and a matched pair, and she sent word for him to bring the equipage around. She would conquer this mood and write to Stratton in the evening to explain her change of decision.

She had not traveled far when she decided the company of a friend would help lift her spirits. She gave the coachman the direction to Althea's home.

Althea lived with her brother on a street near St. James's Square. Clara was brought to the drawing room, where Althea suffered in silence while her sister-in-law chatted with other callers. Althea's eyes lit up when she saw Clara enter. She jumped up to introduce Clara to the ladies assembled. At the first opportunity, she took Clara aside.

"You are a saint," Clara said. "I would go mad if I had to pretend her friends were my friends."

"I do not mind most days, but right now I am very glad to see you."

"Take your leave of them. I have my new carriage outside. We will visit bookshops."

Althea proved extremely agreeable. Fifteen minutes later they stopped at the first shop and entered to count copies.

"Three are gone," Althea said when they were back in the carriage. "Let us check Johnson's on Oxford."

The news there gave them both heart. All but one copy had sold.

As they left the shop, a voice hailed Clara. She turned to see Stratton closing the door on a shop four doors away.

Althea gave her a quizzical look.

"He and I have had some conversation at times," Clara explained. "I should not cut him."

"Of course not. It would be very wrong to cut such a handsome man."

He appeared happy to see her. She could not hide that she was happy in return. She hoped that was all she revealed, and not the rest of what she experienced. Joy and warmth and echoes of sensual thrills suffused her.

Out of the corner of her eye she saw Althea taking it all in.

She made introductions. Stratton knew Althea's brother. Althea remembered Stratton's mother. Finally, Clara turned to her friend. "I have something I must tell the duke. Will you excuse us for a short while?"

Althea smiled sweetly and strolled over to a shop window to admire the wares.

"I cannot go," Clara said quietly. "I know I agreed, and I want to see the race very much, but no matter how I try to arrange it, I see only gossip spreading fast afterward. There is no way to be discreet."

"Discretion be damned."

"You cannot mean that."

"No, I don't. At least for your sake I don't." He looked past her. "Invite your friend. Have her come with you. Is that your carriage there? Plan to go down in it. I will arrange the rest." He looked at Althea again. "You may have to confide in her. Can you trust her?"

"She may be the only person I *can* trust. She is certainly the only person I know who keeps a secret."

He cocked his head. His charming smile sent a tremble down to her toes. "You have secrets besides me? How intriguing. Now I will have to learn what they are."

She called Althea back. "We should continue our errands, Duke. Good day to you."

He took his leave. She and Althea climbed into the carriage. Althea stuck her head out the window to watch the duke walk away. Then she settled in, set her reticule on her lap, and looked right at Clara.

"Is there something you want to tell me, darling? Because I think you have shared much more than conversation with that man."

Chapter Sixteen

Once Adam learned from Clara that her friend would join her, his plan fell into place. He let a small house in Epsom for the ladies to use. Only they would not both use it, in truth.

He shared his genius with Langford and Brentworth that night at a gaming hall while they played the wheel.

"You are daring the devil," Brentworth said. "At least half the ton will be at the Derby Stakes. The roads of Surrey will be crowded with carriages. Her brother is sure to attend. You could find yourself married at the point of a sword."

"Don't you understand? Stratton isn't going to be at the Derby," Langford said. "If you had the woman you wanted alone in a place of privacy, would you interrupt the idyll by wasting a day at a horse race?"

"Perhaps he wants to see the race. Maybe she does."

"I promised she would see the race," Adam said.

"She will not require it if you are not clumsy. Do I have to give advice on that too?"

"Please do not," Brentworth said. "I beg it of you, and Stratton here insists, I am sure."

Langford placed some bets. "I will wager both of you that there will be no nonsense about that race. I am confident that my vast knowledge of women is correct on this. Name the amount."

"One hundred pounds," Adam said.

Langford paused in laying down his bets. "I withdraw the challenge, if you bet that much. Since you have control on the outcome, I must conclude you will ensure you win even if it is against your interests."

"If seduction were my only goal, I would not have to leave London. She wants to see the race, and I am going to considerable trouble to arrange that. So much trouble that even if she insists we forgo it, I will demand we see the plan through."

Langford laughed. *"No, my dear, we cannot stay in bed all day. We must ride to Epsom soon. Stop those caresses. I will not be persuaded by feminine wiles to change the plan."* He imitated Adam's voice.

"Ignore him," Brentworth said. "Look for my stand at the race. We will watch together and toast the winner, which I fully expect to be my horse."

He and Langford began talking odds and competition. Adam watched the wheel spin. Three days until Clara joined him in Surrey. He was sure he would go mad before that.

Clara made a display of entering the house in Epsom with Althea. She stood on the street for at least five minutes while Mr. Brady carried their valises into the house. She greeted several women passing by whom she knew.

"Well done," Althea said once they were both inside and the carriage had rolled away. "I will see you tomorrow morning, early. Now, it is almost two o'clock, and time for your rendezvous. Off with you."

Clara gazed around the sitting room of the house, vaguely noting it looked cozy and welcoming. Most of her concentration was on everything that could go wrong with this adventure. A bad case of nerves had been building the last five miles.

"If my brother learns I am staying here and calls—"

"I will make sure he is none the wiser regarding where you really are instead." Althea took her hands. "Of course, if you prefer to remain here, I will not accuse you of cowardice."

"You would be more generous than I would be with myself. Still, I cannot deny that this is different from the last time. This time I am making a very deliberate decision well ahead of time."

"I think this is the better way. Don't you?"

Did she? It might be more thoroughly her choice, but it was not easier. She would not be able to pretend she had succumbed to surprise or been swept away by kisses in the magical moonlight.

She picked up her valise and walked to the back of the house.

"You should probably bribe the coachman to ensure his discretion," Althea said, walking alongside her.

"I raised Mr. Brady's wages yesterday. I think he knows why."

"If not, he will soon."

They left the house and walked through a small but tidy walled garden to the back portal. On its other side, her carriage waited. She gave Althea a kiss. "I will return in time to accompany you to the race tomorrow." She climbed into the carriage and Althea waved her off. She pulled the curtains halfway closed.

The carriage left the town and aimed west. The roads in this direction showed none of the crowding they had experienced coming down. That crush had slowed travel considerably, enough that at times passengers climbed out and walked to friends' carriages and climbed in. When they had stopped to rest and water the horses, five of her brother's Mayfair neighbors took air among the crowd in the coaching inn's yard.

Stratton's property was near Guilford, in the opposite direction. When they were well away from Epsom, she pushed back the curtains and enjoyed the passing countryside.

After an hour they turned off the main road and up a private lane. When the trees broke away and the house came into view, Clara had to laugh. Stratton's small secondary property was probably one of the biggest houses in the county. Its size was its most ostentatious feature. Otherwise the gray stone and restrained design indicated it was not very old.

Stratton came out while the coachman handed her valise to a footman. After welcoming her and giving the footman instructions to seek out the housekeeper, he had a private word with Mr. Brady. Clara could not see what was said, but she thought she saw a coin being palmed from the duke to the driver.

"Did you tell him about tomorrow?" she asked when Stratton rejoined her and escorted her into the house.

"With tortured precision. He will meet us at a designated place outside Epsom and be waiting from nine o'clock on."

"This will be an unusually lucrative employment for him, I think, since I also paid him extra for his silence."

"Not enough. Nor did he misunderstand my expectations

and my subtle threat when he took that guinea. He is not a stupid man."

A guinea! Whoever knew that sin could be so expensive?

She had not known what to expect when she arrived. Not the formalities that engulfed her. She found herself treated like any guest. A housekeeper arrived to bring her to her chamber. A maid waited there to unpack her valise and to aid her undressing for a rest. Before leaving, the maid promised to wake her to prepare for dinner.

She checked her pocket watch and judged there to be at least three hours before the maid would return. Since she felt no need to rest, being stuck here annoyed her. In the least Stratton could have invited her to explore the house and garden on her own if he did not want her company right away.

She did not know how lovers were treated when trysts were arranged, but she had never guessed she would be bored.

The butler accompanied Adam upstairs. While he went through the predictable steps of being settled in, his mind timed how Clara's own welcome was progressing.

"We have prepared the apartment for you, Your Grace. A footman, Timothy, will serve you. He is experienced as a valet."

"Excellent." *They would be showing Clara her chamber now.*

Adam turned on the landing to ascend to the next level, where his apartment spread.

The butler did not. "Your Grace, we moved everything to the duke's apartment. I hope we did not err."

Her maid is unpacking her valise now.

"Not at all." He accompanied the butler to the door of the chambers last used by his father and steeled himself against an onslaught of memories.

He had not been to Kengrove Abbey since the day his father's remains were transported north. He had not intended to enter these private spaces on this visit. Now, with the butler on his heels, he turned the latch with foreboding.

The doors swung wide, revealing a foreign place. He paced inside, accommodating his reaction. Nothing at all remained of the apartment he knew. Nothing of the last duke. These chambers might have been in another house. *She is inspecting the chambers and the prospects from the windows now.*

He had intended to avoid the memories, but now he felt robbed of them. "What happened here? Who made these changes?"

"The duchess, Your Grace. Letters came from France with her instructions, long ago."

His own books now filled the shelves in the sitting room. His own garments filled the new wardrobe. He entered the bedchamber. Every item of furniture had been changed and the walls repainted and papered. The bed had even been placed differently.

"What did you do with my father's things?"

"They were boxed and placed in the attic."

"And his personal papers?"

"Sent to Drewsbarrow, Your Grace."

"Leave me," he said. "Tell Timothy I will not want him until dinner."

The door quietly closed behind the butler. Adam took one more tour of the foreign apartment. It had been his mother's decision to do this. She must have guessed that he would avoid making changes himself.

She might have told him. Not knowing, he had resisted

coming here since he returned to England. This had been their true home, not Drewsbarrow in Warwickshire. He had grown up here and in London. It might have been years before he used the apartment if it had not been redone.

He concluded that he liked the changes. He would not mind using the chambers because they did not hold those memories. They would be found elsewhere, of course. Eventually he would face them, but not for a long while yet.

Her maid is undressing her and inviting her to rest from her journey.

He removed his coats and rolled up his sleeves. He returned to the bedchamber and eyed one wall. The panels had been painted, but not removed. He placed his palm on one of them and gently pressed.

Finally he found the spot where the panel's edge eased beneath his pressure. A faint click sounded, and the panel swung out.

Good, safe places, the solicitor had said. This was one of them, and there were others.

The first thing he saw was a stack of money. Mr. Leland would be shocked to know that many families did in fact keep thousands of banknotes in their homes.

He pushed those aside, then reached in to see what else hid behind the wall. *She is alone now. The maid has left.*

Five minutes later the contents of the hiding place lay on the bed. They included no jewelry. There were other such safekeeping places here at the Abbey that also should be examined.

He would take care of that later. Right now, other things claimed his attention, like the lovely guest in one of the chambers above.

Chapter Seventeen

She wandered around her bedchamber. The maid had turned down the bedclothes and closed the drapes. She pushed the fabric aside so the light of one window would allow her to see the appointments. This chamber must have been decorated fairly recently since it showed gothic elements still coming into vogue.

The grounds below did not look like a typical garden. Rather, little pools, hills, and plantings created vignettes of great appeal. None of the flower beds looked planned, although she knew great care went into such horticultural designs.

Hands circled her waist. Warmth pressed her back. A kiss thrilled the side of her neck. Stratton's face flanked hers and he gazed out alongside her. "It was my mother's doing," he said of the garden.

She leaned against him and he wrapped her in his arms. "I feared I would be a prisoner up here, and all alone."

"It was my intention to be a considerate host and allow you to rest from your journey." He kissed her neck again. "Then other intentions conquered that idea."

"Your other intentions are far more interesting."

One of his arms moved up her body. His hand stroked

her breast, making her gasp. His mouth pressed her neck's pulse. She closed her eyes and gave herself over to the delicious sensations.

His caresses both soothed and excited her. She no longer wondered about her decision. Of course she had come. For this. For the pleasure and the intimacy. For the chance to feel wanted and cared for.

The touch on her breast aroused her mercilessly. With her back to him she could only accept the way he teased her toward delirium. Her body tensed with anticipation when his other hand began unbuttoning her undressing gown. His slow progress drove her mad with impatience. Firm from her need, her breasts reacted to the slightest stimulation, even the movement of the cloth of her chemise against their tips.

He pulled her undressing gown down, and it pooled at her feet. He held both her breasts and gently rubbed the tips with his thumbs. "Is this what you are begging for?"

She could barely speak, and her mind knew only pleasure and want. As the pleasure grew and spread she flexed against him, her hips pressing his arousal again and again.

Impatience soon plagued her again, until she wanted to cry. She grasped the shoulders of her chemise and pulled them down, so she would feel his touch on her skin. He stripped it down farther, until she was naked in his arms.

Her arousal grew and grew until it became a beautiful power that consumed her consciousness. She let him support her and embraced the abandon. The way he touched her felt too good to bear, and each touch and caress only made her want more.

She ached for what he had done the last time, for his mouth on her breasts and stomach, for his hand pressing up between her legs, for the insanity of having pleasure unhinge her until nothing else existed.

His teeth closed on her earlobe and nipped gently. "I promise that tonight I will take you slowly, but it has been too long and I need you now." His hand slid down her body to her thighs. He turned her enough so he could kiss her. He held her like that and ravished her mouth while he stroked at her pulsating lower lips.

Each long, hidden caress sent a silent reverberation clanging through her entire body, each one stronger and more thorough in gathering her need into a furious demand for something more, something complete, something final.

He moved her and bent her and pressed her back. He no longer embraced her. Instead she felt brocade beneath her hands. She leaned over the thick arm of the divan face down, her hips resting on its high bulk and her legs dangling down its side.

It seemed a while that he left her like that, posed so scandalously. Then he caressed up her back and over her bottom. One firm palm remained on the small of her back, but his other hand sought again the source of her madness.

The sensation undid her. Sharp, deep and intense, it made her scream. She tried to swallow the sound, but she could not.

She felt him then, entering her, first slowly then hard. The intensity centered on his fullness and his thrusts. She knew relief at first, but then a trembling began and grew, one she could not control. The hard tremors frightened her, and his movements only made them stronger. Her body seemed to disappear except for where they joined, and the intensity tightened into something painful but compelling. It twisted tighter until suddenly the tremor coursed through her in a powerful wave of sensation that submerged her.

* * *

Sight returned, but damned little strength came with it. He grasped the arm of the divan with both hands, steadying himself lest he collapse on top of Clara. Limp and silent, she did not make a sound now, but the chamber still reverberated with her howl of joy a few moments ago.

He bent to press a kiss on the small of her back and then on the soft flesh of her bottom. Even now, sated from a staggering release, the eroticism of her pose entranced him.

He fixed his garments, then lifted her to her feet. With a scoop he picked her up and carried her to the bed. She nestled onto the pillow while he drew the sheet over her. She reached out and placed her hand on his arm and looked him over through heavily lidded eyes.

"You certainly know how to make houseguests feel welcome."

"I try my best."

"If that is your best, it is spectacular." She rubbed the fabric of his sleeve between two fingers. "You did not undress, and you appear ready to meet the queen. I, on the other hand—" She looked down at the gentle hills of her body beneath the sheet.

He bent to kiss her. "I will have the maid sent to you in an hour, and a bath as well if you want."

"A bath will be wonderful, assuming I can move by then."

"I will see you later." He turned to leave.

She turned on her side and snuggled the pillow. "I can still feel you. Can still feel what happened," she murmured sleepily.

As could he. He gently stroked her cheek and watched her fall asleep, then sought his own chambers.

Unlike Clara, he did not sleep. He did not even rest. He continued what he had been doing before thoughts of her led him to her chamber.

In the ducal apartment, soon books sat on the floor instead of in their cases in the sitting room. The wall behind one case stood open, revealing a gaping cavern. Its former contents were now strewn on the desk.

He walked past the bag of gold coins and the stacks of papers and headed to the dressing room. He pulled back the carpet and knelt in one corner, feeling with his fingers on the wood. He found the spot he sought and pushed hard. A section of the floor, a foot square in size, bounced up on a hidden hinge. He felt down into the underlying structure of the house.

Learning the locations of these hiding places had been as much a part of his education as learning the history of the Tory party. These secret spots had been built into this house, just as others could be found in most of their other properties. Gold coins often found homes in spots like this.

He groped, sliding his fingers along joists, making sure nothing remained tucked beneath one. His hand closed on a small sack. He dragged it into the light and opened it. Jewelry poured into his palm.

The piece bore no resemblance to that item missing from the last inventory. Nor did its silver, pearls, and purple stones fit the description of anything in any of the inventories he saw. It looked very old. Perhaps it had been stuck down there for generations.

He dropped it back in its hiding place and replaced the section of floor. This had been the most likely house if those missing jewels had been stored and, like that silver necklace, forgotten. Now he would have to search Drewsbarrow, which would take a very long time.

"I trust your friend did not scold you too badly." Stratton poured some wine while he made the observation.

They had dined on a fine meal. They still lounged at the table, enjoying the last of the claret.

A nap and a bath had reinvigorated Clara. She had not even blushed when she came down to join the duke for dinner. She should, however. The afternoon had been a revelation in several ways, not the least being how exciting she found the masterful way he handled her.

Another day she would contemplate what that might mean about him. She would also have to consider what it said about her, she supposed.

"She only cautioned that there would be the devil to pay if there was one slip. I already knew that." Althea had offered a bit more advice that would not be shared with the duke. About the difficulties of having a truly discreet affair. About the danger for a woman never married. She had spoken as if from experience.

"I have an acquaintance with her brother, but confess I had not seen her before you introduced us."

"Althea has an unfortunate history. Unlike my father, hers left her dependent on that brother. When he attempted to marry her off to a man whose favor he wished to curry, she refused and instead married an army officer who unfortunately died in battle. She has been treated like the poor relative she is ever since. A governess would live better."

"She appeared fashionable when I met her. Not impoverished."

"She has a knack with a needle that means she can turn herself out well enough to be comfortable with the friends of her youth. Now, tell me about this house." She changed the subject quickly because speaking about Althea had moved them close to the workings of the journal.

Althea indeed had talent in needlework, but that was not how she maintained her appearance. That was a fiction designed to explain to everyone, but especially to her sister-in-law, the carefully chosen wardrobe additions that would appear from time to time. It would never do to explain that Althea had employment as both a writer and an editor at the journal. Clara paid her for her help, and not enough, considering the role Althea played.

The duke had begun describing the house's history. "Perhaps you would like to see it," he offered.

"Yes, please."

While they toured the public rooms on the ground level, she noticed again and again that, like her bedchamber, they all displayed fairly recent decorating. The rich colors, unlike what had been popular even twenty years ago, enhanced various exotic details. The morning room, for example, gave the impression of an Arabian courtyard with its distinctively pointed moldings, filigree screens, and blue and green tiles on the fireplace.

"I think this is not an obscure property rarely visited," she said.

"It was the one we used the most. We rarely went to Drewsbarrow. This proved more convenient because it is close to town."

She wondered if the reason they rarely visited Drewsbarrow had anything to do with the bad feelings shared with another major family in that county. Probably so. The late duke would not want to attend a county event only to find himself taking pains to avoid the other lord present.

What a tangled mess that disagreement had created. And all over a stupid piece of property. Both families surely had plenty of land.

They mounted the stairs and Stratton beckoned her to a chamber attached to the library. "This was added around ten years ago."

Paneled like the library, this chamber contained no books. Instead a big billiards table took pride of place in the center of the space. She clapped her hands with delight. "Can we play?"

"Do you know how?"

"Not at all. My father began to teach me, but my grandmother insisted it was not ladylike, and he stopped."

"He took you hunting and taught you how to shoot but agreed billiards was beyond the pale?"

"I think it was because others might see me with the cue, but might never see me with a musket. You can teach me, however. I am a very quick learner."

"That I already know." He took two cues from a heavily carved long cabinet and handed her one. "Do as I say, and you will be an expert in no time."

"You mean soon it will seem very normal to me. Very natural."

He did not miss the allusion. "Exactly." He set up the balls, then used his cue to break them up. "One quick snap. See?"

"Perhaps I should practice that first." She gathered all the balls together again and moved to stand beside him. She positioned her cue.

"You must bend in order to aim," he said.

"Like this?"

His palm gently pressed her back. Much as it had a few hours ago. "More like that."

She looked over and up at him. "I think I understand Grandmamma's concern. I would not have yesterday, of course." She tried to do as he had done and failed miserably. One of the balls bounced high enough to leave the table. "Perhaps I should let you take the lead, since you are far more experienced."

He set the balls together again. "We will start simply. If you find you enjoy it, with time I will show you more sophisticated ways to play. There are some interesting techniques that are not for novices."

"You are tempting me to want to do nothing else, if great mysteries await." She bent to aim her cue.

He bent over her and repositioned her hands. "Now, aim for the center of the front ball."

"Should I try a direct and firm thrust or one that is carefully placed and effective due to artistry more than force?"

He laughed. A smack landed on her very available rump. "You are incorrigible this evening. A very bad young lady."

She giggled and eyed her cue's end. "I will have to muddle through if you will not instruct me further."

She opted for less force and more precision. None of the balls bounced off the table, at least.

They played the game, but she only had her turns when she thought he deliberately missed shots. Whenever she went to shoot he helped her, his body covering hers and his long arms teaching hers where to go and how to attack the ball she chose.

"I am going to lose," she said while she dipped low to try what would surely be her last shot. "You are supposed to let me win. Any gentleman would."

He hovered again, his voice near her ear. "I assumed you would be insulted if I deliberately lost. Not that I could have even if I tried, since you refuse to obey my instructions." He moved her hand on the cue's back end. "If you would hold this stick as I said, you would have improved far more by now."

"So I should hold the hilt firmly like this, but let my fingertips caress the tip so it slides through. That does seem more effective. The next time you tell me how to hold a stick, I will listen." She aimed, but her shot did not even hit the ball because again he swatted her rump.

Only this time his hand remained there. "You have a

ribald sense of humor for a well-bred young woman, Clara."

She straightened, right up into his arms. "It must be the wine. Have I shocked you?"

He laughed and pulled her closer. "I don't think you can shock me."

"How disappointing. I tried hard to do so."

"If you are determined, you will probably succeed someday." He kissed her. "I suspect you are accustomed to having your way in most things."

"I am too ignorant to know what my way is yet, in some things."

He held her head to a fevered kiss. "We will rectify that soon enough."

There was no more banter, no more game. That kiss never ended. She clung to him and soared into the excitement he spun as their kisses turned hungry and their embraces grasping. She thought he might lay her down right there on the table. She hoped he would. Instead he released her, then grasped her hand and sped her out of the chamber, pulling her along while he strode up the stairs.

He swung her into her bedchamber and sat her down on the bed. He discarded his coats, then knelt in front of her. While he embraced and kissed her, his fingers found her dress fastenings. Then he sat back on his heels. Eyes hot and face stern, he caressed up her legs beneath her dress. Long, firm strokes made her skin tingle with warmth. He pushed up her skirt.

"Remove your dress while I kiss you." He bent to do just that on her inner knee.

She watched while she hitched her skirt up over her hips, then pulled the dress over her head. Her chemise remained bunched on her thighs. His kisses moved in that direction. Their effect stunned her. So did their path.

He had described this in the park—spoken of kissing her naked thighs again and again, until he finally enjoyed the most private kisses imaginable. Now, as sensual tightness spread through her loins and she pulsed mere inches from his head, she understood as she had not then.

"Are you going to—Are you—" Her breath kept catching with each kiss, and she could not get the words out.

He grasped her hips and moved her closer to the bed's edge. "Yes." He pushed her thighs farther apart. "Lie back."

She sank back on the bed. Kisses, hot and devastating, moved yet higher on her thighs. He touched her, and the pleasure made her delirious. Then she felt the most intimate kisses imaginable, and she went mad until her consciousness crashed around her in an explosion of pleasure.

When sanity beckoned again he stood beside the bed, holding her legs while he thrust inside her. She looked down her body, then in his eyes. She watched the fury rise in him, then own him, and finally bring him to the only ecstasy people ever knew.

Adam stroked his fingertips up and down Clara's back. Naked now, she lay beside him on her stomach, hugging a pillow that supported her head. Her eyes were closed but she did not sleep. His wandering fingertips kept making her smile.

She reached over and placed her hand on his chest, as if she sought reassurance he was there.

"You are beautiful, Clara. Your creamy skin is like silk and velvet. Your hair in this dim light is dark satin, except for a few light flecks where the light finds some of the red strands."

"Do not stop. My pride is devouring your flattery. Normally when I hear comments about my appearance, someone is pointing out the flaws."

"Impossible. There are no flaws."

"What a charming liar you are. I have been told often that my mouth is too large. Surely you noticed."

"I think your mouth is perfect, and erotic."

She opened her eyes. "Erotic?" She puzzled over that. "Thank you for at least not hating it. One *perfect* from you weighs more than a hundred criticisms from others. Still, I think we can agree that the sister offered to you was the more beautiful."

He gathered her up and laid her on top of him, so her breasts and face pressed his chest, not only her hand. She felt good and right in his arms like this, all feminine softness and warmth. Her breath tickled his chest and slowly revived other sensations.

"I do not agree. Even from a distance I thought you the greater prize. As soon as we met I knew it for certain. You are nothing short of magnificent, darling."

She raised her head and looked down at him. A thick tress, freed from its pins, hung down her face on one side. "Do you really think so?"

"I am not one for false flattery." Yes, magnificent. He should tell her more. He should find words to explain how rare she was in the way she opened her whole being during passion. In how she made choices on her own terms. She was not immune to the opinions of the world, of course. The elaborate subterfuge to get her here proved that. But in the end, she *was* here, without guilt or worry, enchanting him with her body and mind.

"You appeared like a visitor yourself when we toured the house," she said.

"I have not been here in years. Since I came back, I have visited the main estate at Drewsbarrow, but not here."

"Yet it is so close to London."

"I was busy with other estate matters. Then I was busy chasing you."

"We never visited the garden. It is unusual in its plan. I will venture out in the morning, before we leave for the race."

"Wait for me, or else stay in the garden proper. I don't want you getting lost."

She laughed. "I do not think that will happen."

"We will go together." He pressed a kiss to her crown. "Do you remember what to do tomorrow?"

"If I should forget, Althea will remember. She is being very protective. Very motherly."

"You must find that annoying."

"Her care for me is disarming. All of her concern comes from a good place. It is not the same as scolds and lectures from family members who are really thinking about themselves."

"If her care is all for you, she probably does not approve of me. Of this."

"She has not said so. Also unlike my family, she does not treat me like an idiot. She assumes that I have already thought of any cautions or warning she could voice."

He knew what those would be. She did not have to itemize the questions that must wander into her mind sometimes. Maybe they did so often. Like right now.

There was no good way to talk about that. Certainly not now and not here. She had to wonder sometimes if she had misjudged his reasons for pursuing her, however.

"Do you not find it at all odd that we are here like this? Everything in our lives would say this was impossible." She spoke in a tone of curious wonder, as if she had heard his thoughts. It impressed him that she broached this subject. She was braver than he was, it seemed.

"Desire makes its own arguments, I suppose."

"Is that what this is? You could leave once that was satisfied. Yet you did not. Unless you wanted to but felt some obligation to stay here with me. Or perhaps you tolerate this other intimacy while you wait for desire again."

Nothing in her voice indicated she sought a particular answer. She merely voiced things she wondered about. Or at least some of the things.

"I felt no obligation. I will admit that I intend to have you again, but being with you is not something I only tolerate until then, Clara."

"Perhaps more than desire binds us, then. Perhaps friendship does too."

It was not the word he would use. If she chose that one, he would not object.

She raised her head again, then glanced down her side. Naughty sparks entered her eyes. "I have not moved, but methinks you just did."

"I have not moved at all."

"Grew, then."

He pretended deep contemplation. "Ah. Yes, I do believe you are correct about that." His cock swelled more and pressed against her stomach.

"I believe desire has raised its head again." She sat up, giggling at her own ribald double entendre. She rested her bottom on his thighs and watched the continuing transformation with fascination. "It is a wonder you did not kill me the first time." She gently poked at him. He swelled more.

She came up and kissed him, deeply, almost savagely. He set her back to where she sat again and took her hand. He closed it around the base of his cock.

"Just like with the cue," she said happily. "Should I handle the other end more gently?"

He told her what to do.

* * *

Clara thought she would never know such pleasure. Even the revelations earlier in the night did not compare. It went on and on, tantalizing her to a release that remained just out of reach.

She hovered over him on hands and knees. His mouth tortured her breasts while the tip of his cock prodded the end of her passage. The satisfaction of absorbing him remained just out of reach, becoming a merciless tease.

Finally she could not stand it. She gave up the one pleasure for the other. She angled back and took him into herself. Nothing had ever felt so good.

Relief did not last long. She moved her hips so she felt him better. She rose, then pressed down to create more sensations.

"Yes. Like that," he said. "To the end, if you want."

It surprised her that he accepted such passivity. She moved this way and that, exploring the sensations, finding the press of his fullness that made her gasp. She made sure she gasped again and again, taking pleasure greedily, fiercely, until she grew desperate. He helped then, grasping her hips and rocking up into her. She cried out with joy at every bruising thrust they shared, until that incredible ecstasy brought its profound relief.

Chapter Eighteen

Adam waited impatiently while his manservant brushed at his frock coat. He had risen later than he intended, and this house servant had taken twice as long as his usual valet to do these duties. Since even now the man's hand shook while he wielded the brush, it was apparent that attending to His Grace had probably been nerve-wracking for the fellow.

He swallowed the impulse to tell him to get on with it and suffered the final efforts. Finally done, he took his leave and went below to the morning room.

No one else was there. He ate some breakfast, then asked the attending footman if Lady Clara had come down yet.

"She arrived some time ago, Your Grace. Almost an hour, I would say. She broke her fast, then went outside."

How like Clara to decide to tour the garden on her own. He went out to the terrace and looked for her.

He could not see her. He peered, waiting for her to emerge from behind a shrubbery or one of the gentle swells of the landscape. Finally a movement caught his eye up on the little hill at the back. Clara stood between two trees on its crest, looking down from that prospect. She did not seem to see him. While he watched, she turned and disappeared.

She had descended the other side. The gardens ended there. At least the formal ones did. Nothing much could be found where she headed, except a little wilderness.

He waited for her to realize that and reappear. Only she didn't.

Cursing her stubbornness, he set off after her. Had he not told her to wait for him? Had he not commanded that she stay in the garden? He strode on. His rancor grew more than it had a right to, but he could not help it. He did not want her straying into that damned wilderness. He sure as hell did not want to have to go in after her.

At the top of the low hill he looked down on the gentle slope toward the trees and brush. This rustic patch was no more than a quarter mile square, but it lacked many clear paths. He could navigate it blindfolded, since he had played here as a boy. A stranger, however, could get turned around.

Cursing again, and thinking that instead of caressing her round, pretty bottom he should have better smacked it less playfully, he went down the slope and entered the trees. He paused to spy for that hydrangea-hued dress she was wearing. When he did not see her, he called her name.

"I am over here," she called back. "By a little pool."

She *would* have found her way *there*. Hell and damnation.

Clara watched the water bubble at one end of the pool. It must be a spring. She rested on her big rock and admired the little clearing. She thought it one of the loveliest places she had seen in years.

She heard Stratton coming. He thrashed closer while

she debated removing her shoes and sticking her feet in the water. Then he was there with her. She felt him to her left while those bubbles fascinated her.

"Isn't this beautiful?" she asked. "So peaceful and serene. It must be perfect in summer."

"Come with me, Clara."

His tone startled her. She looked over. He stood there, a much different man than she had seen the last few days. Dark. Hard. He reminded her of how he had been at their first meeting, when he was angry that she had cut him.

She could not imagine why he was angry now. "Why are you in such a bad humor?"

He did not look directly at her, but more to that pool. "I told you not to leave the garden if you ventured out on your own. You might have gotten lost."

She wanted to laugh. "There is a rough path that brought me here. I think I would have found my way back."

"All the same, I told you not to do it. Now I have told you to come away with me, and you have disobeyed that as well."

"You can hardly be surprised. You already knew I am not much given to obeying commands, especially ones that are not rational."

He abruptly looked at her then. No, not at her. At the boulder on which she sat. His gaze locked on it. He said nothing. While she watched, something else emerged in him and mixed with his anger. It did not replace it. If anything, it made it worse. She could not ignore the change in him, however. His eyes no longer blazed only with fury. They also deepened with sorrow.

She looked down on her boulder, then back at his concentration on it. In the next terrible moment, she thought she knew what had changed him so, and what he saw in his mind while he stared.

She hopped off the rock. "Yes, let us leave. Thank you for finding me. I may have become lost despite my belief I never would."

She walked past him to the edge of the clearing and the start of that path. He remained where he was, far from her in his mind.

She walked back and embraced him, for what little good that would do. That brought his gaze down on her. Her heart twisted at the pain she saw in him. She took his arm with a smile, as if she had not noticed. She urged him out of the clearing.

They walked back to the house in silence. She dared not speak. She had intruded on something private in that clearing that she had no right to see. She wondered if he would ever forgive her for that.

The road from Epsom to the racetrack was only about a mile long, but Clara concluded they could have walked and arrived in half the time it took her carriage.

She had traveled back to the town to rejoin with Althea. The only good thing about the slow journey amid hundreds of other vehicles was her confidence that many eyes saw her with her friend on this Thursday morning.

People of all stations jammed the road. From the finest coaches to the most humble carts, all aimed for the race that would take mere minutes to complete. She looked out her window and realized walking would not have been a good idea at all. Those who used feet instead of wheels had been forced off the road completely and trod in the wet fields and grass alongside.

"I do not mind helping you disguise your true whereabouts, Clara," Althea said. "I think that it means I get to hear whether your tryst is going well, though."

"It went very well. At least until this morning after breakfast."

"Did you argue?"

"We barely spoke at all before I left." She told Althea about her stroll in the woods and finding that pool and rock. "His anger made no sense, until I realized where I was. I think that his father did it there. Shot himself."

"Oh, dear. No wonder he did not want you wandering off on your own."

"I managed to wander exactly where he did not choose to wander himself. I think it evoked memories that remained in him until my carriage rolled away."

She would never forget that look in his eyes in the clearing. Vivid anger and that deeper, soulful sorrow. Her heart knew that grief and recognized it in him. How much worse to have lost a parent the way he had.

"Are we still going to join him in the stand, as he planned?" Althea said.

"I suppose we will find out soon. He said a footman would come for us when we walked down below. If none does, or it is claimed we were not seen . . ."

"We will still see the race, just with a less advantageous prospect."

Clara did not have the heart to tell Althea that seeing the race, about which she had been so excited since Stratton proposed this outing, no longer mattered very much. A sick worry had lodged below her heart. After being so close last night, Stratton's distance this morning unnerved her. Cold formality tinged every word he said. It had been as if they had shared those intimacies in a different world.

Perhaps they had, and entering that clearing had brought him back to earth.

The carriage had not moved in some minutes. Now Mr. Brady opened the door. "We will get no closer." He set down the steps and handed them out. He pointed to the end of a fence along the road. "I'll be right here when you need me. Look for that last post and I'll be standing nearby, no matter where the equipage ends up. I'd not dally much after the race if you want to reach Epsom before nightfall."

Clara thanked him, then she and Althea made their way through the tangle of other carriages and the streams of people.

"I don't see how anyone will see anything," Althea said.

"It appears that they are spreading out near the race-course. It is over a mile run, so better views will be had away from the finish."

Of course, they needed to go to where the race would finish, so that did not help them much. Finally, after considerable dodging and weaving, they found themselves below the large stand where the royal family watched in comfort from on high.

That grandstand was the only permanent building, but other stands set up temporarily flanked it. A few large tents in turn surrounded them.

Clara forced herself not to look up at those stands. One belonged to Brentworth, who had a horse running. It would be his footman who came to invite them up, if anyone did at all.

"Do not look so glum," Althea said. "I am sure that you have put more weight on his mood this morning than is warranted. Should the worst happen, you and I will enjoy the day, and you will stay with me in that very nice house tonight. It is so charming that I am becoming spoiled. I am sure he had to let it for more than two days. Perhaps you and I will stay there for a week before going back."

Clara hooked her arm through Althea's. "That sounds heavenly. We can spend the time plotting out the next three issues of the journal between visits to the spa for long soaks."

They found a spot where they might see something other than men's top hats and ladies' bonnets. No sooner had they elbowed their way there than a liveried footman approached to inform them that the Duke of Brentworth requested their company in his stand.

"See," Althea said while they followed the footman back through the throng.

Clara thought she would not *see* anything until she looked in Stratton's eyes again.

Chapter Nineteen

"We should put forth a bill to have the road from London improved," Langford said. He stood beside Adam while they gazed out over the crowd to the ground that the horses would run. On Langford's other side stood the fashionable and lovely Mrs. Harper. From the way she and Langford traded smiles, Adam assumed Mrs. Harper was a new and accommodating mistress.

Brentworth watched on Adam's other side. Brentworth had left his mistress back in London. Adam assumed that most of the ton did not even know he had one.

Others milled in the stand. As the owner of one of the horses, Brentworth had created a celebration here and invited at least twenty guests to join him. At the back of the stand a table set with silver, tableware and fine cloth held enough food to feed fifty.

Langford and his new lover drifted away to sit on the comfortable chairs provided. They turned their attention solely on each other.

Brentworth glanced over at Mrs. Harper. "I daresay

Langford will be much the poorer before she is done with him."

"They both appear euphorically happy, so I doubt he will mind the cost."

"Langford has looked like that at least a dozen times in my memory. We are all euphorically happy in the first blush of passion. Except you, apparently. You are brooding, despite your efforts to hide it."

"It is passing." And it was. The effect of seeing that place again had been soul shaking, and much worse than he expected. As he stood there it had all come back. The shock and the grief, and also the rage. He had known all of that waited for him out there. He had avoided returning for a reason.

"Perhaps when Lady Clara joins us, it will pass completely. Here she comes."

"I don't know how you can see anything in that horde."

"I have my servants wear livery so I can spot the gold braid on their tricorner hats. Whenever I think of casting off the antiquated traditions, I think of that gold braid and how handy it is for occasions like this."

Adam spotted the hat and the two women behind it. Clara looked up as she started up the stairs. She saw him immediately. Her smile appeared tentative.

He had behaved badly this morning when he found her at that pool. He had spoken too sharply. He had allowed the past to govern his reaction.

She had guessed why. He could tell she did from the gentle way she spoke to him and the manner in which she had urged him away from that place.

He watched her come, her lovely eyes glistening with humor while she laughed at something Althea said. He had been a chaos of dark emotions this morning, but her mere presence had provided what comfort he knew.

She and Althea entered the stand. He and Brentworth went to them, and Clara introduced her friend. They both thanked him for his kindness in inviting them to watch from this elevated spot.

Adam lured Clara aside. He could see the signs of her hesitation with him. The deep intimacy of the night seemed far away.

"Are you displeased that it took so long to find you and bring you here?" he asked.

"Not at all. With such a crowd it is a wonder the footman managed it."

"Then why the tight smile and hooded glances, Clara?"

She remained silent, subjecting him to a long examination. "I am wondering which Stratton I will be with today. The one from last night, or the one from this morning."

"I am always the same man."

"Are you? I was a stranger in that house this morning after we returned from the garden. A stranger to you. In turn, you were a stranger to me. I think I know why, and how finding me at that pool affected you badly. However much I sympathize, I did not care for being packed off this morning with less ceremony or kindness than some whore you found at a tavern." Emotions other than anger colored her little scold.

"You exaggerate. I was not so cold as that."

"I doubt you remember well enough to know. You were thoroughly immersed in your thoughts, and none of them had to do with me."

"Of course you were in my thoughts."

She cocked her head. "Not in a good way, then."

He did not want to have this argument, here of all places. He spoke the words needed to ensure that would not happen. "Then I ask you to forgive me for this morning,

Clara. You did not deserve the way I spoke to you when I found you at the pool and the way I then spoke little afterward. My distraction had nothing at all to do with you."

Only that was not entirely true. It was all of one piece, wasn't it? What had happened in that clearing had sent him away from England and brought him back, and she was not totally separate from it even if he tried to tell himself she was.

She knew that too. He could see it in her eyes.

"Familiarity, even passion, does not change who we are," she said.

It sounded like a condemnation of who he was, and an epitaph for their love affair.

"Althea has suggested that I stay in Epsom with her tonight. Actually she wants us to take advantage of that house for several nights at least."

"You can do that if you choose. However, I hope you do not."

From the smile she gave him, he could not tell what she would do. She turned her attention to the grandstand beside them. "If we stroll near that wall ever so casually, do you think I can ogle the royal dukes without being too obvious?"

"I will introduce you to some of them, so you don't have to ogle at all."

He escorted her over and did so. The royal dukes each had a fine eye for women, and all had known her father. A few appeared surprised to see her in the company of the Duke of Stratton. They chatted for a while and were only interrupted by the shouts from the crowd indicating the race had started. They returned to the front of the stand.

Clara watched the race with a rapt expression. Brentworth shouted his horse on, and all around them a din of excitement grew. When the horses moved out of view, Clara steadied herself by grasping Adam's arm and bent out of the stand as far as she could to keep them in view.

It ended within minutes as the horses charged to the finish. Money began changing hands.

"Almost," Adam said to Brentworth, who scowled mightily at the results.

"That does not save me from this." He felt in his pocket and extracted a stack of banknotes. Peeling off a hundred, he handed it over to a waiting Langford.

"You bet against his horse but ate his food and enjoyed his hospitality?" Clara asked.

"I knew Moses would win. I have been watching him for a year. I even tried to buy him from the Duke of York." Langford grinned down at the banknotes. "It is much like finding money lying on the street. It begs to be wasted on decadent behavior."

"You will think of something appropriate," Brentworth said.

Langford looked over his shoulder at the lovely Mrs. Harper. "I think I will at that."

Down below, the crowd shifted like a huge animal coming to life. It grew tentacles as people walked away in streams. There would be entertainments on the field for those looking to make a day of it, but the main performance had ended.

Still flushed with excitement, Clara peered around the stand. "Ah, there she is." She waved to her friend, who sat near the rear, talking with a woman.

Althea excused herself and came to join them. "Should we look for Mr. Brady?" she asked Clara.

"I suppose we should. I will take my leave of Brentworth." She walked away.

Althea remained. Short, fine and blond, she smiled serenely. "I should explain something, Your Grace."

"What is that?"

"She has trusted you with little reason to do so and much reason not to. If you misuse her in any way, if you bring hurt and humiliation down on her, you will answer to me."

Never had a person so small threatened him so mightily. He would have laughed except she meant it. For all her smiles, she was dead serious.

"I will not do that."

Nodding, she walked over to join Clara. He watched until they both left.

In the stand, the ladies sat to dine at the table. The gentlemen gambled at a makeshift bar set up in front. One of the footmen dealt the cards for vingt-et-un.

"This is far better than fighting one's way through all those carriages," Langford said while he eyed his cards.

"I am glad to oblige. Also, the longer you stay, the more certain I am to win back that hundred," Brentworth said.

"We are not playing each other, but the bank."

"And who do you think provided the bank?" Adam asked.

Langford glanced at the footman and the stack of money in front of him. "Excellent point."

Down below the crowd had much dispersed, but noise could still be heard from the field in which so many vehicles waited. Adam wondered if Clara and Althea had even been able to leave yet.

He also wondered whether yesterday's subterfuge would be repeated or if he should assume Clara would remain with her friend. Probably the latter. Since returning to Kengrove Abbey meant finding out the truth of that, he was in no hurry to leave.

Nor were his two friends. Both were guests at the Oaks and of the Earl of Derby, after whom the race had been named. Derby had joined them and sat at the card bar for a while. The Duke of Clarence, who now had become heir to the crown with his brother George's ascension, settled in for a longer visit. Others came and went. It reminded Adam of boxes at the theater, since other stands also hosted little parties.

The stakes ran high. The wine and whiskey flowed. The men took to talking the way they might at their clubs. With a few raised eyebrows, the ladies left to seek more genteel company. Even Mrs. Harper disappeared. The footmen brought out cigars.

Word must have spread that a fine time could be had at Brentworth's stand, because more men entered. A group shoved the food down the serving table and used its end for better purposes. The footmen kept producing more bottles.

"Luck is with you today, Stratton. You are up, what, two hundred?" Brentworth said.

"Am I? I haven't been counting."

"What ho, I like a man not noting his wins and losses. Mostly his losses," the Duke of Clarence hooted. "Feel free to gamble with me anytime."

Langford had left for a while but now reclaimed his seat. "Your food far surpassed that in Portland's stand. He did not even have champagne."

"Nor do I," Brentworth said.

"Hence my little search mission."

"You visited the enemy camp to see if the provisions were superior?" Adam asked. "That is disloyal of you."

"I had hoped for champagne. Just one glass. Brentworth here does not care for it, so we all must suffer."

Brentworth tipped a glass with far more power in it than mere champagne. "I cannot abide wine that sends bubbles up your nose."

"You never developed the taste. You missed out on it in your youth because your father was the consummate duke, just as you are now. My family, on the other hand, managed to procure champagne all during the war somehow."

"There was only one way to do that, somehow," Adam said. "You have just admitted to buying smuggled goods, Langford."

"Someone had to. Otherwise the roads from Kent to London would have been covered with shipment boxes."

Brentworth shook his head. "We had plenty of champagne in our house during the war. My grandfather laid in a goodly amount when he saw the headwinds, so our cellar remained well stocked. While he was not the—how did you put it?—consummate duke, it is true my father did not hold with enriching smugglers. If you were not in your cups, you would not admit it was done by your family either. It sounds disloyal."

"Not as disloyal as the doings of some of your families, not mentioning any names, of course." The voice inserting this observation came from behind them. Adam turned his head to see the Marquess of Rothborne hovering at his shoulder, looking down with a drunken smirk and moist eyes. Not a young man, the marquess had ruined his health long ago with drinking.

"Excellent whiskey, Brentworth," Rothborne said, waving his glass. "Scottish?"

"Irish, and you have enjoyed it rather too well, I think."

"I heard you had the best, so here I am. Of course, no one told me about your company. I am a bit fussier than you are, I guess. I avoid sitting at a table with a man who only has his title because his father escaped judgment by blowing his brains out."

Rothborne chuckled at his own wit. Brentworth froze. Adam began deciding which friend to have as his second. No one at their table said anything. It seemed none of them breathed much either.

"You are drunk, Rothborne," Langford said. "Apologize, then sit and play. I am losing big, and fate decrees I stop for a spell." He stood. "Here, use my chair. I can ruin my fortune another day."

"I'll be damned before I sit next to him."

With an affable smile, Langford clasped Rothborne's shoulder. He pressed hard, bringing his weight and strength to bear. "I insist you take my chair. *Sit.*"

Rothborne's body slammed into the chair. His face turned red. He slowly turned his head until his gaze met Adam's, right beside him.

"I am sure you want to apologize," Brentworth said from Adam's other side. He gestured to the footman to deal him another card. "Before this hand is finished would be wise. I doubt I can hold Stratton back longer than that."

"Apologize, hell."

Brentworth sighed and shook his head. "And this was such a pleasant day. Now it will end badly, and all because a drunken fool did not know to hold his tongue. I am sorry, Stratton. As host I feel responsible."

"It had to happen eventually. If not this drunken fool, then another one. I have grown somewhat accustomed to killing them." He turned his gaze back on Rothborne and hoped this particular fool would come to his senses in the next two minutes.

Langford bent low to speak in Rothborne's ear. "Lest you are so far gone as to forget how this works, let me remind you. Stratton here must now call you out. Your pride will not let you stand down, even when in the morning you awake sober and realize you will die soon. It was not a small insult to his honor, and he was an expert shot by the time he was fifteen."

"I won't die, he will, with more honor than his father at least."

Another tight silence claimed the men around the table. Adam noted that a few of the others in the stand watched now. Hell.

"Rothborne, you give me no choice but—"

"Apologize." The Duke of Clarence, who had been watching with rapt attention, spat out the command. "Am I to explain that I sat here while a duke and a marquess arranged a duel? Stop being an ass, Rothborne."

"But I—"

"I said apologize now, or I will have George call you to the palace like a schoolboy and send you down to the country. A few years' rustication might do you good."

Rothborne looked miserable. His chin went down to his chest. He muttered something. Langford, still bending close, looked over at Adam and shrugged.

"We cannot hear you," the Duke of Clarence said. "You threw insults loudly enough. You can speak clearly now too."

"My apologies, Stratton. I am not myself today." He barely got it out, his voice was so strangled.

Langford released his hold on Rothborne's shoulder but gave him a very hearty clap on his back that shook the man's body. "Ah, there we are. Now, stay and play a round or two, so everyone can see what good friends we all are."

Rothborne played two rounds, then rose and staggered away. Langford retook his chair. His gaze met Adam's in one meaningful exchange. Adam said nothing. He would thank both Langford and Brentworth later.

"We appreciate your help," Brentworth said to the royal duke.

"Yes," Adam said. "You spared me considerable unpleasantness."

"I couldn't have him ruin a fine day when I am enjoying such good whiskey. Irish, you say?" He drank a swallow.

"I will have a case sent to you," Brentworth said.

"No need, no need. My physician has me mostly drinking barley water these days. Although I would not mind some of that champagne your grandfather squirreled away, if any is left."

"Brentworth will tell me the vineyard and vintage, and I will have some sent from France," Adam said.

They played on. Adam stayed because to leave now would look bad. He joined in the camaraderie, but the close call with Rothborne weighed on him.

There *would* be another fool eventually. Even if by some miracle he cleared his father's name, he doubted it would stop.

Chapter Twenty

Clara watched dusk fall, then the night gather outside the windows. She began to think Stratton would not return tonight.

She had only herself to blame if that happened. She had given him no promise that she would come here as originally planned. When they parted, she was not sure that she should.

Yet here she was, feeling less confident in her decision by the minute.

He had been very kind at the race. Very charming. She did not doubt his apology was sincere. Time had cleared the worst of his mood, too. She still sensed that shadow and saw it in his eyes, but not with the intensity of the morning.

Dangerous. She had forgotten that people said that about him. He had not seemed dangerous to her. Not in the ways the gossip meant. This morning, however, when he appeared in that clearing, that word fit all too well.

Had he been there that day? Had he seen the result? She suspected he had. He had been lost to her, to the whole world, while he stared at that big rock. Lost to himself too.

She looked around the chamber in which she lay. Althea

had urged her not to come. *If he needs you he will find you*, she had said. Althea thought that like most men, Stratton would want to be alone if he lost a battle with himself.

Althea had probably been correct.

Adam entered the house near midnight. It had been a hellish day. The only good thing had been seeing Clara. Their time at the race shone as a bright spot surrounded by storms. There was a painting in the gallery like that, a landscape of a cloudy day with beams of sunlight pouring out from the clouds, illuminating a few farms in the middle.

Eventually, of course, the clouds would close in over those farms too.

It had taken two months for someone to force a challenge out of him here in England. As expected, it had not been a man who bore any responsibility for what had happened years ago. Rothborne might have known what anyone of his station knew or heard in private gossip, but he was drunk so often that his voice had no influence, and his befuddled mind could never form an argument for action.

He mounted the stairs. On impulse he approached the chamber Clara had used. In the moment before he opened the door, a soulful hope twisted in him. In the next instant it died. She was not there, of course. Why would she be? An apology did not absolve him of the cold way he had treated her this morning. He had not blamed her, not in words, not even in his mind, but she had seen what was in him and probably guessed that he did blame her family. *Familiarity, even passion, does not change who we are.*

He walked to his apartment, grateful now that it had been totally changed so nothing of its previous occupant would haunt him. His manservant slept on a chair in the dressing room. He wanted no fawning servant imposing on him now. He jostled the fellow awake and sent him on his way. Then he shed his coats and sat down to pull off his boots.

The second one hit the floor loudly. He stripped off his shirt.

Another presence intruded on the space. He felt it before he looked. When he turned his head, he saw Clara at the threshold to the bedchamber, wrapped in a sheet. Her bare shoulder indicated she was naked underneath.

She looked beautiful there, washed in the pale golden light from the small lamp. She seemed to be emerging from the shadows, barely visible but elegant and soft.

"I thought you remained in Epsom," he said.

"I decided not to."

"I cannot imagine why."

Her brow puckered a little. "I am not sure I can either."

He reached out. "Come here. Leave the sheet."

She dropped the sheet and came to him, naked and beautiful. He drew her onto his lap facing him, so he could hold her against his chest. Her warmth soothed him. Contentment spread like a long, physical sigh.

Her face nuzzled the crook of his neck. "Was I wrong? Did I make a mistake?"

"I am grateful you are here." He caressed down her back and over her hips and the round swells of her bottom while she lay against him. Her breaths quickened in the musical way her arousal sounded.

He should take her to bed and show his gratitude by giving her every pleasure she ever imagined. He should express his affection with slow lovemaking. Instead hard and desperate desire exploded in him,

He lifted her to her knees and moved her to straddle him. He used his mouth on her breasts and stripped off his lower garments. She braced her arms against the chair back while he pushed her ruthlessly toward the abandon that would deny him nothing.

He put his hand to her until she reached the edge, then watched as her release shattered her. Its tremors shook through her powerfully. Beautifully. While she dwelled within them, he wrapped her legs around his waist, stood, and carried her to the nearest wall. With thrust after furious thrust he exorcised the memories and resentments that haunted him.

"This is a very nice bed." Clara made the observation well into the night. It was the first words spoken since the ones in the dressing room. Only now, a good hour after he had carried her to this bed and taken her a second time, had they both calmed enough for any conversation. This seemed a safe topic.

"It is, isn't it? Nice and big, so I feel appropriately ducal. It is all new. I was surprised by its appearance when I arrived."

Any number of responses came to mind, but each one of them led back to his father. So she said nothing.

The bed in question looked disreputable right now. They lay under the sheet stripped away in the dressing room. It barely covered them, dragged here as it had been and thrown haphazardly. The maids would wonder what had happened. Then again, probably they would know.

She lay against his chest, sated and, if truth be told, a little sore. She did not mind that. Her spirit had known what was in his while it happened. His releases had been about much more than carnal pleasure.

"I almost had to challenge a man today," he said. "A drunk, dim-witted fellow. He would not restrain himself.

At least twenty men heard what he said, so I could not pretend I did not."

"Yet you did not challenge him." She made a statement but sought reassurance. There was no guarantee the dim-witted fellow was not very good with a pistol.

"Langford and Brentworth tried to intervene, but it was the Duke of Clarence who saved the day. Thank God he likes disobeying his physician by drinking Brentworth's whiskey, or he might have left earlier."

"It is said he is called Silly Willy." Her father had told her that. She left that part unsaid.

"I know, but not by me after today."

They lay there in peaceful silence, both awake, his hand sliding up and down her back as if stroking out the rhythm of his thoughts.

"He died there, in that clearing. But I think you guessed that."

His words broke through the night. Her breath caught.

"It was one of his favorite places. He and my mother would go there. I think sometimes they bathed in that pool, not that I ever saw it."

She dared not speak. She would allow him to say what-ever he wanted to say, although already her heart wept at what was coming.

"He had been melancholic for months. I did not know all of it yet, but I knew enough because I had not been spared either. That day I suggested we go riding. It was my attempt to distract him. When he was not at the stables at the agreed-upon time, I knew. I just knew. So I went look-ing for him."

She closed her eyes to try and contain the anguish she felt for him.

"He must have been sitting on that stone, but he had fallen beside it. It was what the ancient Romans did, to save their families and fortunes, when disfavor fell on them. To save their sons. I felt an unholy anger that day, mostly at him. I still do, which seems unfair."

"That anger is common when those we love leave us." She knew this from her own experience, and she had not even lost her father in the manner he had.

He pressed a kiss to her crown. "I had not been there since that day. Until this morning. That was why—"

"You do not have to explain." She stretched and kissed him.

He stroked his fingers through her hair and held her head to a deeper kiss, one heavy with emotion. Then he pulled the sheet over her shoulders and tucked her back under his arm.

She rested there, drowsy now, her heart drenched with layers of emotion.

"I did not have to explain," he said. "But I wanted to."

Chapter Twenty-One

Brentworth noticed Adam's distraction. "I can see I am boring you."

"I am hearing every word. You just confided that you have a new mistress. I am waiting to learn her name but wondering if you plan to share it."

"I think not now. What the hell are you staring at? You look like a tiger eyeing his prey." He turned his head to search the crowd in the ballroom. "Bad enough you talked me into attending. You know I dislike crushes like this, and Lady Prideux knows no restraint in her invitations. You could at least occupy me with conversation."

"I needed you here. He may cut me, but he will never cut you."

"Who is he?"

"Hollsworth. Come with me."

Adam took three steps before realizing Brentworth had not followed. He looked back to see Brentworth's severe face at its most ducal.

"I am going nowhere," Brentworth said. "Not unless you are forthright about why I am going wherever there is. And before you say a word, let me make as clear as a bell's toll that I will not agree to be your second if you challenge

Hollsworth. He is an old man, and a duel would be the same as cold-blooded murder."

"Do you think I am capable of that?"

Brentworth sighed. "Of course not. It is just—" He sighed again. "Lead the way. Try not to force me to lose an old friend tonight. My father knew Hollsworth for decades."

"I do not think you will lose his friendship tonight."

"I was not referring to that particular friendship, Stratton."

Adam led the way through the crowd to the terrace doors. "It is damp tonight. Heavy fog. I do not think we will have much company."

That fog hung low enough that Hollsworth's lone form barely showed near the stone balustrade.

"What is he doing out here? Ah, he has a cigar," Brentworth whispered. "He is having the devil of a time lighting it, though. He won't stay long."

"Invite him to join us." Adam removed two cigars from his coat.

"You will never get those lit in this weather."

"Invite him. I will get them lit."

Brentworth made a display of peering through the mist. "Hollsworth, is that you there? Join us. You and I can share a wager on whether my companion can raise a flame."

Hollsworth peered in turn. "Brentworth. I did not see you there. If you can provide a flame, you are better than I. Damnable fog."

He sidled over. Only when he reached Brentworth's side did he see Adam. Resigned dismay showed behind the thick spectacles.

Adam used his match on the underside of the terrace's balustrade and lifted the flame. Hollsworth made use of it quickly, then Brentworth. It went out before Adam even attempted to light his own cigar.

"This is much better than that crush in there," Brentworth said.

"I hate it myself," Hollsworth said. "My wife always wants to attend, but I plead off when I can. At my age, balls hold no interest. They are for the young, like you two. A chance to eye all those young girls."

"Normally we would be doing just that, but the terrace drew Stratton here instead."

"Well, there is nothing like a good smoke, I agree."

"It was not the chance to smoke that drew him. It was you."

Hollsworth calmly puffed. He did not look pleased. Then again, he did not move away.

"He does need to know," Brentworth said. "I am sure you agree."

"If he is looking to fight someone, I do not have a name for him."

"I only want to know the accusation against my father," Adam said. "It cannot have only been a vague rumor."

Hollsworth looked down at the glowing end of his cigar. He looked over at Brentworth. Brentworth strolled away, to the other end of the terrace.

"One hears things," Hollsworth said.

Adam was sure Hollsworth heard more than most. He was the kind of man everyone treated as a friend because he never spoke enough to make enemies. Had he been at the race in Brentworth's stand, and sat to play cards, within fifteen minutes most of them would become unaware of his presence.

"I learned some jewels might have been involved."

Hollsworth nodded. "Rich ones, belonging to your

family. Valued in the thousands, by some accounts. Well, people talk. Who is to say the value? They found their way into the wrong hands while the Corsican was on Elba. French hands. They were used to help finance the new army."

"How is this known or claimed?"

"After the war, questions were put to those involved. The usual methods. Not by us, of course. We are more civilized."

"Of course."

"Two officers in the know spoke of this."

Adam's mind rebelled at absorbing this. The rumors had not been baseless. "Who received them? To whom were they sent?"

"Marshal Ney." Hollsworth puffed deeply, and a cloud of smoke swirled into the fog. "He was a friend of your mother's father."

Hell. Damn. Ney was the highest-ranking officer to join Napoleon's Hundred Day campaign, and the only one to die for it.

What had his father said when presented with this story? How had he explained sending anything at all to Ney? And if he did it—he could not believe he allowed that thought into his head—why? Because his mother asked him to help an old family friend?

The questions kept coming, a chaos of them, filling his head and emptying his soul.

"Did Ney corroborate any of this before his execution?"

"Not a bit of it. That proved inconvenient. We were very interested in where the money came from, as you can imagine. It took more than those jewels to raise that army, unless a bushel of French jewels joined them. The investigation continued for several years in France. And here."

Adam had known how it ended but not when it began.

Early, it seemed. Long before the questions and suspicions took enough effect to be visible in his father's mood and distraction.

"You can understand why the government had to take a look at all of it," Hollsworth said softly. "It was to be very quiet. Very secretive. Well, that never happens, although very few learned much of the details. It would die down for a while, then voices that mattered would insist it be pursued and . . . well . . ."

"Which voices?"

"I'll not give you names, I said."

"I think I know anyway."

Hollsworth's cigar, half-smoked, gave up then. Its glow dimmed, then died. "Every man has enemies. Even a man like your father."

"You don't."

Hollsworth chuckled. "There is something to be said for being forgettable." He threw the cigar into the garden. "Your father did what he thought he should do. Perhaps you should leave it at that." He walked toward the terrace doors.

Brentworth came out of the fog. "Did you learn anything?"

"Nothing good." The notion of going into that ballroom sat poorly on him. All that bright gaiety . . . The damp fog suited him better.

All the same, he joined Brentworth in walking across the terrace.

"I think I did you no favor, if it was nothing good."

"You did me a great favor. Thank you. You were right when you told him I needed to know." He opened the French window. "Now tell me about this woman who seduced you. Don't look at me like that. You are not so green as to believe it was all your idea."

* * *

Clara sat on the divan in her sitting room, with Althea beside her. A portable desk, such as travelers used, rested on the cushion between them. Althea had it facing her, with a pen in the inkwell. Lady Farnsworth, Lady Grace, Mrs. Clark, and Mrs. Dalton sat with them. Lady Farnsworth had called for the sherry again, and even instructed Mrs. Finley where to find it.

If she ever had her women's club here, Clara expected afternoons in it to be much like the one they all shared right now.

"The goal," she said, "is to plan the next two issues of *Parnassus*. We have here a list of subjects and lengths. We need to determine the manner in which the areas will be addressed and which contributor will do it."

"Will there be poetry?" Mrs. Clark posed the question in her usual tentative voice. She rarely accepted Clara's invitations to join in these meetings. Although Mrs. Clark always had the good excuse of her millinery business, Clara thought the real reason was that the woman did not feel comfortable sitting like this with others born so high above her.

Today, however, Mrs. Dalton attended as well. A gentry matron of considerable girth and a cloud of pale hair, Mrs. Dalton provided expertly researched history essays that she signed Boudica's Daughter. She had befriended Mrs. Clark and had taken to having all her bonnets and hats made in Mrs. Clark's shop.

"Of course there will be poetry," Mrs. Dalton said. "What a question."

"There will be indeed. I am already receiving examples left for the journal at a few of the bookshops. Perhaps you will take them and choose our next ones, Mrs. Clark?" Clara opened the little desk and retrieved a sheaf of papers.

"How do we know they are not written by men?" Lady Farnsworth asked.

"You have only to see the handwriting to know," Althea said. "I suppose some man might be dictating to a woman in order to hoodwink us. However, the sentiments in most of them do not appear to be male."

Mrs. Clark appeared both pleased and flustered that she had been asked to choose the next poems. She peered at the top one with interest.

"Now, as to the travel essay," Clara said.

Lady Grace cleared her throat. "If we are willing to take on a new contributor, we could have an essay that would probably cause us to triple the printing."

"What sort of travel essay would that be?" Althea asked.

"A lady's journey through the Continent with a person of the highest position. We could allow it to be written as a confidence shared with the author if she did not want to use her own name."

"Am I correct in assuming the person would be the late Princess Caroline?" Lady Farnsworth asked sharply. "I thought so. That means your contributor would be Lady Anne Hamilton. Since Anne has already written indiscreetly once about Caroline's situation even while the poor dear was alive, I do not doubt she will agree to do so again, now that she is dead. As for whether it would be wise for *Parnassus* to publish it, I leave that to others to decide."

Her tone made it very clear her opinion of such a rash move.

"If you prefer I not ask her, I will not, of course," Lady Grace said.

"I want to think about this," Clara said. "Mrs. Dalton, do you have the subject of your next history essay?"

"I think it will be on a Roman woman of nobility. Everyone likes reading about the Romans."

"They like reading about the orgies, you mean," Lady Farnsworth said. "Find a way to include that, and we will triple our printing without resorting to Anne's betrayal of poor Caroline's memory."

Mrs. Dalton's expression fell. "I am not sure I know enough about Roman orgies."

Clara laughed. "No orgies are necessary, Mrs. Dalton. You should not say such things, Lady Farnsworth. She thinks you are serious."

"And you think I am not?" Lady Farnsworth smiled mysteriously.

Clara was about to move to the next item when Mrs. Finley entered the chamber and hurried to her side. She bent to her ear. "A carriage is drawing up outside. Your *brother's* carriage."

Althea overheard. She stood and looked out the window. "Here she comes."

Clara knew who *she* was.

"Ladies, we are about to have a visitor," Clara announced. "Please chat about something else until she leaves. Anything else." She reached over, snatched the poems from Mrs. Clark's hands, and returned them to the desk. Althea picked up the desk and placed it on a shelf.

"She is in here?" the dowager's voice could be heard saying. "You say she has callers? Then I will join them."

The dowager appeared in the doorway. She paused, surprised by the group of women who had all unaccountably called on the same day. Using her parasol like a walking stick, she paced over and took them all in. "Cakes, I see. You are a generous hostess, Clara." Her gaze lit on the decanter. "Are those spirits?"

"Sherry," Clara said. "Would you like some?"

"I should say not."

"Perhaps you should, but is that in fact what you are saying, Hannah?" Lady Farnsworth drawled.

That brought the dowager's attention on her. "*Dorothy*. How odd to find you here."

"I daresay Clara welcomed my call at least as much as she welcomes yours, *Hannah*."

Her grandmother did not miss the insinuation. "Well, what a nice little party." Face pursing, she looked around for a seat.

"Please, ma'am." Mrs. Clark shot up and offered her chair.

Her grandmother accepted, only to turn once she sat to give Mrs. Clark a long, hard inspection.

"Please join us over here, Mrs. Clark," Clara said, indicating the spot where the portable desk had recently been.

Clara made introductions. She only gave her visitors' names and hoped that her grandmother did not take to quizzing them on their histories. Lady Grace of course already knew the dowager, as did Lady Farnsworth.

"Do not let me interrupt," Grandmamma said. "Continue on."

"We were discussing the sad history of the late Princess Caroline," Lady Farnsworth said. "I am sure you have views on that, Hannah."

Indeed she did. Given the stage, she produced a soliloquy. From the way Lady Farnsworth's smile tightened, Clara guessed that *Dorothy* disagreed with every word *Hannah* said.

"You are most severe, Hannah. Yet you befriended her at first, only to turn against her when her profligate husband did." Lady Farnsworth sipped her sherry. "I suppose you did not want to risk losing invitations to his obscenely excessive parties by standing up for a friend."

The dowager momentarily appeared dismayed at the direct attack. She recovered quickly. "I was never her friend, Dorothy. Your memory fails you. Perhaps it is all that sherry."

"My memory is excellent, Hannah. In fact, I was present when you tried to arrange being one of her ladies-in-waiting. Would that she had agreed. It would have given you something to do besides terrorizing everyone."

The dowager's eyes narrowed dangerously. "By *something to do*, I suppose you mean writing naïve essays on politics that are published in journals of suspicious origins, like you do these days."

"If you knew anything about politics, you would know the essays are far from naïve, and the journal is above reproach. But, yes, I mean *something* like that."

Clara and Althea exchanged desperate glances. Mrs. Clark saw it, sitting as she did between them. She leaned forward and picked up the plate of cakes. "Would anyone like another one? They are delicious."

"I would." Lady Grace took one. "Say, did anyone hear any details about that little drama in Brentworth's stand at the race? It is said that Rothborne insulted Stratton and only one of the royal dukes prevented a challenge then and there."

The dowager's attention swung to Lady Grace. She looked as shocked as if someone had slapped her.

"This is news to you, it seems, Hannah," Lady Farnsworth purred. "I do not know why. Eventually someone would start talking, and Stratton would start dueling. One does wonder what Rothborne said. I trust he did not name names. Goodness, what a problem that would be for *some* people."

Lady Grace looked from one woman to the other. "I do

not think names were named." She took a big bite out of her cake.

Lady Farnsworth gathered herself and stood. "Well, it is only a matter of time before someone does. I must go, Clara. I have dallied too long over your hospitality, and I have *something to do*." She almost shouted the last words right in the dowager's ear as she passed.

Clara saw Lady Farnsworth to the door.

"I am sorry our meeting was interrupted."

"I'm not. I would not have missed it for anything. I will write to you with some ideas for my next essay."

Lady Farnsworth's departure gave the others a good chance to take their leaves too. One by one they escaped, until only Clara remained in the sitting room. Not alone, unfortunately. Her grandmother had chosen to remain.

"What a dreadful woman Dorothy is. Beyond the pale." Her grandmother had retreated into rigid hauteur. "I can't understand why you received her. She has no notion of propriety. She is loud and overbearing and voices opinions as if speaking for God Himself. It is a wonder anyone can bear her company."

Clara barely kept a grin off her face. "Well, she is gone now. How nice that you stayed."

"I had to stay. I came for a reason. I heard you attended the Derby. With a friend. Not Dorothy, I hope."

"No. With Mrs. Galbreath." She pointed to Althea's spot on the divan. "She is a widow. Her late husband was in the army and died at Waterloo."

"It would be better if you did not spend too much time with her if she is a widow. You do not want Stratton thinking that you have been privy to an experienced woman's confidences."

Clara just looked at her. Her grandmother actually appeared chagrined.

"Yes, well, speaking of Stratton, I was told that you visited Brentworth's stand, and Stratton was there."

"I did, and he was."

"You have seen quite a lot of him."

"Not a lot at all."

"Enough that there is talk. The best kind of talk. The world is waiting, so to speak. If he does not declare himself soon, it may reflect badly on us."

Clara liked that "us."

Her grandmother clasped the hilt of her parasol beneath both hands. She leaned forward, using the parasol for a support. "Here is what I think we must do. I believe that your brother should call on Stratton and put the question to him."

"What question would that be?"

"Inquire as to his intentions, of course. As the male relative responsible for you, it would be appropriate for Theo to seek confirmation of honorable intentions. It may be just the nudge Stratton needs."

Clara pictured that meeting. She saw Theo puffed up like some *paterfamilias*, putting the question to Stratton. Then she heard Stratton telling Theo not to worry, since a proposal had been made weeks ago.

He had promised not to reveal that, hadn't he? She surely had remembered to extract that reassurance from him, right?

"Grandmamma, I must insist that you not encourage Theo to quiz Stratton in any way. Such a conversation suggests that Theo does not trust Stratton, and in turn implies that he questions the duke's honor. After all of your efforts to become friends with him, it would be unfortunate if things only became worse instead."

Her grandmother chewed over that, frowning. "Normally I would disagree. Two gentlemen having such a conversation is very commonplace. However, after what

Grace said about there almost being a challenge—" She speared Clara with a sharp look. "Were you there? Did you see this?"

"I was well gone by then."

"That is unfortunate. I would so like to learn exactly what happened."

"You could ask Stratton."

"Ask the duke? I think not!" She stood. "What a reckless notion. Really, Clara, sometimes I do not understand my son's insistence that you were as clever as I am. Now, I will go." She aimed for the door, where Mrs. Finley waited to escort her. "Ask Stratton, indeed."

Chapter Twenty-Two

"I need to go down to Drewsbarrow," Adam said. He had arranged for Clara to visit him at Penrose House, his London home. He and Clara had indulged themselves upstairs when she arrived, and now they satisfied other appetites at dinner.

"You seduce me, then leave me so early in the affair? I think you are too sure of me when I have given no cause for such confidence."

Her eyes reflected her displeasure at his announcement. He liked how she did not hide her reaction to his pending absence. The sophistication she showed others did not extend to him anymore.

"How long will you be gone?"

"A week perhaps."

"That is not too long. Long enough for me to flirt with other men, however. I will have to review my invitations and choose some good ones."

He reached for her hand and entwined his fingers through hers. "It is far too long, but necessary."

"Then of course you must go. I will miss you, but I have matters of my own to attend that will make the days fly by."

He had on occasion wondered how she passed her time.

Her arrival in the hackney today reminded him of her use of them in the past and of meeting her on her own in town far from Mayfair when she still lived in her brother's house.

"More mysterious doings?" he asked. "What matters require your attendance?"

"The normal woman things."

"What sort of woman things? You do not make many calls now, and you are not buying an extensive wardrobe."

"Women do not only make social calls and shop. We are often busy people. If men are unaware of that due to lack of interest, we do not mind."

"Because men would object? That is what you are implying."

"They might. Most women have some man who might think he can interfere. I, of course, do not."

I answer to no one, including you. He understood she had sound reasons for refusing to marry, both emotional ones and practical ones. Only now it entered his mind that Clara might be involved in something that she feared a husband would forbid.

What could it be? Reform work that took her to dangerous areas? Radical demonstrations that might turn violent? Whatever it was, the ability to come and go at will without any interference might be why she now lived on Bedford Square.

"I hope you know that I would not try to stop you from doing something that truly mattered to you, Clara."

She smiled sweetly, but he doubted she knew that at all.

Their meal done, they retreated to the library. "I love this chamber." She held out her arms and made a little twirl in its center, looking up. "It was my favorite as soon as I saw it when you gave me the tour before dinner. No one would guess looking at the house's exterior that its library had a dome."

"At night, if you look through those windows set into it, you can see the stars on a clear night, or even the moon."

She threw herself onto a divan beneath the dome and gazed up. "You can! How wonderful. The lamplight from down here does not reach it, so the windows are quite black."

He strolled to a desk and retrieved a box from its drawer. "I have something for you."

He sat beside her and handed her the box. The ruby necklace, so long in the giving, lay inside. She lifted it. The lamplight created deep sparks in the stones.

"It is beautiful. And thoughtful." She undid the clasp and set it around her neck. "It is also too generous."

"I do not think it generous enough. It is past time for me to express my . . . affection for you."

She did not seem to notice the slight pause caused by that catch in his words. She looked down, admiring the jewels lying on her chest.

To express my love for you. That was what he had almost said. The word emerged on his tongue without thought or choice. He stopped because such declarations required both of those things. He did not want to sound like a man who professed love easily, without meaning it, even if he had been that man in the past sometimes.

Now he wondered how she would have reacted if he had been less careful.

She reached behind her neck to unclasp the necklace. "It is stunning. I will have a special dress made to wear with it as soon as I can flaunt jewels again. I must find an event appropriate to their richness. One that my grandmother will not attend."

"Do you think she won't like them?"

"She will love them. This necklace is to her taste. Add four or five more stones and she would love it all the more. I don't want her to see it because she will question me about how I came by it."

He set his arm around her shoulders. "Tell her your lover gave them to you."

She laughed. "Or better yet, tell her *one* of my lovers gave them to me. Oh, I can picture her now, suspicious that I goad her but wondering and worrying if I tell the truth."

He kissed her temple. "Or even better yet, tell her that I gave them to you."

Her mirth subdued, she fingered the gold setting of the largest ruby. "She will be relentless then in trying to force a proposal. You must promise me that you will never tell her there has been one already, insincere though it was."

"I will not give her cause to browbeat you, but . . . we could both do much worse, darling."

"You certainly could do much better."

"I do not think so." He turned her face so he could look in her eyes. "I must marry eventually. You know that. You can choose to continue as you are, but I cannot."

Her expression shattered. "Of course I know it. It is unkind to remind me now, right after giving me that gift."

"You are right. It was unkind and clumsy." He kissed her cheek and tasted moisture. He never expected to see Clara cry about anything, least of all him.

He pulled her on his lap to embrace and kiss her until pleasure made her forget any unhappiness.

A half hour later they lay entwined on the carpet, under the dome, catching their breath while they gazed up at the stars speckling the black in the circle of windows at its base. She wore only the necklace and he nothing at all.

"Come down to the country with me," he said. "You can

stay at the Grange and ride over to Drewsbarrow every day to be with me."

She did not respond at once.

"Of course, if your mysterious doings will not allow it—"

"It sounds scandalous," she said with a naughty smile. "Shocking. A whole week of unfettered passion. Why, some might call that decadent. What kind of woman do you think I am?"

"An enchanting woman. A beautiful woman." He kissed her. "A rare woman."

She laughed. "Those were excellent answers."

"I can keep going."

"Please do."

He continued praising her, with his words and then with his hands and mouth, until she agreed to try and join him down in Warwickshire.

Clara did not believe she could leave town for a week without her family knowing it. She would have to tell them but find good reasons that called her there. The next morning she wrote to her grandmother, explaining that she had to go down to Hickory Grange to meet with the steward about some tenants on her property. She offered to bring back anything that her grandmother requested.

A letter arrived in the next post, from Emilia. *I was told you are going to Warwickshire. Please do not stay there long. I will be left with a different chaperone during your absence, which means I will have no fun at all.*

That evening a letter from Theo arrived, asking her to bring back a favored waistcoat that he had left behind.

No response came from her grandmother. No scolds. No complaints. No objections. How odd. Perhaps she schemed to use this time to send Theo to Stratton, to put the question to the duke. If so, Theo would be unable to do so.

Packed and ready, the next day she and Jocelyn climbed into the carriage with Mr. Brady at the reins. Two days later they pulled up in front of Hickory Grange's manor house.

She let Jocelyn settle her in while she met with the steward that afternoon. She had not lied about having business with him. She used the same one as Theo, and together they rode to the farms in question and discussed the improvements that he felt two houses needed.

They finished early enough that she debated her plans. She had intended to ride over to Drewsbarrow in the morning, but right now she was halfway there already.

"Please tell the housekeeper and butler that I decided to continue riding," she told the steward. "I should be home by dusk, but in any case they are not to worry. If night or weather catches me, I will stop at a neighbor's house."

He rode away charged with her message. She turned her horse east. Stratton would be surprised to see her now, but in the best way.

She had never visited Drewsbarrow. She had never even spied the house from a road. As she rode toward it, its appearance struck her as appropriate to its name. A thick grove surrounded it on its hill, filled with tall, old oak trees. People of the county often still referred to it by the old name for the hill from centuries ago. Back then it was called Druids Barrow, or grove of the druids.

No druids greeted her. Only servants. The house, constructed of stone, rose tall, wide, and formidable. Little decoration relieved its mass. Any thoughts that it might not be a comfortable place disappeared as soon as a footman admitted her. Old-fashioned luxury waited.

The servants had never met her, but they knew who she was. Her footman did not even look at her calling card. "You are expected," he said. "I will bring you to His Grace at once."

Through cavernous chambers and echoing halls they traipsed. All the rich paneling, beamed ceilings, thick tapestries, and heavy fireplaces made her feel like she toured one of Queen Elizabeth's castles.

Finally, in what seemed a deep corner of the ground level, the footman opened a door. A simple office lay on the other side, one with plaster walls and a timbered ceiling. Wooden boxes piled high with papers and scrolls lined a long table. Only when the footman announced her did a dark head emerge on the other side of that wall.

"Lady Clara. What a happy surprise." Stratton stood and came around the table. He bowed. She curtsied. He sent the footman away. As soon as the latch clicked, he grabbed her. "Damn, I thought you would never get here," he murmured between kisses. "I had given up hope for today."

"I can only stay a short while before riding back." She looked at those boxes. "What are you doing?"

"Digging through family papers sent here from Kengrove Abbey."

His father's papers, she assumed. "You have spent four days here doing this?"

"No, first I opened every hiding place in this pile, to see what they would yield. There are a lot of them."

"Did you discover any treasures?"

"Not the one I sought." He took her hand and led her out of the room. "I know you have been out for hours, but I have been buried. Let us take some air."

A door to the grounds was not far away. It gave off into

the grove. Once outside she looked up the severe stone face of the house. "It could use some new decorating."

"Do you think so? You do not favor my great-grandfather's taste?"

She laughed. "It is all very dark."

He shrugged. "It was all but abandoned after my father married. They made their country home at Kengrove Abbey, not here."

"They did not come here because of us, you mean."

"Yes."

She hated how that old argument had hung on for years, affecting not only the generation that started it, but the next one as well. And the current one, she had to admit. She wondered if anything could truly end it. Perhaps if they all agreed to say nothing about it to children born hence, it would eventually die.

He backed her against one of the trees and gave her a long kiss. "How long can you stay?"

"Not long enough for what you are thinking."

He laughed. "Am I so obvious?"

"I read your mind in your kiss. I promise to ride over early tomorrow so we have many hours with each other."

He kissed her again as if that hardly mollified him. With a sigh of resignation, he released her and took her hand. "Come inside and I will show you some of those hiding places. There is one that could house several people inside the walls."

Jocelyn set out her green riding habit. "This will have to do for today. Or else the black. I need to mend the blue one."

"This will do."

Jocelyn began to help her dress. "There is a bit of talk

among the servants about you are riding every day, all day. The women fear you will harm yourself somehow, with all the time in a saddle. The men remember how you did this after your father passed, and worry that you are again lost to grief."

"And you?"

"I think you are not riding all day at all."

"Just keep those thoughts to yourself."

"Of course."

"And reassure the servants that I am healthy and happy and well beyond deep grief. I do not want anyone feeling obligated to write to London with concerns."

"I will take care of it."

Dressed and ready, she once more aimed her horse east.

She doubted she would ever again know such grand days. She and Stratton had turned time upside down. They spent the morning in bed and, after the first two days, when late afternoon had found them still there, then dressed and ate and played like children. One fine day he took her to a little lake where they bathed. Another they met in an archery contest. Yesterday they brought pistols and muskets and practiced shooting. And of course they had kissed. Again and again they had kissed.

He told her stories too, about how his father had met his mother when she was a girl, then returned to France to marry her and bring her back before the troubles started there. He showed her the family graveyard where two older brothers were buried. Both had died as infants, which made his survival like a miracle. He described Paris in the years right after the war, when it seemed all of society from all over the world arrived to stroll in the Champs-Élysées.

Not once did he mention his father's death or the cause of it. She began to think that perhaps, just maybe, it would not take another generation for the old memories to fade.

They might do it together. They might forever find common ground, if they tried.

A groom waited to take her horse, as always. A footman opened the door. No formality greeted her, however. She strode to the stairs and went up to Adam's apartment. Old-fashioned like the whole house, at least these chambers had been redone in the last century. Gilt carvings festooned the bed's massive headboard with abandon. The moldings dissolved into arabesques of leafing tendrils. The entire apartment presented an environment of excess and decadence.

He still lay abed. The drapes had not even been opened. She went over and sat on the bed, and he unfastened her habit. She stripped it off, and her chemise, and climbed into bed with him.

"I wish you could stay here and be spared all this dressing and undressing," he said after a kiss. "I would have you all the time then."

"We would have to pay the devil not to be found out. Besides, I have taken to not wearing stays, so the dressing part is easier now." So was naughty play later in the day if they chose.

"What is the worst that could happen if we are discovered? Your brother demands I marry you?"

That probably was the worst that could happen. This morning, after the heightened familiarity of this week and the depths of their intimacy, it did not sound so bad.

"We would stay here together and ride and swim and shoot during the day and be scandalous at night," he said. "You could redecorate this old pile and renovate the gardens, and I could reclaim my place with the estate and the county."

"It is sounding very domestic."

"Isn't it? It all has great appeal to me." He glanced sideways at her.

It had appeal to her too. Mostly because he left out the parts that did not.

"Or if you won't stay, you could ride like Godiva and be spared any dressing at all," he said.

"That would be a fine sight for the tenants."

"They would be in awe. There you would be, riding out of the mist in the early morning, your hair flying behind you, all creamy on that black horse. You would look like something out of a myth or a dream. Legends would start. Hundreds of years hence farmers would tell about the naked fairy who came with the spring."

"What an imagination you have. You should be writing poems or novels."

"What can I say, you inspire me." He pulled her close to him. "I am far better at creative pleasure than poetry, however. I am wondering if you might be too."

He proved what he meant. His mouth aroused her with devastating precision. She had no defenses anymore with him and succumbed quickly to whatever he did. This morning she had arrived so eager and full of joy that one smoldering gaze might have left her breathless. As it turned out, he had much more in mind.

His kisses moved in a hot trail down her body. She knew what he would do, but he moved so slowly that she moaned with impatience. He did not move down her body, either, but bent to kiss her stomach, and lower.

Hot breath on her mound. A firm hold on her hip. He turned her to her side, then turned himself as well so they faced each other upside down. He lifted her knee over his shoulder and sent her screaming into delirium. Even in her daze she realized this odd position allowed her to caress him. She took his phallus into her hands to give pleasure in return. The more she pleased him, the more he gave her, until finally she used her mouth too, first with kisses, then with more, while his tongue astonished her again and again.

Adam rose from the bed while Clara slept. He went to the dressing room and pulled on trousers, boots, and a shirt. He left just as his valet hurried in, carrying one of his banyans. He returned to the bedchamber, picked up Clara's riding habit and chemise, and laid them on the nearby chair. He placed the banyan on top of them.

He left the apartment through the dressing room. "Do not disturb her. Leave hot water here, then make yourself scarce. I will be in the old study."

He went down the stairs and wound through the chambers to the beamed room with the boxes.

Since he arrived he had examined every hiding place once more, looking for the missing jewelry. Nothing of such value had been found. Then he had begun the long chore of looking through his father's personal papers. He faced those boxes again and pulled one toward him.

When the butler at Kengrove Abbey packed all of this, he had begun with the most recent papers and worked backward through time. That meant the oldest material had been on top, and Adam's examination had moved forward through the years. If he did not sift through quickly, it was because each letter revealed something about his father. Even the reports from the stewards opened little windows.

The most interesting items had been letters from his mother, written before they married. Sent from France, she reported on the mood abroad in her country and expressed her concerns. Not love letters as such, they read as warm and affectionate communications between friends. He had set those aside to give to her when next he saw her.

He sat behind the boxes and removed a big stack from one of the last ones. Within ten minutes he realized that he had before him the papers from the last year of his father's life. There were a lot, and many letters from other lords. He unfolded each one and read it.

In some, people begged off a party his mother had planned. In others, peers pointedly set aside the rumors and wrote on about bills to be discussed. The tone began changing, however. One man wrote to break their friendship. Another bluntly referred to the smell of treason. Then for several months, there were no letters at all.

Finally he found the reason why. A long letter in a fine hand began with regrets over the difficulties an old friend faced. However, it then gently gave bad news. *Marwood sent a man to France, unbeknownst to anyone, I assure you. No minister approved this mission, and more than one is angry for the interference and the earl's insistence on stirring once again this cauldron of innuendo. Unfortunately his man found the pawnshop at which the jewels were sold and retrieved a description that, along with the pawnkeeper's explanation of their heritage as given to him, ties them directly to you. It is all around town, and I beg you to remain in Surrey until the worst passes. I regret that I must inform you of this, but you need to know. It is time, old friend, to discover what you can about these events so you are not impugned for others' actions.* It was signed *Brentworth*.

It touched him that the last Brentworth had remained a friend to the end and even assumed the rumors were untrue despite new evidence to the contrary. The last sentence loomed large, however. *If not you, then who?*

There was only one other possible who. The most likely

who. Had his father asked her and learned that indeed she had done it? Had he chosen a path to ensure she would never be asked, by him or anyone else?

Adam stared blindly at the letter a long time. The revelations in it emptied him out until only a dark hollow existed in his heart. He had assumed he would find proof the accusations had all been wrong. As for the who—

"What do you have there that makes you frown so seriously?"

He looked up. Clara stood just inside the door. A ribbon bound her hair at her nape. She wore the banyan and, he guessed, nothing else. It was much too large, and the sleeves covered her hands. The bottom pooled around her feet. If any servants had seen her, she would never know it. They all had orders to fade away if the lady visited.

Her eyes held naughty lights that said she wanted to play. They faded, one by one, as she gazed at him. She walked to the end of the table and looked at the pile of papers in front of him. "Your father's papers."

"I am going through the last group." He set the stack back in the box. "I will bring these with me to London and finish there."

"What was that you were reading, Adam? You looked far away and almost lost."

He looked down on that letter, not even folded again now. "It was a letter he received that explained what he faced." He held out his hand. "Come along. I will have breakfast sent up to my chambers."

She did not take his hand but instead kept looking at that box. "Have you learned anything from them?"

"A few things, yes."

"Did you learn that my father played a role?"

He wanted to lie, desperately. Had she asked an hour before or an hour later, he probably could have. "Yes."

"I think you always suspected that. I feared you would learn you were right. It is why my brother fears you and my grandmother is so eager to make peace. Not because of some old argument over a piece of land. Because of this." She looked at him with a gaze both sad and defiant. "Do you think of my father when you see me?"

"Not any longer. Not since very early. Please believe that."

"I am not sure I do. What if you discover he is to blame for all of it? Or did you already? He is dead and you cannot challenge him. Do you take what little revenge you can through me?" Her voice rang with both fury and hurt. "When you are with me, perhaps you are thinking *Look what I am doing to your darling daughter, you scoundrel.*"

"That is not true. Do not say that." He reached for her, but she slipped away. Her back to him, she hugged herself.

He moved behind her but restrained himself from the embrace he longed to give her. "When I am with you, I think how I would like to live here with you, as I said this morning."

"Here? A few miles from his home? From my family home? You will never give this up, ever, if you live here, with the grave of a man you blame mere miles away. As for me, am I to abandon them? Cross the great divide and never look back?"

He dared one touch on her arm. She did not thrash at him or jump away. "We can make peace, just as your grandmother first proposed. There would be no need to cross a divide if a bridge is built."

She turned, angry still, and looked at him. "What were you reading when I arrived, Adam? Something bad, I think. Very bad, if you do not want to speak of it."

"It confirmed some things I had already guessed and told me others I wish I did not know."

"Was it enough for you? Are your questions answered? Are you now finished with this? Because if you are not, there will be no bridge that stands long, and no place for me in your heart that I can trust."

Was he finished? Was it done? He wanted it to be. With his whole soul, if it meant he could have her.

Her expression smoothed. She reached up and laid her palm on his face. He would remember forever the look she gave him, as if she sought to memorize his face. "You must see it through, of course. This is your legacy as surely as these lands. What a fool I was to fall in love with you, knowing that. And yet, I find I am not sorry, even knowing what I now will suffer."

"Clara—"

She touched his lips with her fingertips. "Do not. Please, do not. I think you would lie if you had to, and that would be too sad." She lifted the hem of the banyan and walked to the door. "Please stay here until I am gone."

She slipped from view. His mind went black and he slammed his fist into a wall. Then he sank down its length until he sat on the floor, and the hollowness filled with anguish.

Chapter Twenty-Three

Clara opened the letter. She knew what it would say. She knew Adam had sent it.

Come to me it read.

Similar letters arrived three times a day. They had continued for a week. Only the first one, written upon his return to London, had been more expansive. *You fell in love with me, you said. As I have with you. To discard love when we find it is a great sin. Come to me.*

Each letter made her want to cry. Each one also lit a tiny flame of uncertainty.

Could she do it? Would love let them separate themselves from the past? Even if that past included his belief that her father had wronged his so severely?

It would mean believing in him more than common sense warranted. More than she had any person, really. Would love let her see deeper than normal or make her blind?

Mrs. Finley announced that Althea was arriving. Clara tucked the letter into her writing desk with the others and removed a stack of banknotes and a bag of coins.

"Do you have it all?" Althea asked as soon as she entered.

"I visited every shop the last two days. Here it is. Three

copies remain at Ackermann's, but he expects them to sell and told me to increase the order to twenty next time."

Althea opened a sheet of paper at the table, then moved the inkwell over. "Let us proceed, then, so our ladies see the fruits of their labor."

Althea's paper listed all the women who had contributed to the last issue of *Parnassus*, from Lady Farnsworth down to the women who carried the copies to the shops. She read out the amount each should receive, and Clara counted it out.

"Mrs. Galbreath, ten shillings," Althea read as the last name.

Clara took a five pound note and placed it beside the others. Althea glanced at it, then at Clara. "That is not ten shillings."

"Indeed it is not. I think it is the correct amount, however. Your list was in error."

"We agreed to ten shillings almost two years ago."

"We agreed before it was known if we would sell a single copy. You do more than half the work, Althea. I could not do this without you, let alone contemplate a regular schedule of publication. In fact, I think you should be a partner in the law, not only one in responsibility."

Althea's big smile made her glow. "I think so too. Where do we sign?"

Clara laughed until she cried. She wiped her eyes. "Oh, that felt so good. I was beginning to think I would never laugh again." She took a deep breath. "I will have my solicitor draw up an agreement and we will sign as soon as it is prepared. Now, take that banknote before I decide it would pay for a nice ball gown."

Althea grabbed the note and stuffed it in her reticule. "If you deliver the money to those who live near here, I will do so with those who live near Mayfair."

"You will have to be more discreet than I will."

In Althea's always organized way, she placed pieces of paper naming each stack, then tied coins into little sacks with the papers inside. She grouped the Mayfair stacks on one side and the east London stacks on the other.

"Now," she said, "I want to celebrate and do something decadent with my earnings. I think you should come with me to Berkeley Square and indulge in an ice."

"Mr. Brady can take us, then bring you home before we return here." Clara went to the reception hall to call Mrs. Finley and tell her to send word down to Mr. Brady.

She and Althea tied on their bonnets. "I am so glad you are joining me on this little debauch," Althea said. "While we indulge ourselves at Gunter's, you can explain why you feared you would never laugh again."

Clara dipped her spoon into her ice, then savored its cold, rich sweetness. It helped soothe the sadness that came on her when she explained her break with Stratton to Althea.

From their tiny table, she could see the other wares that made Gunter's famous. Cakes and bisquits and other desserts lined the counter of the confectionary shop. Marzipan could be had too, crafted into artistic tiny sculptures of animals and flowers. A decadent sweet smell permeated the premises.

"Of course if you could not trust his motivations, there was nothing else to do," Althea said.

"That is what I told myself."

"It would be horrible for it to go on, only to learn he had deceived you all along."

"Terrible. Only—he is not one for deception, it seems to me. To say so is unfair."

"So you do not think you would have discovered that?"

She thought about it. "There was the chance I would, I suppose. I rather think not."

Althea set down her spoon. "If you believe he would not deceive you, why do you doubt his motivations in pursuing you? You are contradicting yourself, darling."

She shoveled a large spoonful of ice into her mouth. Too much. It hurt.

"How can I marry a man who carries such hatred for the father who loved and protected me? And he must hate him, if he learned my father encouraged the accusations against his own. For an instant, when he looked at me that day, I think he hated me too, or at least hated the ghost he saw standing behind me."

Althea raised her hand holding the spoon. "Stop, please. Let us go back to your first sentence. Did you say *marry*?"

"Did I?"

"I am sure you did. Have you been considering it?"

"I suppose so, a little."

"Did he propose, even a little?"

"Oh, he proposed the second time we talked to each other. It was a sly form of revenge. He has all but admitted as much."

"Did he ever propose again?"

She poked her spoon repeatedly into the remaining ice. "I suppose so."

Althea reached over and patted her arm. "You suppose a lot of so. Is heartbreak making you a little dim-witted?"

"I suppose so," she muttered.

"Clara, your mention of marriage makes me change my opinion of him and makes me better understand your current sorrow. If you considered marriage at all, you must care deeply for him. I believe you should learn if there is a possibility for happiness with him. You should be very sure before throwing away a chance for that."

"He said much the same thing," she said when they finished. "Or rather, he wrote it."

"Then perhaps you should see him one more time and speak honestly with each other."

That night, after much debate, Clara picked up her pen. *I will call on Wednesday afternoon. You must tell me everything. There will be no kissing.*

It was not cowardice that made her delay that meeting with Adam, she told herself. She did not dread what might be the final, unalterable break with him. Not at all. She did not spend most nights fighting against impossible hope that wanted to take hold in her heart. She could not see him right away because she had things to do, that was all.

The next day she set out early to pay her contributors. She called on Mrs. Dalton first. Mrs. Dalton presided over a household near the river. Her husband and she let the modest home only for the Season, after which they would return to their property in Kent.

Mr. Dalton did not know his wife was Boudica's Daughter, so Clara arrived at one o'clock, ostensibly to pay a call. While she and Mrs. Dalton chatted about society gossip, the little sack moved from Clara's reticule to Mrs. Dalton's ample bodice.

No such sleight of hand proved necessary with Mrs. Clark. She greeted Clara at her shop and took her to a tiny office, where they transacted business.

"If you have the payment for the others, I will see they get it as before," Mrs. Clark said.

"I would like to bring it myself, if you would supply their directions."

"That is good of you, but it may be better if I do it. Their streets are not fitting for a lady like you."

"I have a coachman with me. I think I will be safe enough. If you brave those streets, I can too."

Mrs. Clark did not like it. All the same, she wrote down the directions. "You watch yourself now, Lady Clara. There's pickpockets and worse about. Don't let your man leave the carriage, whatever he does, and tell him to have his whip at the ready."

"I promise to be alert and cautious, Mrs. Clark." Before she left she admired some of the bonnets in the shop. When she embarked on an orgy of sartorial excess, she would have to order some here.

Mrs. Clark's warnings proved less charming and more sensible when Clara's carriage rolled into the neighborhood where one of her delivery women lived. Mr. Brady did not want her to step out of the carriage when they found the sad house of Mrs. Watkins. Clara insisted, however, and knocked on the door.

It went without saying that no servant answered, but instead Mrs. Watkins herself. A young girl accompanied her, grasping her skirt.

"Milady. What brings you here? Did that shop man claim I did not take him the books? If so, he is lying so as to rob you. I did, most certainly, and—"

"There has been no complaint, Mrs. Watkins. I came to bring you this." She handed over the sack of coins.

The girl heard the sound and her eyes widened. Mrs. Watkins flushed. "My apologies. I was just surprised to see you here on my doorstep." She looked behind her. "Won't you come in?"

Clara could see the chamber and the makings of a dinner being prepared. A cot hugged one wall. Mrs. Watkins and her family appeared to occupy only this one room and not the entire house.

"I do not want to intrude, and I have more errands to attend to," she said, to spare the woman the difficulty of trying to host a visitor. "I just wanted to bring that to you and tell you how much I appreciate your help."

Mrs. Watkins beamed. "My pleasure, milady. I'm glad to do it anytime."

Clara returned to the carriage. Mr. Brady could not get her in it fast enough.

"Bedford Square?" he asked through the window.

"I am afraid not. We next go to St. Giles."

"Lady Clara, I don't think—"

"St. Giles, Mr. Brady."

She gazed out at Mrs. Watkins's home while they rolled away. *Parnassus* might be a lady's avocation for her, and others like Lady Farnsworth and Lady Grace, but for Mrs. Clark and Mrs. Watkins, and even Mrs. Dalton and Althea, the small earnings they gleaned from the journal mattered. In some cases quite a lot.

Chapter Twenty-Four

Adam pulled on the oars, hard. His body felt no pain because all of his concentration remained on thoughts in his head. They flashed to the rhythm of his rowing.

Clara wanted to hear all. She believed he could never see her as separate from the rest of it, from her family's actions, from his duty to extract some justice. He might convince her otherwise. *All*, however, also included the recent revelations he learned from that letter.

That led to a terrible place, where his thoughts had lived for days. If he had not lost Clara, he might have had a better sense of where his duty lay. He never expected to face a choice between his two parents, but now he did.

Let it all lie as it did, and his father's good name remained dishonored. Try to rectify an injustice, and it would mean asking his mother questions no son should ever put to the woman who gave him life.

He pulled harder, his whole body stretching, his shoulders knotting from the effort. Wednesday, Clara had said. Tomorrow. *Are you now finished with this?* Perhaps he could be. If she did not forsake him entirely, he might be.

Shouts came to his attention. He looked around. Behind him, arms hailed him.

"You won, damn it," Brentworth shouted. "Do you plan to row to Richmond?"

He set up his oars while he judged the currents, then turned the boat and made his way to shore.

Brentworth and Langford had already donned their coats. Servants who had followed along the shore began rowing the boats back to where they had all started the race. Others held the horses. Adam's bow hit ground, and he jumped out.

"Hell, you rowed as if your life depended on it," Langford said. "We did not even have a wager."

"The exercise suited my mood and helped me think."

"You are doing too much of that these days." Langford wiped his head with a towel. His curls emerged all the more reckless. "Let us partake of some ale so your brain might find some ease."

A tavern waited across the road. The three of them sat at a table and Langford went to bring back some pints.

"He is right," Brentworth said. "You are too much in your thoughts. You look angry. It makes men nervous. Last night at White's the card room almost emptied when you arrived."

"I didn't notice."

"Of course you didn't."

Langford returned with the ale. "Are you telling Stratton that he is casting a pall on the entire Season with his infernal brooding?"

Adam drank his ale, then set it aside. "I learned something. Several somethings. I now wish I had not."

Neither friend prodded him. They just waited.

"I found a letter from your father to mine," he said to Brentworth. He described what had been written.

Langford whistled. "So the earl would not let it rest when others had chosen to. There is no way to seek satisfaction with him dead, not that any jury would accept this as just cause for a challenge anyway."

"That is not what haunts you, is it?" Brentworth asked.

"No."

"Have you written to her and asked about it?"

Langford grasped the direction the conversation had taken. "Oh, hell. Yes, of course." His expression turned frankly sympathetic.

"I have written the letter and had a copy made of a drawing of the jewelry in question to send along. I have not sealed and mailed it. In fact, I find myself avoiding the desk on which it lies."

"Hell of a thing," Langford muttered. "Small wonder you have looked like a man eager to thrash someone the last few days. If you send that letter you ask her to admit that she—that his death—I don't think I could do it."

"Can you live with not sending it?" Brentworth asked. "Live with not knowing, and allow it all to remain as it is?"

"That is the question that absorbs me." Adam gestured to the publican for more ale. "Let us talk of other things, so I do not look like a man hoping for a fight. Tell me how it goes with your ladies."

He had raised Langford's favorite topic. His friend did not fail him.

At one o'clock, and still thinking about the conversation she would have with Stratton the next day, Clara called for her carriage and had Mr. Brady bring her to the City for an appointment with her solicitor.

Mr. Smithers greeted her himself. A young man fairly new to the law, he had been delighted to obtain such a distinguished client. She had gone to a great deal of trouble to find a lawyer who both came highly recommended and whom she trusted to resist anyone's attempts to learn her private business. When Theo learned she had moved her private affairs to someone other than the family solicitor—who had informed Theo about her troubling decisions, out of concern, of course—there had been quite a row.

Now Mr. Smithers patted his blond hair, plucked his cravat into new creases, and smiled obligingly across the table in his chambers. He handed her the document he had prepared at her request that would give Althea half ownership in *Parnassus*.

"You will see that she must pay you a shilling, so there is what we call consideration. However, as equal owners, you will share in any profit. I trust Mrs. Galbreath understands that she will also be equally responsible for any debts."

Clara read the contract. There would be no debts. *Parnassus* had a benefactor who paid any costs beyond those covered by the subscriptions and sales.

"If you send me the copies, I will have them signed."

"Very good, Lady Clara."

On impulse, she raised another matter. "I am curious about something. If I marry, what that is mine remains mine?"

She surprised him. "Are you thinking to marry?"

"No. I am just curious."

"I ask because there is a simple answer that may satisfy you. However, should you plan to marry, rather longer explanations might be wise so you understand thoroughly your situation. The simple answer is that all that is yours remains yours. However, your real property would be your husband's to use and profit from during his lifetime. He could replace the tenants, or build villas, for example. The income would be his."

"So I would lose control of the land. I thought as much but wanted to be certain."

"Yes, and also the house you recently purchased. Had you used your legacy to buy dresses instead, those would be personal property. The house, however, is real property."

"I knew about the land, but to also have some man given leave under the law to poach my house seems very unfair."

Mr. Smithers chuckled. "*Poach* is an amusing word to describe it. Be of good cheer, however. A husband could use it or let it. He could not, however, sell it without convincing a judge you freely agreed."

That pending meeting with Stratton kept looming large in her mind and heart. As long as she was here . . . "I have another question. Are you familiar with the property that was contested for years by my family and that of the Duke of Stratton?"

"My goodness, yes. The case is somewhat infamous, even if it began well before my time. It is the sort of story older lawyers tell younger ones over port."

"Can you learn the details of how it was finally disposed? The when and how of it, I mean. I ask because I was told that my father may have taken advantage of the situation, and I would like to have proof that he did not."

"So you can present that proof to the person who disparaged him?"

"Possibly."

He jotted on a paper. "There are records, of course. Nothing that happens legally in the courts is a secret. Finding such records can be difficult, but it is what lawyers do. I will look into this at once so you can put the gossip in her place. Although the most recent disposition is of course known to you."

"Are you saying it was sold?"

Mr. Smithers looked over, confused. "Goodness no. Having gone to such lengths and waited so long to secure it, selling it would be most odd."

"Extremely odd. Then what did you mean by its recent disposition?"

"I see you do not know. My apologies, but I thought you did." He leaned toward her and offered a reassuring smile. "Not to worry. It remains securely in the family, Lady Clara. You own it now. It is the property left to you by your father."

Exercise, fresh air, and friendship turned Adam's mood around. He still faced a hard choice, but his head had cleared. He decided he would wait a few days, then make a decision about that letter ready to go to Paris.

Later that afternoon, he set the letter and other documents related to it aside on the desk in his study and busied himself with estate affairs. In particular he continued an ongoing communication with the house steward at Drewsbarrow about reviving the house's appearance. All those timbers and gold really had to go. The steward's last letter had implied it might be money ill spent, since no one much used the house. Adam penned a letter making clear that was going to change.

An hour of writing letters left him thinking that it might be past time to employ a secretary. He was debating how to proceed with that when a commotion began in the house and grew in intensity.

Suddenly the door to his study crashed open. Clara stood there. Behind her shoulder the butler made expressions and gestures of apologies.

A better day became a wonderful one when Adam saw her. She had indeed come to him, finally, a whole day before she had promised to.

Unfortunately her expression indicated her unexpected arrival might not be good news. Her blue eyes glared like jewels that could cut iron. Her posture remained rod straight. Her black ensemble encouraged the impression of a force of destruction. She was about as angry as he had ever seen her.

He thought she looked glorious.

He got up and walked toward her, gesturing for the butler to go away. "What a wonderful surprise, Clara." He reached toward her.

She strode past him, into the study. "Do. Not. Touch. Me." From her tone, she might as well have added *You. Miserable. Scoundrel.*

"I see you are in a fine humor today."

"I was. Until an hour ago." She turned on him. "You can wait until tomorrow to tell me the rest, but today I demand you tell me this. Did you know that I had inherited that contested land? You know which land I mean. The land that started the years of unpleasantness between our families."

Damnation. He had spent days marshaling explanations and promises about their fathers, their families, his duties, his love for her. He had not expected this to come up, least of all now.

She peered at him. "Do not try to lie. I know you now very well. I will be able to tell if you dissemble in the least."

Hell. "Yes, I did become aware of that."

"When?"

"I am not sure just when. Sometime—"

"When?"

Shit. "I realized it after we spoke that first day. I rode back to Drewsbarrow much the way you rode over during our time together there." *Our glorious, passionate, loving time together there.* "I recognized a few landmarks, like the town and the mill. And I realized why your father and grandmother wanted me to marry Emilia, not you."

She strode back and forth, angry and, he knew, hurt. "So you decided you would show them, didn't you? You would make sure that old argument ended in your family's favor. Marry me and that land would become yours."

"No, it would become *ours.* It would be a fitting end to the whole matter, don't you think? No family wins, and no family loses. Your grandmother claimed to want peace."

"I think you saw a way to turn the tables on her. On my father. I think you enjoyed the idea of besting them at their own game."

"Since it undermined his careful plan to ensure that land would forever remain out of my family's hands, I definitely enjoyed knowing that."

"What do you mean, careful plans?"

"Why in hell do you think he bequeathed you that property, Clara? There had to be other lands not entailed that would have suited you just as well. He believed you would never marry. He counted on it. Theo might sell it, maybe even to me, if he ever found himself caught in financial trouble. You never would because it would be your source of independence."

She wanted to disagree. He saw that in her scathing glare and tight posture. Adam counted on her being too smart to miss how very neat that plan had been.

She looked down on the desk and its papers. "Were you in here making your own plans on how to ruin his good name the way he did your father's?" She still sounded angry, but at least she no longer looked ready to shoot him.

"My last letter discussed decorating at Drewsbarrow, if you want the honest answer."

The worst of her fury left her like a dark specter flying out of her body. "Tell the steward not to use blue too much. So many people use blue." Looking weary now, she walked to the door. "I will go now. My carriage is waiting."

He strode over and pressed his hand against that door so she could not open it. "You are here now. I cannot let you go on the chance you will return tomorrow."

She stood there, her hand on the latch, her back a mere inch from his body. He drank in her scent and closeness like a man deprived for years.

"I cannot let you go, Clara, because I fear if I do I will never see you alone again."

She turned. "You are braver than I am, if you force this conversation now."

"Not so brave." Not brave at all. Desperate. "I will send your carriage away. Do not move. Do not leave."

He sent word to her coachman. When he stepped back in the study, she was sitting on a bench in front of the garden window. She had removed her black bonnet, and the afternoon sun found those subtle strands of copper in her dark hair. She did not appear eager to see him again.

"Do you have any sherry here?"

"I can send for some, or I have brandy on hand."

"I suppose brandy will do."

He opened the cupboard that housed it and poured two glasses. She tasted tentatively, thought about it, then shrugged. "It will do."

"You were making calls today," he said.

"What makes you think so?"

"The black."

She looked down at her dress. "I visited my solicitor. That is how I learned about the land. As I think about what you said, about my father's plan, I think you give him more credit for nefarious plotting than is fair. My grandmother changed her mind, you see. When she concluded you preferred me to Emilia, she decided that would do as well."

He set down his glass, and went over to her, and knelt on one knee in front of her. He wanted to say he was wrong and swear that he never thought about land or fathers or anything at all where she was concerned except heartfelt emotions. *I saw you and decided to marry you.* It was not the entire truth.

"Your grandmother decided that because that old argument and that land was the least of it. She knew I had more recent causes to want an accounting with your family. More serious reasons. I will not lie and say my interest in you was always separate from that, Clara. I desired you from the start for the woman you are, but I also saw at once how knowing you might benefit me as I sought to learn the truth."

"And did it benefit you?"

"In small ways at first. And then, soon, I no longer cared if it did."

She searched his face, his eyes, looking for the signs of lying, he assumed. He counted on her knowing him very well, as she claimed.

He ventured a touch on her hand. When she did not resist, he took that hand in his. "At Drewsbarrow you asked if I could let it go. If I could ever be finished with it. For you I can, and I will."

Her hand turned palm up, so she held his. "I said you must tell me everything. I do not think you want to."

"If I will be finished with it, maybe you should be too. Do the details matter once we put it all behind us?"

She smiled sadly and squeezed his hand. "What were you reading when I found you in that room that morning? What did you learn about my father and yours? I think we both need to learn what is between us if we are ever to truly be finished with it."

He hesitated. He considered arguing. Instead he rose and went to the desk, and came back to hand her a letter. "It was from the last Duke of Brentworth."

She read it. Her gaze returned to the top and she read it again, slowly. By the time she finished, tears brimmed in her eyes.

Chapter Twenty-Five

Oh, Papa. She could barely believe what Brentworth revealed. For her father to have gone to such lengths to ruin a man . . . He might have held that gun that took the last duke's life.

This was not the man she knew. Not the father who taught her to ride and spent hours with her after her mother died. Not the man who allowed her to become the woman she was meant to be. That man was generous and loving and good, not this vengeful, cruel person who needed to win so completely it meant a man died.

Grief swelled in her, as raw as it had been right after Papa died. It inundated her heart, only it was worse this time because she did not even have refuge in memories she could trust. She closed her eyes until that wave of emotion ebbed.

She let the letter fall on her lap. It gleamed brightly against her black dress. "No wonder you looked so serious and lost that morning. I find myself thinking I should beg your forgiveness in his name."

"It had nothing to do with you, or with me. Nothing to do with us. Not directly, and not in the future."

He looked very sure of that. Determined. He gestured

at a small stack of papers on the corner of the desk. "You said you want to know everything. You know what matters already, but if you need more, there is a letter there to my mother that explains it all, including what few questions remain. You can read it if you want, now or later."

"Perhaps I will. Later." She reached out to him. He came over and she urged him to sit beside her. "Did you mean it when you wrote that you loved me, Adam?"

"I am insanely in love with you. I even wrote a poem about you."

"Is it any good?"

He laughed. "It is terrible."

"I still want to read it."

"It will make you laugh."

"More likely it will make me cry. No one has ever written a poem about me."

"I am sure there are dozens tucked away in drawers throughout London, unbeknownst to you."

She adored him for really believing that. She took his strong hand between hers and raised it to her lips. "Did you describe me kindly?"

"I described you adoringly."

"Even my mouth?"

"It includes a scandalous line about your mouth."

"Oh. It is *that* kind of poem."

"A very loving that kind of poem."

She moved closer yet, so their faces were an inch apart. "Aren't you going to kiss me?"

"You wrote there would be no kissing."

"That was at tomorrow's meeting."

"Well, then." He raked his fingers into her hair and held her head to a thorough kiss. "Come upstairs with me, before I make shocking use of the carpet in my impatience."

He spoke of impatience, but he showed none. Not in

leading her to his bed. Not when he undressed her, and not when he laid her down and covered her with his body. He took his time with every kiss and every caress. He murmured words of love in her ear while he gave her the sweetest pleasure. First in English, then in French, his words gave voice to the emotions filling her own heart too, until the pleasure and love were one and the same, each stronger for the power of the other.

Their joining became a precious intimacy, one not to be rushed, the first ever after acknowledging their love. The sight of him, the feel of him—she knew she would remember all of it forever, from the first press of his fullness to the image of him braced above her to the love-drenched ecstasy at the end.

She held him to her afterward, with her arms and legs wrapping him. She could not have held back her love even if she wanted to. Free now, no longer bound by questions or guilt or worries, it moved her to where she quietly wept with happiness.

Late that night, Clara slipped from the bed while Adam slept. She pulled on her dress and half fastened it so she would at least be covered. Taking the lamp, she went down the stairs. The household had all gone to their chambers except the footman at the door, and he slept at his post.

She made her way to the study and sat at Adam's desk. She set the lamp close to her and lifted those papers from the corner.

She did not have to read any of these, but she wanted to.

The letter to his mother lay on top. It was four pages long. Not a single word had been crossed out. She guessed he had written several drafts that would show many changes, and this was the final version.

It felt odd reading his words to this mother she had never met. He addressed her with a son's informality, even intimacy. His love for her came through, even if he never used that word. Paragraph by paragraph he told her what he had learned about the events leading up to his father's death. On the fourth page he explained the revelations discovered by the man sent to Paris at the behest of the Earl of Marwood.

That evidence had been damning in Brentworth's letter and was equally damning here. Adam did not try to qualify any of it. Jewelry owned by them had been sent to France. *Only one question remains*, he wrote. *Did he send it, or did you?*

He did not ask for an answer. He made no accusations. That question just sat there, before he added two paragraphs with information about the estate.

She set the last page down. He had not sent this. It did not yet bear a date. This might have been written days ago. She pictured him anguishing over sending it, trying to decide if he needed to know or even wanted to.

Her heart broke for him. He had come back to England to clear his father's name. How horrible to discover that he only could do so if he found he could betray his mother instead.

She wiped her eyes of the tears welling up in them and set the letter aside. A page of notes labeled *Hollsworth* faced her. It included some of the information already found in the letter. She expected everything else in the stack would as well, but she flipped through anyway.

At the bottom she found a drawing. Two, actually, but of the same object. A necklace and diadem. Heavy and old-fashioned, they filled their pages. She thought it a beautiful set. This must be the jewelry that had disappeared from the family inventories and that Adam thought had ended up in France.

She moved the drawing closer to the lamp, then closer yet. She stared at it a long time. She stood, walked away, and looked out the windows into the night while she battled a profound sadness. Then she collected herself, returned to the desk, and folded one of the drawings. She returned to the bedchamber.

His dream shook. No, his body did. He opened his eyes to darkness.

Clara jostled his shoulder. "Light will break soon. I must go, Adam."

He circled her waist with his arm and pulled her down on him. She fell with a squeal and tried to extricate herself. Black crepe covered his face while she fought him. She had already dressed. Well, that was easy enough to rectify. He groped for the fasteners of her dress.

She reached behind her back to slap at his hand. "Stop being naughty."

"You do not have to go. Who will care or know if you stay? That housekeeper who brought me to your chamber our first night?"

She escaped his grasp, sat on the edge of the bed, then turned to hold his arms down, pressing with her weight.

"I seem to be imprisoned," he said. "If you stay, I will let you bind me properly and do your worst."

A flash of curiosity showed in her eyes, but she shook her head. "I have things I have to do this morning."

"More mysterious doings?"

"Very mysterious."

"If I ever convince you of marrying me, you will have to tell me about them."

Suddenly serious, she cocked her head. "Will I? That argues against marriage, it seems to me."

"I will tell you about any such doings I have too, so it is fair at least."

She looked down at his chest and bent to give it a kiss. "You are proposing again. Are these settlement negotiations?"

"I hope so."

"Would you promise I can keep the use of my house?" She asked right away, as if she already had a list in mind.

"As long as you do not bring lovers there. Or anywhere, of course."

"Can I have at least half of my income from the land, to use as I choose?"

She pressed her advantage now, but he was in no condition to truly negotiate after last night. "I have no need of that income."

"Can I continue with my circle of literary friends? Those bluestockings, as you once called them?"

"I would never deprive you of friends." That might be too generous. This was Clara, after all. "As long as they are not revolutionaries or criminals."

She raised her eyebrows. "Criminals?"

"I am just eliminating the impossible, darling."

She decided to let it pass. "And no matter what else you should learn, do you promise that you are finished with this quest you brought back with you? Do you promise that you will never seek revenge?"

"I have already said so."

She released his arms and sat straight. "Then I will marry you, Adam." She laughed quietly. "Those words almost made me choke, but it seems I got them out." She leaned down and kissed him. "I will marry you because I love you too much not to, it seems. So much that I can never be contented again without you."

He wrapped his arms around her and held her to his body. They remained like that long enough that he decided she must stay. Again he felt for her fasteners.

Again she slapped him away. She stood. "You should write to your mother and tell her to come home, I think. I am sure that you will want her at the wedding. Now I really must go. I will tell the servant at the door to find me a hackney."

Two thoughts crossed his mind after she left, while he drifted back to sleep. One was that writing this letter to his mother would be far easier than the last one, which he would never send now.

The other thought was that as soon as they were married, he intended to find out about Clara's mysterious doings.

Chapter Twenty-Six

The Decadent Dukes sat in their usual chairs in the upstairs chamber at White's. Adam had just told the others about his nuptial plans.

"We will announce it in a fortnight."

Brentworth congratulated him graciously.

Langford did too, but with little enthusiasm. He gazed around the chamber. "I suppose this is over now or will be soon. The Decadent Dukes will be no more."

"Why? I am decadent still, just with one woman."

"It won't be the same. There is nothing decadent about being bad with your wife. If we continue, we will have to change our name." He pondered it. "The Dour Dukes. The Despondent Dukes . . ."

"In time I expect it will be the Domesticated Dukes," Brentworth teased.

"Take that back. I cannot bear the thought of it."

Brentworth laughed. "The Dutiful Dukes."

Langford covered his ears with his hands. "I refuse to hear it."

"You could continue alone and be the Debauching Duke."

Langford brightened. "That isn't so bad."

Brentworth turned to Adam. "Have you met with her brother yet?"

"This afternoon. He was so happy he almost wept. He believed a duel was inevitable and only a marriage alliance would save him."

"If he knows half of what you know, he worried for good reason."

"Clara reports that her grandmother is also elated."

"I am sure, since she probably knows all that you do," Langford said.

"So you decided to leave it all as it stood after all," Brentworth said. "Just as well."

Yes, just as well. He had faced a devil's choice. He understood his father better now, and why he had ended it as he had.

"Let us go out," he said. "It is too fine a night for this chamber. Langford, you can lead the way. We will visit your favorite lairs."

Langford was on his feet at once. "Follow me, and we will reclaim our name. There is a most interesting party taking place tonight that you will both find a revelation. After that we will visit a new pleasure house that opened near Covent Garden. Stratton, you can remain in the gaming salon if you choose. Unless, until you marry you believe you can visit the more interesting chambers. There is one in which a woman shackles a man and uses a whip and a feather to—"

"It sounds inventive, but I will remain in the salon."

Clara climbed out of her carriage at Gifford Hall. As soon as she did, the door opened and Emilia ran to her and embraced her.

"Theo told me. Everyone is so excited and happy. I

think Stratton rather frightening still, but if you like him this is wonderful news."

"I do like him. Very much." Clara linked her arm through Emilia's and they walked together. "Perhaps you can visit us, if you like. Should Grandmother ever become a trial."

"Do you mean it? Here in London?"

"At any of his properties. You will always be welcomed as part of our family, Emilia. It is important to me that you know that."

"I am so glad. My one sorrow since I heard was that we would not see each other so much anymore. This way we shall."

Inside the house, Clara went to the morning room at once. Emilia trailed along.

"Has Grandmamma not yet come down?"

"She is still in her apartment," Emilia said. "She chaperoned me last night at the theater. She had a wonderful time, since so many ladies stopped by to pay their respects. I am not surprised she slept in."

Clara pictured her grandmother holding court in the family box at the theater. Of course she had a wonderful time with all of that groveling proving her place in society.

"I will go up to see her," Clara said.

"You know she does not like that."

"This cannot wait."

Emilia thought better of joining her and stayed in the morning room. Clara mounted the stairs slowly, not looking forward to this meeting. She had not seen her grandmother since she wrote and told her of her pending engagement to Stratton. Five letters had come in reply, in fast succession, praising her in the first, and listing long series of instructions in the others.

She faced the door to the dowager's apartment for a solid minute before knocking. Margaret opened it and led the way to the dressing room.

The dowager sat at her dressing table, dressed and ready. She looked over at her visitor and her whole expression lit. "Welcome, Duchess. I am delighted to see you, although it took you a good long while to come. Sit, sit. Margaret, have some coffee sent up. Lady Clara and I have much to discuss."

"Please do not, Margaret. I will not be here that long."

"Oh, tosh, of course you will stay. In fact, I have had your apartment made ready. It is best if you move back here until you marry."

Clara did not argue. She wanted Margaret to leave, and this provided a reason.

"August would be good, I think," the dowager said. "Ideally we would wait until the year of mourning is over, but I think we can wink at that. Or even July, if that would not be too rushed. Most of society is still in town in early July. It goes without saying that it must be a special license, but I doubt Stratton would have it any other way . . ."

Her grandmother chattered on, moving from one plan to the next. Clara spent her time finding her courage to say what she had come to say.

"You are probably relieved," she finally interrupted.

"Pleased, that is certain."

"No, *relieved*. You so worried that Stratton might harm Theo. Remember? It was your reason for trying to form an alliance through marriage. So he would not find a reason to challenge Theo."

"I am sure I did not say it quite that way."

"You said it exactly that way. As did Theo. You indicated it had to do with that old argument over property. I thought it bizarre that you believed he would kill a man over that ancient disagreement. And you said I did not know everything."

"Did I say that? I don't remember. Nor can I think why I would. Now, about your wedding garments—"

"You know why he came back. Why he fought those

duels. What he intended to discover. That was why you were afraid."

"I am sure that I do not know what you—"

"He has learned what you feared he would learn, Grandmamma. About how my father revived the accusations and even sent a man to investigate. He says he knows everything."

The dowager fussed with the bottles and cases on her dressing table, holding her expression firm and her composure strong.

"Except he is wrong," Clara said. "He does not really know everything, even now. I think I do, however." She stood, walked over to her grandmother, and placed a sheet of paper on the table in front of her. "As do you."

Her grandmother looked down at it. Her color rose. She picked it up and waved it. "What nonsense is this?"

"It is a drawing of jewelry."

"I can see that."

"That set belonged to Stratton's family. Only I saw it here when I was very young. Right here, in this very dressing room. It was in that drawer with your paints. I even wore it. Then I stared at it in a looking glass while you whipped me. Do you remember? I have never forgotten."

Her grandmother's arm dropped. The drawing hung limply from her hand, then fell to the floor. She turned her body and faced Clara. She looked afraid.

Clara's heart clenched for her. This woman was often an interfering harridan, but she was also family.

"I love you, Grandmamma, but not enough to pretend ignorance about this. A man killed himself over this deception. The man I love believes one of his parents committed treason. So I must put the question to you. How did jewelry that I saw in your possession find its way to France to help pay for Napoleon's last army?"

Chapter Twenty-Seven

Adam rode to the entrance of Gifford House and handed his horse to a waiting groom. To his surprise, Brentworth rode in right after him.

"I hope you did not forget to bring the special license," Brentworth said after dismounting.

"I have no license yet."

"You can't get married without one."

"I am not getting married today."

"How odd. I received a letter yesterday from the dowager requesting my attendance today to *bear witness*. Her exact words."

"Since I came at her request as well, let us go in and see what whimsy drew us here."

They were brought to the drawing room. The dowager sat there, resplendent in black. Her grandson did too, looking bored. Clara also waited, along with an older woman.

"What is Lady Farnsworth doing here?" Brentworth murmured to Adam.

"Perhaps she will bear witness too. It would be like the dowager countess to find a way to arrange a wedding without my consent."

After greeting Adam and Brentworth, the dowager turned to Clara. "Are you quite satisfied now?"

"I am."

Face pursed, the dowager surveyed her company.

"Should you not begin, Countess?" Lady Farnsworth asked.

The dowager glared at her, then composed herself. She looked at Adam, or rather at his crown, not his eyes. "I asked you here, Duke, in order to explain some family matters to you. Why my granddaughter insisted you also attend, Brentworth, is beyond my understanding. As for Lady Farnsworth, that is utterly incomprehensible to me."

"She wanted witnesses so no one will ever believe your claim that Stratton lied about what you are about to say," Lady Farnsworth inserted. "Should you ever decide to recast any of it later, that is."

"Please, Lady Farnsworth," Clara whispered. "Let us allow my grandmother to do this her own way."

"That way will take two hours," Lady Farnsworth muttered.

"Not at all," the dowager said. "I have no desire to prolong this. I will get right to the heart of it. Stratton, neither of your parents sent that jewelry to France. I did. Not to support that Corsican, I assure you. However, it was not them, but me."

Adam hoped his expression remained bland, but he suspected not. Such a public admission cleared his father's name and answered the remaining question in one sentence. Clara rose and came to sit beside him. She smiled at him sweetly, delighted by his relief and astonishment.

"If not to support that army, then why?" Brentworth asked. "If you do not explain that, the world will damn you no matter what the real reason was."

"She assumes her word will be enough," Lady Farnsworth said. "Don't you, Hannah?"

If looks could kill, the swords in the dowager's sharp glance would slay Lady Farnsworth on the spot. She then closed her eyes, as if to steel herself. "The real reason is embarrassing. I must ask that my grandchildren hear it with generosity in their hearts." She glanced at the earl, not Clara. Theo no longer appeared bored, but concerned.

"When I was a much younger woman, I formed a tendre for a young man. A Frenchman. This was before all the trouble there. I met him while visiting that country, and I fell in love."

"But you only went there with Grandfather, so—" Theo caught himself. His expression fell in shock.

"Thank you, Theo, for articulating that which I had hoped might not be said." She cleared her throat. "Of course, that love was doomed. I returned here, and life went on. That young man survived the revolt in France by straddling the fence as best he could, but in the end, of course, that proved impossible. When the Corsican came to power, he was one of the ones banished for opposing the emperor and sent to a penal colony."

"You seem to know a lot about what happened to him," Theo said suspiciously.

"How fortunate we are to have you here, my dear boy, to provide statements of the obvious." She sighed with strained forbearance. "While love does not last, I kept his memory in my heart. So after Napoleon's defeat, I sought to release him from that prison by bribing certain government officials in Paris. The jewels were sent with the understanding they would buy his freedom. Regrettably, I was betrayed, and they were used for other purposes."

"It is understandable you would not want to admit to this when questions started," Adam said.

Something like gratitude softened the dowager's face. She looked at him with tears in her eyes. This explanation had humiliated her. It had diminished her, and she felt it clearly.

"I do not understand, however, how you came to have that necklace and diadem," he said. "I am almost positive the ones in question were owned by my family."

"Your mother gave them to me. She wore them once, and I admired them, and she made a gift to me of them."

Lady Farnsworth leaned forward, toward the dowager. Her eyes narrowed. "Tell him why, or I will. Some of us already know this part, after all."

"I have no idea what you mean, *Dorothy*."

"It was not a gift, it was tribute, *Hannah*," Lady Farnsworth said. "She made you that gift so you might cease your cruelty. So she might not be cut left and right, and ignored, and she might be received as the duchess she was. She gave them to you so you would take your boot off her neck."

The dowager's face turned to stone. She did not look at Adam or anyone else.

"Are we done?" Brentworth asked. "I have heard enough, should any questions ever arise in the future. I will take my leave now." He bowed to the ladies.

"I will go out with you," Lady Farnsworth said. "I daresay Stratton will be glad for our absence. He no doubt has much he would like to say in private. I know that I would if I were he."

The door closed on the two of them.

"Do you have anything you want to say, Adam?" Clara asked quietly.

The dowager still sat straight and tall. Her face showed no emotion. Such a woman would know the cost of what she had just done. She would be the one cut left and right now. Her power was over.

"I have nothing I need to say."

"Well, I do," Theo said. "Did Father know about this? He sent that man to France who said it was all Stratton's doing. Did he lie about that?"

The dowager's face crumpled. She closed her eyes.

"I think we will never know. If he did, it was to protect his mother, Marwood. I am not sure you or I would have done differently," Adam said.

Clara took his hand in hers and squeezed it.

"I will leave now, if you do not mind," the dowager said, rising. "I think that, come autumn, I will retire to the dower house. I have thought for some years that I might like that."

Adam and Theo stood until she left.

"Please sit, Theo," Clara said. "I have something more to explain to you. Grandmamma already knows what I am about to say."

"There is *more*?" Theo dropped into his chair with dejected exasperation.

"Regrettably, yes. There will be talk, of course. And in the way of talk, some of it will be wrong. Her friends will try to turn it so it sounds less bad. Ambiguities will arise."

"I assure you I am well aware of the scandal we face."

"That is the least of my worries. Rather, I cannot have there be any further questions about Adam's family. None. So the story of this unhappy deception will be published. The accurate story. Everyone will know it is accurate because if it were not, Grandmamma would bring suit for libel. Which she will not."

This shocked Theo anew. "What gossip sheet do you plan to give it to?"

"Not a gossip sheet. A very respectable journal. One that will permit me to see the text to ensure it is correct. One that will treat Grandmamma as kindly as possible. It will emphasize how her initial motivations in sending the jewels to France were noble and generous."

"It will kill her. She just said she was retiring from society. Isn't that enough? And what of our father's name and memory?"

"I cannot have men insulting my husband, Theo. I will not risk that the day comes again when his hand is forced and there is a duel. And that will happen, you know it and I do, unless this is thoroughly and finally finished because the true story is clearly known by all."

"She will be finished too. I hope you know that," Theo snapped.

"*She* already knows it, Theo. She knew it even while she explained the truth to me."

Theo slumped more in his chair. Then, distracted and not looking at all a boy anymore, he stood abruptly and left the chamber.

Adam raised Clara's hand to his mouth and kissed it. He urged her up and sat her on his lap. "Thank you, darling. I am not surprised you were brave enough to do this, but I am still astonished, and very grateful."

"It is not hard to be brave for you. As for my family, it is always best if the truth wins, I think."

"How did she come to admit all of this to you?"

She gently stroked his lips. "If I told you that her conscience would not allow her to keep silent any longer, and she wanted to remove the shadow from your father's name, would you believe me?"

"I would believe anything you told me." He kissed her, and the light and gratitude in his heart poured through him freely. And the love. Most definitely the love. "What is this respectable journal to which you will provide the story? I don't know of any that would allow you to control the writing of it as you described to Theo."

She wound her arms around his neck. She kissed him deeply. Greedily. Erotically. He ceased caring about the day's revelations or anything at all except having her naked in his arms, beside him, below him . . . One with him.

She looked in his eyes and smiled mysteriously. "Ah, yes, the journal. Explaining that will take a while."

"Later, then." He kissed her, savoring the warm clarity in his soul that remained a novelty after five years of shadows. "For now, just let me hold you and love you. There will be time for explanations later."

Watch for the next in
Madeline Hunter's Decadent Dukes Society series:

A DEVIL OF A DUKE

by
Madeline Hunter
New York Times bestselling author

*The Duke of Langford meets his match in the
beguiling and resourceful Amanda Waverly,
who may or may not be behind a string of
jewelry heists in Regency London.*

On sale in May 2018!

Connect with U s

Visit us online at
KensingtonBooks.com
to read more from your favorite authors, see books
by series, view reading group guides, and more.

Join us on social media

for sneak peeks, chances to win books and prize packs,
and to share your thoughts with other readers.

facebook.com/kensingtonpublishing
twitter.com/kensingtonbooks

Tell us what you think!

To share your thoughts, submit a review,
or sign up for our eNewsletters, please visit:
KensingtonBooks.com/TellUs.